SHELDON MAJORS AND THE CHASE

SHELDON MAJORS AND THE CHASE

Written by

Jason G. Waters

Edited by

Alexzandria Waters

CASTLE
BY THE SEA

"A small town can be just as cruel and cold as the big city. People can torture you all they want, but in the end, it is the person holding the pen that has the last word."

I dedicated this book to anyone who has ever struggled with who they are and where they belong. It is also dedicated to mothers who mothered the best they knew how. May you forever live in our hearts and minds, and until we see you again…

Prologue

Abandonment

It was a beautiful day, not a cloud in the sky—one of those moments where you cannot tell whether it is morning or afternoon. A young boy walked up an overgrown dirt lane to an abandoned house. Typically, one would hear the wind blowing through the trees and smell the fresh country air. A place that always had a sense of peacefulness that one longs for in life. However, on that day, something was off. No birds were singing, no wind in the trees, no sounds at all, and there were not any of the typical country smells.

The young boy walked up the path and realized he was alone. He did not see his brother anywhere. During the summertime, he and his brother often played in the abandoned house. Since his brother was nowhere to be found, he proceeded up to the old, abandoned house to find him.

It was an old two-story house built in the late 1800s. The paint had been worn away by wind and rain many years ago. All that was left were weather-worn, dull gray clapboards. The front of the house faced west, and the back faced east towards their house, which was about a mile away. Normally, a mile away did not seem far, but for a kid, it seemed extremely far away. The boy was trying not to panic.

The boy walked up to the back of the old house. He proceeded past the water well with an old hand pump, from which he could still draw water. To his left, he saw an overgrown garden where grapes were the only edible thing still growing. He knew his brother would not be playing in the garden, so he turned his attention back to the house.

The boy walked past the old well and up to the enclosed back porch. The porch still had an old, wooded screen door. The screen was made of metal, which was now rusted and partially torn. As he opened the screen door, it creaked from age and lack of lubrication, giving the boy an eerie feeling. He stepped onto the back porch as the door slammed shut behind him. The lack of sound in the air intensified the slamming of the door, causing him to jump.

He proceeded across the porch and opened the back door into the kitchen. He stepped into the abandoned home and called out his brother's name. There was no answer, only an uncanny stillness. The inside of the house was just as unmaintained as the outside. Wallpaper and paint were peeling off the walls. Dirt was thick across the hardwood floors as he walked through the kitchen and into the dining room.

He continued through the house, now yelling out his brother's name; his voice did not echo through the empty house like it usually would but fell flat. Something extraordinary was happening. The boy pressed on into the living room that had ugly brown paneling, puke green shag carpeting, and an old rotary phone that still hung on the wall. The boy's heart jumped as he saw a frail-looking older man with dirty rags for clothes. The older man looked like he had not bathed in a while.

The old man sat quietly in an old rocking chair in the middle of the room, staring out the window.

The boy asked the man, "What are you doing here?" The older man continued to rock, staring out the window without acknowledging the boy.

Again, the boy asked the old man, "What are you doing here?" This time, the old man pointed a long, crooked finger to the window.

He walked to the window to see what the older man was pointing at. He looked out the window past the dirt and film from years of not being cleaned. The boy unmistakably saw backwater rising, which had already flooded the lower fields, and seeing all the rising water made his heart start to race. He had forgotten entirely about the strange man rocking in the middle of the room.

The boy backed away from the window and frantically began to search again for his brother. His mind started to race. *What if the water continued to rise? We could go to the second floor and if needed the attic.* First, he must find his brother.

He ran out of the house and headed to the barn. *Maybe he was playing out there.* He arrived at the barn but did not find his brother. His heart leaped when he saw his mother's blue and white Suburban parked in the field. His Mom was here, and she would save them, but the vehicle backed up and headed out through the field. He was sure she saw him. He threw his hands in the air, waving them and yelling for her to stop. He wondered why she was leaving him. He started to run after the vehicle, but the vehicle only got further and further away, and the boy realized he could not keep up. Feeling abandoned, he dropped to his knees on the dry brown corn stalks and began to cry. He gave up trying to catch the vehicle.

The young boy woke up panting and covered in sweat. He realized that it was only a dream, but it would haunt him for years. That young boy's name was Sheldon Majors.

Chapter One

Small Town, Anywhere

A black bird was flying high in the sky, circling, searching for food. It was a warm August morning, and below, you could see a small-town square. In the middle of the town square stood an old courthouse built in the late 1800s, next to which stood the old jailhouse. The bird swooped down and caught a mouse running across the courthouse lawn.

The town square consisted of two squares; an inner square paved with old bricks and an outer square paved with asphalt. The inner square provided parking for the courthouse and local businesses. On the south side of the inner square, most of the kids ended up parking and chatting after cruising up and down the main strip. The outer square handled traffic flow and was lined with local businesses. On the north side of the square was a gas station, an old church, a video arcade, and various other businesses surrounding the outer square, but on the south side was where all the action took place. That is where this story will begin.

Sheldon and his Mom just pulled into the GIA parking lot, one of only two grocery stores in Albion. His Mom asked him to come with her to the store to pick something up for dinner. Sheldon was in a great mood. He had recently started working at the grocery store, which made him feel like he had a purpose and fit in with others.

Sheldon got out of the car when he heard some redneck boys, parked across the street yelling, "FAAAAAG! QUEER!"

"Yea, we are talking to you, fagot," Laramie said, sneering at Sheldon.

"What are those guys yelling about?" His Mom asked.

Sheldon only shrugged his shoulders, pretending he had not heard them. Though embarrassed as he walked alongside his mother, he hid it well.

As they proceeded into the store, he could see Laramie Miller glaring at him from across the street out of the corner of his eye.

Sheldon was having difficulty admitting to himself that he was attracted to guys. *Do they know his dirty thoughts last year about one of his teachers at school? Mr. Ackles with his plump lips, piercing green eyes, and that nicely shaped firm butt.*

They would always surface regardless of how much he pushed the thoughts away. Sheldon would sit in class and daydream about his teacher. Wondering what it was like to be at his place, wake up next to him, and have dinner with him. Sheldon had such a crush on his teacher that he even went out and bought a sweater just like the one he wore.

All his efforts to get the teacher's attention were futile because the teacher was already sleeping with one of his fellow classmates and later fired. Sheldon was disappointed that he would not get to see him this year.

Sheldon was helping his mom pick out bananas when a new face caught his eye. He was a young man who appeared to be about the same age as Sheldon. He had never seen this boy before.

The first thing he noticed, aside from his strut, was his square jawline and wavy brown hair. He also had on a T-shirt and basketball shorts that said, "Los Angeles." This guy piqued Sheldon's interest. As he came closer, he saw the boy with deep blue eyes and long dark eyelashes.

Before Sheldon knew it, he was staring. The boy did not take notice; he was clearly on a mission but unsure where to go. Sheldon seemed to have a new obsession.

When Sheldon and his mom got home, they carried in the groceries while his brother Levin played video games in his room.

§

Sheldon grew up on a farm with his mother, father, older sister Susan, and younger brother Levin. Susan was seven years older, and Levin was a year younger. On the farm, they raised pigs, cows, chickens, and horses.

Since Susan was away at college and no longer lived at home, this left Sheldon and Levin to help out around the farm. The two had to ensure the animals were fed and watered, and they cleaned out the pig pens.

In the summer, their father would force them to help plant crops that usually consisted of corn and soybeans. When a field was growing crops or for the pasturing of animals, the grass would grow tall. Then, the field would be mowed, and the dead grass would be used for bailing hay. Sheldon did not enjoy bailing hay because it made you sweaty and itchy.

Their neighbors would also hire Sheldon and Levin to help with their fields. The job was strenuous, but it did give them some money to spend.

Their dad's hay bailer was broken a few summers, so the bailing had to be done by hand. The process consisted of doing it with just a pitchfork, a wagon, and a couple of horses, which was highly challenging for Sheldon and his brother, trying to pick up dead grass with a pitchfork and throw it over their head into the wagon while trying to not get it all over them. Boys, being boys, would get to play and try to make light of such a mundane and sweaty task.

In the fall, they help harvest the crops. In the winter, they would glean the fields for any corn the combine failed to get, or the corn stalks that the wind had blown down. Their hands would be cold from digging the corn out of the ice and snow. The gloves would become soaked through, causing their fingers to become numb. They were not allowed to stop and warm up, but the sooner you got that field done, the sooner you could go home.

Sheldon and his brother made the best of their lives on the farm. When the weather was nasty, they would play in the hayloft, which was the second floor of the barn, which was used to store the hay for the winter. They would build forts and mazes and play for hours. After their parents stopped raising chickens, they took the old hen house and made that into their playhouse.

One time, they even built a tree house. They had a lot of good times in that tree house. That was until Levin fell out of it and broke his arm. That was the end of their tree house. They would run and play in the ditches and creaks near their house.

Also, in the summer, Sheldon would lie in the swing in front of their house and get lost in his books. If he wanted total seclusion from everyone, he would climb up into the hayloft of the barn, lie in the straw, and read for hours. These books would take Sheldon away from his sad, lonely world into a world filled with excitement, adventure, and sometimes romance.

Susan was going to college to be a social worker, which made sense because she was a great listener who knew how to solve other people's problems. She was great at pointing out what Sheldon had accomplished and not dwelling on the things he had yet to accomplish.

When Susan would come home to visit on breaks from college, Sheldon would tell her how he was doing in school and what was new in his life. He would only talk to her about how other kids at school treated him for being feminine. He told her about a boy named Laramie and how he bullied him in school. Sheldon did not even feel comfortable talking to his Mom about how the other kids treated him at school.

§

That night, everyone in the house was pulled out of a sound sleep by the sounds of sirens drawing closer and closer to their home. They got out of bed as fire trucks flew past their house.

As they came down the stairs, they saw a bright, glowing light beaming in through the bathroom window. When they looked out, they saw the glow was coming from the abandoned old house they owned up the road, which was engulfed in flames. They all scrambled to get dressed.

Sheldon and his brother felt grown-up when they ventured away from their home to explore that old, abandoned house. This was a place where they would explore and make their own adventures.

Sheldon and Levin sat silently in their parents' Suburban, parked just down the driveway. They both felt a lot of emotions; it was like the house they lived in was burning down. They could see the firefighter trying to put out the flames as their parents talked to the firefighter.

They could smell the burning wood even with the windows and doors of the vehicle closed. "It's unfortunate to see it on fire like that," Sheldon finally broke the silence. "I have so many memories of this place. We played there for hours, making up all kinds of stories, playing house, hiding, and seeking or conquering each other's camp. Remember my scary dream about the homeless man in the living room and all the flood water."

"Yes, but your scary experience was only a dream. Mine was real!" Levin exclaimed. "I will never forget that day. I got up…"

§

It was early Monday morning, and Sheldon was getting ready for school when Levin came rushing into his room out of breath. "You look like you have seen a ghost," Sheldon remarked, looking curiously at Levin.

"I had left my schoolbook at the old house, and I need it today at school," Levin explained, still somewhat out of breath. "And…"

"Why did you take your book up there?" Sheldon interrupted him to ask.

"I wanted to get some reading done while we were there playing," Levin replied. "I got up early and rode my bike up there to get the book."

The old house was so big it had two back and two front doors. Levin went in the back door on the north side and straight to the living room, where he left the book. He liked reading in the living room because it was one of the rooms that had carpet. The carpet was softer to lie on than the hardwood. The living room was well-lit, which made it great for reading. However, the book was not there, and he was confident that was where he left it.

He heard a sound coming from upstairs and decided to investigate. He headed to the back set of stairs that led to the second floor. As he went up the stairs, he noticed the house was silent. The only other sounds were the echo of the stairs creaking with each step and birds outside. When you are alone, you tend to notice more prevalent things. Levin noticed the smell of old wood, musty carpet, and years of being heated with a wood-burning stove. He assumed that the noise was a raccoon.

He reached the second floor and stopped to listen for the sound again. At this point, he had forgotten entirely about the book. The upstairs had no hallway to get from one end to the other, so he had to walk through the bedrooms. He reached one of the middle bedrooms and discovered the book in the corner. He thought it was a peculiar place for his book but assumed Sheldon had been messing with him and put it in that room. He crossed the room, grabbed the book, and as he turned to leave the room, he heard what he thought was a baby crying. He convinced himself he was hearing things and continued back through the rooms.

He was headed towards the stairs when he heard a baby crying again. He stopped in his tracks. That was weird. He really must be hearing things. He listened closely to see if he heard it again. He went to take a step, and the unmistakable sound of a baby started crying again. He thought it was too weird not to investigate where this sound originated. He moved back through the bedrooms towards the sound, which was getting louder and louder. The closer he got to the attic door, the louder the sound.

"Tell me you didn't go upstairs!" Sheldon exclaimed, interrupting the story with wide eyes.

"Be quiet and listen," Levin chortled at Sheldon, annoyed at being interrupted.

Levin tried to open the attic door quietly, but it creaked as it opened. At this point, it was evident that the baby was crying from the dimly lit attic. He proceeded up the stairs as calmly and quietly as possible to investigate.

By this point in the story, Sheldon was biting his nails and listening intently.

His brother got to the top of the stairs and scanned the area to see what the sound was and where the sound was coming from. In the corner, he could see something standing there. His heart seized as a dark figure stepped out, holding a crying baby. He froze in place for a split second.

He had seen enough. He bolted down the stairs and out of the house like his ass was on fire. Levin peddled his bike as fast as his feet could go. He did not even take the time to look back to see if someone was following him.

Levin and Sheldon just stared at each other for a moment. "Are you for real?" Sheldon choked out. However, he knew his brother well enough that the look in his eyes said it all.

"Will you come back with me to see what that was?" Levin asked with a pleading look on his face.

"Are you crazy?!" Sheldon shrieked, looking at Levin as if he had lost his mind. "I'm not going back there! Plus, we have to get to school!"

Just then, the bus driver honked the horn, and this bus driver waited for no one. One honk, and she kept on moving. Sheldon and Levin rushed to grab their book bags and flew out the front door.

§

"Oh wow, I had forgotten about the crying baby," Sheldon commented thoughtfully, staring back at the house engulfed in flames as the walls began to collapse. At this point, the firefighter had given up on saving the structure. Now their goal was to keep it from spreading to the wooded area.

"So many memories here," Sheldon added as a tear ran down his face."

Emotions made Levin uncomfortable. "Speaking of fires," Levin stated trying to change the subject. "Remember when you set that field on fire to get out of working?"

"I didn't set the fire, you did!" Sheldon exclaimed as he turned his head to look at Levin. He then laughed at the look on Levin's face when he realized he was joking. "I will never forget that day…

§

Sheldon, Levin, and their dad were clearing a section of mowed grass along the highway. They were collecting the hay for their horses. Sheldon and Levin had stopped for a drink of water.

"Do you want to finish this quickly?" Levin asked with a devilish look on his face.

"How?" Sheldon queried with a furrowed brow.

Levin pulled out a book of matches. "This is how; we will wait till a car goes by. I will toss a lit match into a pile of hay. Then I will say the car threw out a cigarette butt," Levin plotted as he kept an eye on their Father.

"Yaaa, then we can go home early!" Sheldon quietly exclaimed as his face lit up with excitement.

Sheldon set off to distract their dad while Levin spotted a car coming. As the car went by, Levin struck the match and tossed it in a pile of dead grass near the road, but nothing seemed to happen. He didn't think it was going to work when suddenly a small amount of smoke appeared, and then all hell broke loose.

The grass was so dry it literally burst into flames, immediately scaring the horses, who took off running along the highway with the wagon in tow. Sheldon's eyes got as big as pop bottles. "Whaaaa the…" Sheldon uttered. He could not even complete a sentence.

The fire spread rapidly. Their father took off after the horse while Sheldon flagged down a woman in a passing car. The lady came to a stop beside him.

"Oh, Lord Jesus, there's a fire!" The lady exclaimed.

"Can you take me to the church down the road to call the fire department?" Sheldon asked.

"Of course, get in," The lady instructed him.

Sheldon paused just before he got into the car, *Wait you're not supposed to get into a car with a stranger, but there is a fire! Get in!*

As the lady drove him to the church she asked, "What happened?"

"A car drove past. Next thing I knew, there were flames everywhere," Sheldon answered, trying not to look the lady in the eye.

"Thank the lord no one was hurt!" The lady exclaimed, looking in the rearview mirror.

The lady dropped him off in front of the church. Sheldon ran in and asked the people working in the church to call the fire department.

Sheldon came out of the church and the lady was already gone. He started to walk back along the highway, he could smell and see the smoke filling the air. The sounds of sirens were getting closer and closer. Sheldon could see that the fire had spread quickly across the field to the trees that were engulfed in flames.

Their father explained to the firefighter that a car had gone by, and shortly after that, the flames had started. There were no more questions and no further discussion. They never played with fire like that again.

§

As the sun set, sobs could be heard coming from an old storage shed behind Sheldon's house. In the back, lying over the top of an old, worn-out deep freeze unit, was Sheldon. He tried to stay positive, especially when teased. He acted like it did not bother him, but sometimes things got too much. Like yesterday when he was called a Fag while walking into the grocery store.

By this point, he was crying uncontrollably. "Whyyyy Whyyyy?!" Sheldon cried out, looking towards the sky. Why can't I just be normal like everyone else?" he asked, sobbing through his tears. Why did these guys have to single me out, call me names, and why does it matter to me?" He cried so much that his throat began to hurt.

He laid his head back down on the freezer and sobbed uncontrollably. Sheldon raised his head with tears streaming down his face. "Why do I feel so alone? Why do I have to be so different? Why can't I just fit in like everyone else?"

For as long as he could remember, he knew he was different, and people would never let him forget. However, he never let those differences keep him from living his life but sometimes he would find himself trying to be what others wanted him to be.

Through his sobs, Sheldon heard his Mom calling his name. He whipped his face as he tried to put on his best happy face and went to see what she wanted. His Mom had good news. His cousins were coming to visit soon and might be staying indefinitely. That night, Sheldon was excited about his cousins coming to visit and about the hot guy he saw in the grocery store. Thinking about those things helped to distract him as he drifted off to sleep.

Chapter Two

The Chase Begins

Sheldon sat on the bus, staring out the window. It was Monday morning, the second week of his sophomore year. The school had just purchased new buses, and he enjoyed the smell of the new leather seats. He had tried to read a book but was distracted by his thoughts and nervousness about the new school year.

During his freshman year, Sheldon had made friends with a few senior girls, Tammy, Susie, Joanie, and Alsea, whom he met in choir class. Tammy Lowry was the most popular girl at school, meaning Sheldon was immediately in with most seniors. Tammy took Sheldon in like he was her little brother. Tammy's boyfriend Trevor would defend Sheldon when the other kids tried to bully him. Sheldon looked up to Trevor with great admiration. He thought this must be what it was like to have an older brother, which was a wonderful feeling. Trevor coincidently happened to be the school quarterback, so everyone respected his authority. No one bothered Sheldon as they did in junior high.

Sheldon was the only freshman invited to the senior prom. Susie's boyfriend had bailed on her at the last minute, so she asked Sheldon if he wanted to go in his place. Sheldon was excited to go to the prom and hang out with his senior friends. Sheldon had never been to a formal dance before, so the preparations were challenging, but he succeeded and looked sharp in his tux. They danced all night.

His senior friends graduated and went off to college. He had become concerned that it would not be long before the taunting and teasing would start since he no longer had the protection of his senior friends.

Since kindergarten, Sheldon and his brother have ridden the bus to school every day. This year, Sheldon will get his driver's license. As he thought about taking driver's education, he smiled.

Today, Sheldon was one of the last to get off the bus. He exited the bus and noticed his brother Levin was already ahead of him. As Sheldon walked up the sidewalk, someone caught his eye. He saw a handsome-looking guy standing near the building. This mysterious new guy turned to greet someone, and that is when Sheldon got a good look at his face. As he got closer, he realized it was the guy he had seen at the grocery store, and his heart leaped. The guy had a sharp jawline, prominent brow, and sexy full lips. In a school this small, everyone knew everyone. The new guy was walking with someone but could not see who. Then the crowd parted, and he could see it was his brother Levin. How did his brother know this guy? He was determined to find out but did not want to raise suspicion.

Sheldon's last period was a work program, which meant he got to leave school and go to work. When Sheldon was fifteen and a freshman, he received permission to work part-time at a local grocery store. Sheldon continued working there throughout the summer. After the seventh period, Sheldon would go to his locker and put away his books. He would get out whatever he needed for homework that night. With the books in his backpack, he headed to the main hall leading to the school's entrance. The main entrance faced Main Street, which takes him straight to work. As he turned the corner to the main hallway, he saw Laramie Miller. He was chatting up some freshmen girl. They had yet to see Sheldon, so he quickly turned and went in the other direction. He was not in the mood for any trouble, so he decided to cut through the gym instead.

As Sheldon walked across the gym floor, he noticed how strange it was to be alone without lights. The gym was eerily quiet and did not seem as big of a space in the dark. He could see the exit sign on the opposite side of the gym. He headed for the exit when he suddenly heard a sound, causing him to stop dead in his tracks. The sound seemed to be coming from behind the bleachers like someone was behind it, or maybe it was a mouse; no, it sounded too big to be a mouse. The gym was too dark to see anything. He decided he did not want to stick around and find out, so Sheldon took off as fast as he could and flew out the gym doors.

Sheldon rounded the corner of the building when he practically ran over someone. He turned to see the new guy standing there. Sheldon could tell immediately this guy was not expecting anyone to come out those doors and quickly hid his cigarette. Sheldon turned and started walking backward, slightly out of breath, as he looked the new guy up and down. This time, he was able to get a better look at himself. Not only did this guy have a handsome face, but a fantastic body. He wore a shirt with the sleeves cut out, and you could see his biceps, triceps, pecks, and abs. This guy had the body of a quarterback and deep blue eyes.

"You didn't see that," The new guy commanded with a dimple smirk using his charm.

"See what?" Sheldon played dumb and returned the guy's smirk with a cheesy smile.

The guy was still smiling as he turned to go back inside. Sheldon could see the V shape of his back muscle, followed by a killer butt. Sheldon could not help but daydream about that butt the whole time at work. As he bagged the groceries, he almost put eggs on a loaf of bread. He made it his goal to find out more about this guy.

When Sheldon got home from work, he was relieved that his brother had already finished the chores. Having a job, going to school, doing chores and homework can sometimes be overwhelming. He found his brother in his room with his nose in a book. Sheldon popped his head into his brother's room to thank him for completing the chores. The brother grunted in acknowledgment and kept reading without looking up from his book.

"Hey, who was that guy you were walking with this morning," Sheldon inquired matter-of-factly.

His brother looked up from his book thoughtfully for a moment. "Oh, that was Chase, a transfer student," Levin answered plainly and continued reading. Sheldon, not wanting to seem suspicious, left it alone, content with a name to the face.

The next day at school, Sheldon kept an eye out for the new guy, but he was absent from his classes. After lunch, Sheldon walked to his locker to get a book for his next class. Lyssa Mallozzi, whose locker was next to his, was digging for something in her purse. Since Lyssa's last name began with an MA like Sheldon's, they had been seated next to each other most of their school careers.

Suddenly, there was a burst of giggles, which caused Sheldon and Lyssa to stop what they were doing and look to see what was going on. "Give me a break," Lyssa scoffed as she rolled her eyes. "You would think these senior girls had never seen a pretty boy."

When Sheldon spotted Chase, Sheldon could not stop staring. "Not you, too," Lyssa groaned as she threw her purse over her shoulder. "You realize he is a freshman?" Sheldon was still staring as Lyssa slammed her locker, trying to get Sheldon's attention. "You people are pathetic!" Lyssa shouted as she headed to class. The fact that Chase was a freshman never crossed his mind, but it explained why Chase was not in any of his classes and how Levin knew him.

§

After weeks of classroom training, Sheldon passed the written part of the exam to get his driver's license. He was excited to start the behind-the-wheel training. However, he was intimidated by the instructor, Coach David, who always favored the athletes. Sheldon was to meet in the teacher's parking lot for training.

After lunch, Sheldon made his way out of the building and towards the parking lot. Sheldon didn't want to admit it, but he was pretty nervous. Sheldon crossed the parking lot looking for the driver's ed car and spotted someone leaning against it. When he got closer, he recognized that it was Chase, and his heart skipped a beat.

"Wha…What are you doing here?" Sheldon clambered to get the words out.

"Uhh…Driver's training," Chase laughed with his head cocked to the side and a half smile on his face.

Linda, who was in Sheldon's grade and had taken the class together, showed up, breaking their gaze at each other. "Linda, are you okay?" Sheldon asked when he noticed she did not look well. "You don't look so good."

"Yea, you're looking a little green," Chase added.

Linda bobbed her head up and down, trying to say yes, but she quickly turned and lost her lunch. After spitting and trying to get it all out of her mouth, she grumbled, "I know we have to do this to get our license," Linda grumbled as she stood back up, wiping her mouth and looking slightly less green. But I don't think I can." Linda pulled back her blond hair and spewed more of her lunch over the parking lot.

"So that's what the school lunch looks like the second time around," Chase joked, trying to make light of the situation.

"You're going to do well," Sheldon encouraged as he tried not to laugh, feeling bad for her.

"What's going on here?" A voice boomed across the parking lot, and they turned to see Coach Ted walking towards them. Sheldon quickly looked to Chase for support.

"She must have eaten something bad for lunch," Chased answered, trying to downplay the situation so the coach would not give Linda a tough time.

Coach Ted gave them all a severe look. "All right then, let's get started," Coach bellowed. "Who wants to go first?"

No one said a word and just looked at each other, hoping the other would volunteer. The three had been expecting Coach David to give them their behind-the-wheel driver training, and they were unfamiliar with Coach Ted .

"Sorry, I guess I should explain what's going on," Coach Ted said as he cleared his throat. "Coach David has broken his leg and won't be able to give you behind-the-wheel training." He turned to Sheldon, "You will drive first, Majors, but… before we start, we need to go over some rules."

He read through the rules: "Always check your tires, and make sure you adjust your seat and all your mirrors. "Sheldon was trying to pay attention, but all he could think about was what the heck Chase was doing there with his sexy lips. Chase had his arms crossed, and Sheldon stared at his biceps.

"You think you're ready, Majors?" Coach Ted interrupted his daydream. "I think so, Coach," Sheldon's voice sounded shaky but confident. He could not believe he would have to go first while

Chase watched.

Sheldon walked around the car, checking the tires. While everyone else got into the car, Sheldon adjusted his seat and checked the side mirrors accordingly. He started the car and began to put it in drive. "I'm going to stop you right there," Coach Ted interjected. You're not ready; you forgot to check your rearview mirror and ensure everyone has on their seatbelt," he instructed as he wrote something down on his clipboard.

Sheldon watched him writing. *What the fuck did he just write down?* Sheldon nodded his head in agreement. He adjusted the review mirror, noticing Chase looking back at him with humor in his eyes. Sheldon quickly looked away and then looked back again. "Does everyone have their seat belts on?"

In the rearview mirror, Sheldon could see Chase holding in his laughter. "Sir, Yes, Sir!" Chase shouted.

By this point, Linda was feeling more at ease. Sheldon's nerves had settled a bit, even though Chase being in the car amplified them. Coach Ted instructed Sheldon to turn right onto Main Street. Sheldon turned on the turn signal and proceeded to make a right turn. After a few blocks, Coach had him take another right, taking them into a residential area with less traffic. While Sheldon drove, Coach Ted proceeded to talk to Chase. "So, De Longpre, do you think this season will be good?"

"Well, coach, if we can get our offensive line to work together and the wide receivers would stop dropping the ball, I think we will stand a chance of having a winning season," Chase hypothesized.

Sheldon tried to follow their conversation. *What language is he speaking, and why is the coach asking him? Also, why do they seem to know each other so well?* He kept glancing in the review mirror, watching Chase's lips move. He wondered what it would be like for his lips to touch them. They were driving slowly when the car suddenly stopped; Sheldon had not even touched the brake. Couch had used his brake on his side to stop the vehicle. "Boy, are you trying to kill us? Can't you see there is a stop sign up ahead?" Coach shouted at him.

The car had stopped about fifteen feet from the stop sign. Sheldon was confused, he might have been a little distracted, but they were still far from the sign.

"You see, right there is a classic example of distracted driving," Coach scoffed. He seemed excited to use Sheldon as an example. Tell me, Majors, precisely what were you thinking about that was so important? Hum? I am waiting. We are all waiting since it was all our lives you just put at risk. Tell us what was so darn important?"

Sheldon's mind was racing. *Was he joking? He cannot be for real. I think he is deadly serious with the look on his face, and he is not letting go of that brake, but what can I tell him? I sure as hell can't tell him what I was thinking.* "I was thinking we hadn't checked the turn singles to make sure they are properly working," Sheldon blurted out the first thing that came to mind. *God, there is no way he is going to buy that excuse.*

The Coach looked at him with a severe expression. "Wow, I believe you're right," the Coach acknowledged, seemingly caught off guard. Now pull this car over next to the curb so we can thoroughly inspect the lights on this car."

Sheldon pulled the car to the side of the street and parked it. Coach Ted got out of the vehicle and had Sheldon tap the brakes and turn on and off the headlights. Then, he requested Sheldon to turn on the right turn single and the left turn single and leave the hazards on. Coach instructed Chase to take the driver's seat next. Sheldon could not help but feel relieved that he could be the passenger for the time being.

"I can't believe he bought that flimsy excuse," Chase smirked as he passed Sheldon, and they traded places. "I know better," Chase winked at him.

What did he mean by that, and did he just wink at me? The coach did not seem to care that Chase did not adjust his mirrors or signal before pulling away from the curb. "Take the next left," Coach instructed Chase. "Didn't your family move into where the old Chalcraft house used to be?"

"I believe so," Chase replied. "It was an empty lot when my dad first got here."

"Take another left here," Coach instructed.

As the car turned, you could see a new, beautiful two-story home that had been built on the corner where Chalcraft's house used to be before it had burned down.

"Did your dad build this himself?" Coach asked Chase.

"Yea, which is kind of his thing," Chase responded. "He owns his own construction company."

"So, this is where he lives," Sheldon muttered.

"What did you say?" Linda asked as she turned to look at Sheldon.

"Nothing," Sheldon replied with a dismissive look on his face. Sheldon had forgotten she was even in the car because she had been so quiet, and Chase had distracted him.

Knowing where Chase lived and where he laid his head down at night brought a little joy to Sheldon's day. However, he was not quite sure why it mattered. Sheldon realized they were down the street from his job as they drove past the house. Coach asked Chase to pull the car over because it was Linda's turn. Linda sighed nervously and slid down in the seat. Linda was having a lot of anxiety over this whole behind-the-wheel training. Sheldon remembered that in class, she aced every written test and knew the rules of the road handbook from front to back.

Linda and Chase both got out of the car. Sheldon suddenly realized Chase would sit beside him, and his heart started racing. Sheldon suddenly got butterflies in his stomach, and his hands were sweaty. He noticed that Chase even smelled nice as he got into the car. Also, Chase seemed relieved not to be in the driver's seat.

He wanted to say something to Chase, but everything that came to mind seemed ridiculous. He pondered if he should say anything while Coach instructed Linda on what to do next. The Coach gave Linda just as hard of a time as Sheldon. She was highly nervous. She put the car in reverse and gunned it. They jumped backward suddenly; luckily, no one was behind them. The Coach was not expecting that even after years of experience, probably because it happened so fast. However, the coach was patient with her. "Okay, let's try this again," Coach requested calmly. "Just make sure to put the car in the drive this time and check to make sure it's ok to pull away from the curb."

Not long after Linda's rough start, she drove better than Sheldon and Chase. Coach continued to talk to Chase. Sheldon was tuning in and out of the conversation they were having. He did catch that Chase was in Coach Ted's morning driver-ed class, which had to be combined with the afternoon class for behind-the-wheel training since Coach David had broken his leg. Chase was a year older than the rest of his class because his birthday was the first of September, and Chase missed the cut-off to start school. For that reason, he was able to get his license before the rest of the freshman class.

Before Sheldon knew it, they were already back at school, and their first day of behind-the-wheel training was done. "Next time, we are going out on the open road and learning about maintaining speed and how to use the passing lanes properly," Coach Ted instructed as they exited the car.

Driver's training flew by too fast. Sheldon enjoyed being in Chase's presence. Chase's arm would brush up against Sheldon's, or their hands would happen to touch, and chills would go up and down Sheldon's spine. Chase would smile at him like it was nothing. Sheldon could not help but wonder what was going through his mind. Sometimes, he could tell Chase was lost in his thoughts, too.

After eight weeks of behind-the-wheel training, Sheldon passed the test and got his driver's license. He was itching to drive his baby blue Chevy Nova convertible to work instead of walking. Plus, it meant this winter, he would not have to walk in the snow to work.

On Saturdays, when Sheldon had to work, he would go out of his way to drive by Chase's house. It was like he had become somewhat obsessed with Chase. He was unsure why, but the idea of seeing or even a glimpse of him—would make his day. Sheldon often drove by Chase's place and never saw him outside, but it had been a cold winter. He began to think he did not live there.

Then, one spring day, he saw Chase in the yard tinkering with some old vehicle. It was a beautiful spring day. The flowers bloomed, the temperature was a perfect seventy degrees, and the birds sang. Sheldon had gone to town to get a few things at the grocery store and decided to drive by Chase's place. It had been a while since he had done it, and he thought, what the heck? Sheldon's heart leaped at the sight of Chase bent over his car's engine. Chase's pants were tight against his butt. Sheldon did not know it, but Chase looked up and saw him drive by. Chase walked down to the street to confront him.

Sheldon circled the block to get one more glimpse before he headed home. Chase was standing between the sidewalk and the curb when Sheldon drove by again. As Sheldon turned the corner, he was going slower to catch a better view, but this time Chase stepped out into the street shouting, "What? What do you want?" Sheldon panicked and hit the gas, causing the tires to squeal in his haste to get away. Sheldon could see in his rearview mirror that Chase was in the street with his hands in the air. Sheldon flew down a side street, taking the next right turn. "What is wrong with me? Why am I obsessing over a guy? Am I gay?" Sheldon yelled at himself aloud for the first time.

This moment was the first time Sheldon started to admit aloud to himself that he might be gay, and to acknowledge that to himself was hard, let alone to say it aloud. His upbringing taught him to hate gay people. That being gay was a sin and an abomination against God. He felt so embarrassed that Chase had seen him stalking him. He decided then that there would be no more driving by his house. He headed straight home. *What if Chase tells his brother Levin? You only have to get through the next couple of weeks. Then it will be summer break.*

The next day at school, Sheldon had not seen Chase all morning. He began to think that he was in the clear. Then he spotted Chase at the end of the hall talking with his brother Levin. Oh god, please do not be telling my brother. Sheldon quickly hid behind some upperclassmen and went past them unnoticed. Whatever they were talking about, they were both so focused on their discussion that they had not noticed him. *Maybe if I avoid Chase, I will get through the next few weeks, but no one will know. Out of sight, out of mind, Chase might forget what happened.*

That night, when Sheldon got home from work, he was nervous about entering the house. He sat in his car for a few minutes. *Did Chase tell my brother, who in turn told Mom, and then they would disown me and kick me out of the house?* Sheldon pulled himself together and walked through the back door of their home. His Mom was the first to greet him. She asked him how work went and said she would make him a plate for dinner if he were hungry. So far, nothing out of the ordinary as he proceeded to his room. He put his book bag away and changed out of his work clothes. He passed by his brother's room and popped his head in to say hi, or at least that was what he told himself. His brother responded with his usual grunt without looking up from his book. Still nothing out of the ordinary so far; we are in the clear, he thought. After eating his dinner, he returned to his room to get some math homework done for tomorrow. He was solving an algebra problem when Levin popped his head in Sheldon's room. "How's it going," Levin asked, causing him to jump.

"Good, but I hate math," Sheldon wryly responded.

They both laughed, and Levin agreed, though he was good at math. Levin was still lingering at his door. *Shit, what is he about to say to me?* Levin cleared his throat. "Chase De Longpre asked me today if you were my brother, and at first, I almost said no but said yes anyway," Levin explained while he played with stuff on top of Sheldon's dresser. "I asked him why, and he just said he was curious." He turned his attention back to Sheldon, "Please don't do anything embarrassing. He has probably heard you're a weird freak or something."

Sheldon threw his pillow at Levin, who ducked as the pillow flew past his head and into the hallway. It knocked a picture off the wall and sent it crashing down the stairs. "It was Sheldon, not me!" Levin screamed so his mom would know it was not him this time. Levin didn't want to get blamed for breaking anything, so he took off downstairs. As he ran, he bent over to avoid another object being tossed at him.

Sheldon did well at avoiding Chase during the last two weeks of school, and the incident seemed forgotten. Everyone focused on the end-of-the-year finals and what they were doing that summer. Sheldon was excited for the start of the summer. *I'm out of the woods and want to put the past week's events behind me.* Sheldon turned on the radio and dressed for bed. As he climbed into bed, he heard Martina McBride singing, *Safe in the Arms of Love.* Lying there, he thought back to the times he was in the back seat of the driver's ed car, and Chase's hand would brush up against his. The feeling Sheldon got from his touch was so powerful. Whenever he thinks about it, he stops and tries to think of other things. But he could not shake the feeling that the Chase had just begun as he drifted off to sleep.

Chapter Three

Seven Hills

The sounds of birds chirping woke Sheldon, and before he opened his eyes to greet the day, he lay there listening to them. Also, he could hear Reba singing Little Rock in the background. Levin was already up and playing his favorite tune. "It's the second week of summer break. What happened to sleep in," Sheldon grumbled to himself as he pulled the pillow over his ears.

Their parents had separated. Their dad moved out, and they sold the farm. Mandy and the boys stayed in the family home and started working at a local horse ranch, which gave Sheldon and Levin more freedom to enjoy their summer break. They could sleep in as late as they wanted and did not have nearly as many chores. They had more time to read and explore the remains of the burned-out abandoned house up the road from their home.

Sheldon suddenly remembered his cousins were in town, which excited him enough to get out of bed. Levin heard Sheldon stirring around in his room and knocked on his door. "About time you woke up," Levin remarked as he walked into his room without waiting for a response. "Come on, let's ride our bikes over to Uncle Bob's and see what Ninnie and Jimmy are up to."

Mandy had two older brothers. Ted was the oldest, and Bob was a year older than her. Bob traveled the world selling generators. He and his family never lived in one place too long. They lived in several states, such as Louisiana, South Carolina, Georgia, Oregon, and California, and other countries, such as Germany and Japan.

They would visit the family regularly for holidays.

Sheldon and Levin were always excited when they came to visit. Their cousins were a bit on the wild side. They were far more experienced about the world and life in general. Plus, they always had the most incredible stories to tell and bring fascinating new things. For example, once, when they were younger, their cousins brought these books where you traced the outline of a figure or object on trace paper. Sheldon thought that was the coolest thing he had ever seen. However, with the arrival of their cousins came their Mother.

Their Mother, Letty, was the strictest person Sheldon and his brother had known aside from their father. When Aunt Letty was present, there was no talking with food in your mouth or elbows on the table during dinner. If she caught you with your elbows on the table, she would walk over, grab your wrist, and slam your elbows down on the table. If you talked with your mouth full, you got one warning the next time you left the table without finishing dinner.

When Sheldon and his brothers went to town with Aunt Letty and their cousins, they learned that you do not touch anything while in the store. Just before entering a store, Aunt Letty demanded they always keep their arms crossed and not touch a single item. One time, Sheldon wondered what would happen if they did touch something. Would she even know? Sheldon got his answer quickly. The youngest of their cousins, Jimmy, touched a pack of baseball cards, and as soon as they got to the van, he got the beating of his life.

While growing up, Sheldon and his brothers were not allowed to have friends over, let alone have a sleepover, so it was quite a treat when their cousins were in town to visit. Those times were some of his best childhood memories. At bedtime, someone would have to give up their bed to their Aunt and Uncle, which meant they would all be sleeping in the same room. After a fun-filled day of catching up, it was hard for them to wind down and immediately sleep. They would giggle even after their Aunt yelled, "Lights out!" After one warning, Aunt Letty would come in and spank whomever she thought was giggling. Aunt Letty put fear in anyone.

After years of traveling, Uncle Bob decided to retire and settle down. They bought a home closer to the family. He and his wife got local jobs to keep themselves from being bored, extra money to travel, and to save for their kids to go to college. Sheldon and his brothers loved the idea of their cousins staying permanently. That would mean they would go to school together and spend more time with them.

§

Sheldon and his brother arrived at their cousin's new place. They dropped their bikes and ran up to the front door. They pounded on the door with excitement. Jimmy opened the door and invited them inside. Sheldon immediately noticed a lot of unpacked boxes stacked everywhere. Even though there was clutter everywhere, their house was newer and more modern than their own.

"You came; that is awesome," Ninnie greeted them excitedly as she ran down the stairs. "Let me show you around," She requested as she grabbed Sheldon's arm.

"I was just about to take them outside and show them my new skateboard." Jimmy interrupted.

"No! Now, don't be rude, Jimmy," Ninnie commanded. "Let's show our guests around and offer them something to drink first." It was freaky because you could see a hint of their Mother in how she spoke to Jimmy.

Jimmy turned his back to his sister and mocked her by mouthing the words she just said to him as he stormed out through the garage door. He requested, "When you guys are done here, meet me outside," as he turned to close the door.

There are four cousins. Laynardia, Shawndrea, Ninnie, and Jimmy. Laynardia was the oldest. She was four years older than Sheldon and was away at college. They mostly hung out with the three younger cousins. Shawndrea was a year older than Sheldon. Sheldon and Ninnie were the same age. Jimmy and Levin were the same age, too. Sheldon and his brother enjoyed hanging out at their house because they had better games. They had a Nintendo, board games, and other electronic devices. That afternoon, their cousins were bored, and Shawndrea got an idea.

"Hey, let's go on a country cruise," she suggested with a look of anticipation as she urged them to say yes. Our parents will not be home from work for hours."

Sheldon was immediately onboard. Ninnie thought differently. She knew how Shawndrea always had a way of finding trouble, or trouble seemed always to find Shawndrea.

With much persuasion by Sheldon, Jimmy, and Levin, Ninnie gave in with a few conditions. "Okay, but we have to drive slowly; there is no speeding, and everyone must wear seat belts," Ninnie requested.

"Why do I always have to be the voice of reason here?" Ninnie grumbled under her breath.

They all piled into the green van. They flew down the highway with the windows down and the wind blowing their hair. Shawndrea turned up the radio, and they sang along to Jon Bon Jovi's *Blaze of Glory*. Shawndrea turned down the radio. "Do you all want to go on an adventure?" She asked.

Sheldon looked at Ninnie. "Don't look at me," She replied. "I have no idea what she is talking about, and whatever she thinks is not going to be a good idea."

"Oh, come on guys, don't be a stick in the mud," Shawndrea taunted. "It will be fun, come on!"

"No!" Ninnie shouted.

While everyone else shouted, "Yes!"

"Ding. Ding. Ding, looks like we have a winner!" Shawndrea chimed. "You're overruled, Ninn."

Shawndrea took the next left and flew down a gravel road, leaving a trail of dust behind them. Ninnie looked at Sheldon with a so-help-me look as she shook her head. "Oh lord, help us all," she prayed, looking worried. "Cause her adventures never end well." Ninnie kept looking over at the speedometer as she gripped the armrest of her seat like it was her lifeline.

Black Velvet came on the radio. "Oh my god, this is my song. Turn it up!" Ninnie demanded unexpectedly.

Ninnie started to sing along with the radio at the top of her lungs. They all joined in. Ninnie finally started to relax and seemed to be enjoying herself. They all laughed and were having an enjoyable time as the van sped down the road. "We're almost there, guys!" Shawndrea shouted. "Here we go!"

Suddenly, something seemed to take over Shawndrea. It was like she was possessed or thought she was a daredevil. She shoved the gas pedal to the floor and shouted, "This is gonna be fun!" Just before they went over the hill, she yelled, "Hold onto your knickers!"

Their stomachs dropped as they flew over the top of the first hill. As the vehicle came back down, they could not see the road. They could only see trees. Everyone in the van screamed as the van mashed back down, and gravel flew everywhere. They were all laughing except Ninnie. As they approached the second hill, Ninnie shouted, "Wait, how many hills are there?!"

They approached the peak of the second hill, and Shawndrea shouted again, "Hang on!"

They all shouted holy shits and oh my gods as their stomachs dropped again. They crashed down as gravel flew everywhere. "How many fucking hills are there?!" Ninnie yelled again.

At first, Shawndrea ignored her question and laughed like a mad woman. They approached the third hill. "Hang on… Oh, and there are seven hills!" She finally shouted.

Sheldon and Ninnie looked at each other with fear as the van flew through the air. "I'm too young to diiiiiiiiiieeee," Ninnie cried out. "This is entirely your fault!" Ninnie yelled at Sheldon, "You said, 'Yeah, let's go for an adventure.' 'Oh, ya, an adventure sounds like fun!" Ninnie mimicked them.

They approached the fourth hill. "If we make it out of this alive, you are all going to die!" Ninnie yelled as they flew through the air again. "Oh lord, if we wreck, please don't damage my beautiful face," Ninnie prayed.

They crashed back down. Sheldon thought that by this point, Shawndrea would have slowed down, but despite Ninnie's pleas, she seemed to have only sped up. As they approached the fifth hill, Shawndrea cried out again, this time laughing even louder. "Haaaaannng on!"

"This is it; we are really going to die," Sheldon mumbled. He had become concerned, too. It was fun at first, but now it seems dangerous.

Just as they came crashing down there was a car directly in front of them. Shawndrea quickly responded and swerved the vehicle, barely missing the oncoming vehicle. Ninnie was no longer shouting but shrieking, "Pull this God damn car over now!"

Meanwhile, Jimmy and Levin were in the back, loving every minute of it and laughing their butts off. As they flew over the sixth hill a pair of head lights appeared behind them. The car flew up on the rear end of the van. "I think it's the guy we almost ran into," Jimmy shouted from the back of the van.

"Almost ran into… Ha!! No, he got in OUR way," Shawndrea grumbled under her breath. The car started honking and flashing its lights as they flew over the last hill. "Hang on, guys, we have to get the fuck out of here," Shawndrea shouted with determination in her voice as she punched the gas pedal to the floor.

She took the next right as fast as possible, which seemed almost on two wheels, and headed for the highway. The highway would bring them back home. They got to the highway, but there was so much traffic that they had to wait for a break in the traffic. Suddenly, the guy from the other car was at the driver's door, trying to pull it open.

Shawndrea started yelling at the guy, "What the fuck is wrong with you?" The guy was close enough she got a good look at him. He was a young man mid-twenties. There was something about the way he screamed at her that got her juices flowing.

"What the fuck is wrong with you?!" He yelled back at her, still pulling on the door. "You're a crazy fucking driver!"

The word, crazy set Shawndrea on fire. She jumped out of the van and screamed, "Crazy, huh? How about you come closer and call me crazy?" As the word crazy came out of her mouth, she threw what was left of her Dr. Pepper in his face. "Maybe your mama should have taught you some manners on how you should speak to a lady."

Ninnie murmured under her breath, saying, "Oh god, here we go. You don't call a crazy person crazy."

The next thing you know, Shawndrea has the guy thrown up against the van and yelling, "You wanna see crazy? Huh? Okay, here is crazy!"

Shawndrea put the guy in a lip lock. Ninnie had gotten out of the van to save the guy from her sister. "What the hell! Only my sister can rub her legs together and get a crazy man to calm down enough to want to fuck!" Ninnie marveled with a chuckle.

Ninnie walked up to the two of them, who were already in full-on make-out mode. "Break it up, break it up; she is young enough to be your daughter!" Ninnie commanded as she pulled Shawndrea off the guy.

"How old do you think I am?" The guy asked, confused.

"Frankly I don't give a fuck how old you are," Ninnie snarled.

"When you're ready for that and more, give me a call," Shawndrea flirted as she backed away from him, licked her lips, and winked at the guy.

"Ya Ya enough hot pants, get in the van you have caused enough trouble for one day," Ninnie ordered as she shoved Shawndrea towards the van.

"What the fuck were you thinking?" Ninnie asked as they got into the van.

"What?!" Shawndrea exclaimed. "I was just having a little fun. Besides, he is not old enough to be my dad."

"Look at the van, it's covered in dust!" Ninnie cried out. "How are we going to explain this? We have to go to the car wash."

They left the scene of whatever had just happened and kept looking behind them to see if they were being followed. Heading into town, Sheldon could not help but think, what if they ran into Chase? He had not really seen Chase since his own little incident. They headed straight to the car wash.

"Ok, Jimmy you get the brush, Shawndrea you're in charge of the quarters and I will man the power washer nozzle thingy," Ninnie instructed like they had done this a million times.

"How about I man the power washer thingy and you do the quarters?" Shawndrea requested.

"Oh no, no, no, the last time you managed to get more water on us than the van cause a cute guy drove by," Ninnie argued as they pulled into the car wash bay. "Little Miss hot pants here, tends to get distracted and starts to spray water everywhere, but where she is supposed to. Just like a horny little freshman in the back seat that sprays his load before he has landed in the intended target."

"What the fuck, Ninn? I told you that in confidence, not for you to blab that shit in front of everybody!" Shawndrea exclaims as she exits the car, yelling around the van at her. "Besides, it was his first time. Who could blame him? Look at how hot I am. I could make any guy explode just looking at my naked bod," she said with a dramatic gesture up and down her body as Ninnie stared, gagging.

"Please, we do not need any visual images here," Ninnie pleaded, putting one hand in the air. "You win. Take the damn nozzle. It's all yours. Let's get this done and get home!"

As they were cleaning the car, Sheldon remembered when Aunt Letty showed him how to drive their manual pick-up. On the farm they had driven tractors a short distance, but had never been allowed to drive a vehicle before.

Aunt Letty drove the truck and trailer through the field as they loaded the trailer with bales of hay. Two people stacked the bales, and two people threw them onto the wagon to be stacked.

Aunt Letty extremely intimidated Sheldon. She called him over to the truck and asked if he wanted to learn to drive. At first, he did not know if she was joking or serious. "Yeah, that would be awesome," Sheldon cheered.

She told him to jump in the passenger seat and watch as she shifted the gears several times. For being such a forceful and aggressive person in life, she was patient and good at teaching Sheldon how to drive. Of course, she decided to teach when they were in the field picking up bales of hay. As they stacked the bails, the driver had to be careful not to take off too fast, or they would topple over, and you would have to start again. Anyone who learned to drive a manual knows that the first few times can be jumpy. The added pressure of the fact that everyone was watching. No biggie.

"Slowly let out on the clutch and, simultaneously, give it a little gas." Aunt Letty explained as she demonstrated.

Sheldon was repeating what she said when suddenly there was a bang, bang, causing him to jump. "Okay, Mom, let's move," Jimmy called, tapping on the roof.

Aunt Letty repeated in a nice, soft tone while demonstrating how to take off. She showed him a couple of times. "Are you ready? Do you think you got it?" she asked him.

"I believe so," Sheldon replied nervously.

They switched places. *Should I be doing this? What if something goes wrong?* He looked at Aunt Letty, and her smile made him feel more confident.

"You've got this," she told him. "Just remember what I showed you. With your foot on the break and the clutch, release the parking brake and put it into first gear. Take your foot off the brake and put it on the gas. As you press ever slightly on the gas, you slowly release the clutch."

Sheldon tried to do as instructed, but he released the clutch faster than he gave it the gas, and the truck lunged and died. When this happened, one of the hay bales came off the top and almost landed on Jimmy. "Hey! Are you trying to kill me back here?" Jimmy screeched.

"Oh, pipe down back there," Aunt Letty yelled back at him. "Jimmy, stop being so dramatic."

"Dramatic?" Jimmy asked looking around at everyone else. "Did you all just see how close that came to my head?!"

Sheldon thought Aunt Letty was going to be mad instead she just laughed. "It will do him some good and teach him to be on his toes," She scoffed, still laughing." It's ok Sheldon, let's try it again."

Sheldon tried it again, this time making sure not to let the clutch out too fast. It could be confusing at first to have the left foot do the opposite of the right. But he was successful the second time, and the truck slowly rolled forward, and they all cheered. It was good to see his Aunt smiling and laughing for a change.

When she was like this, Sheldon could see the real person under that tough exterior. "See, Sheldon, you can do anything you want to do. You just have to seize the moment, don't be afraid to ask, and don't be afraid of failure," she explained to him. We all fail from time to time, but the trick is to learn from your failures and don't be afraid to try again."

Sheldon was suddenly jerked out of his daydream by water hitting him. Ninnie had decided to hide behind him and use him as a shield. "Shawndee! I told you not to spray us!" Ninnie yelled.

"And I told you never to call me Shawndee," Shawndrea yelled as she shoved Sheldon out of the way so she could continue spraying Ninnie.

"Aaaaahhhh, that is cold! Stop!" Ninnie screamed as she was trying to catch her breath.

They were all laughing as the water came to a stop. "Now see, we are out of quarters, and soap is still on the car!" Ninnie shouted, thoroughly annoyed.

"I want to drive back!" Sheldon unexpectedly blurted out.

Ninnie turned to look at him. "Well, okay. Way to be assertive. You just might make it in this family after all," Ninnie commended him.

They all laughed as they got into the van.

As Sheldon drove, he couldn't help, but smile even though Jimmy and Shawndrea were having a disagreement about something, it was nice being part of a family. Sheldon and his brothers learned a lot about life from their cousins. Granted one of the things they learned was how to cuss, but being part of a family was the most important thing.

Sheldon turned the radio to a country station as someone moaned, "Ugghh, Country nooo!"

"This is my song, turn it up!" Levin shouted.

You hear Reba singing, *Little Rock*. They all started singing along with the radio…

Chapter Four

The Deep End

Saturday morning, their cousin's green van pulled into Sheldon's driveway. Their cousins excitedly jump out. "Come on, we are going to the swimming pool!" Jimmy yelled. Sheldon and his brother had never been to the pool, so Sheldon was excited but scared simultaneously. They had already finished their morning chores, so their mother agreed to let them go after their cousins convinced her to agree. Sheldon and his brother grabbed their cut-off shorts, and their cousins looked at them, shaking their heads. "You can't wear cut-off shorts to the pool!" Shawndrea said she chased one of their kittens, trying to catch and pet it, but it ran under their porch. "Come on, get in the van, and we will swing by and get a couple of Jimmy's old swim trunks."

They headed into town with the windows down and the music blaring. Sheldon could not help but be grateful that his cousins were in town. Their cousins always listened to what Sheldon and his brother called weird music. However, listening to their type of music showed them a different side of the world, outside the farm and small-town life.

Growing up, his cousins always talked about the different states they lived in and other countries they had traveled to. One of Sheldon's favorite places to hear about was California. He would always daydream that one day, he would go to California, a place he had always heard so much about. Sheldon's favorite song growing up was *All the Gold in California* by *The Gatlin Brothers*; something about it fascinated him.

They pulled into the pool parking lot, and Sheldon could not help but feel nervous. He saw some of his classmates and started to think this was not a good idea. Sheldon never quite fit into one group at school. Instead, he floated between clicks.

Sheldon refused to make eye contact with anyone as they walked into the pool area, though you could hear whispers. "What are the Majors boys doing here?"

Sheldon's brother and cousins had already headed for the pool's deep end. Sheldon was afraid of jumping into the deep end. He started in the shallow end and worked towards the deeper end. Sheldon had managed to get waist-deep when a shadow loomed over him. "Is everything okay over here?" The figure asked standing over him.

"Yeah, I'm good," Sheldon responded without looking up as he nervously ran his hands across the top of the water.

"You realize you're still in the shallow part?"

Sheldon tried to look up to see who was talking to him, but the sun glared in his eyes. The figure moved slightly to his right and blocked the sun out of Sheldon's eyes. He could now see who was talking to him. Sheldon froze when he realized it was Chase, and his heart started to beat faster. *What is he doing here at the pool?* He had been avoiding Chase since the whole driving past his house incident. Sheldon searched for the words to respond to Chase's question. What could he say that would not sound lame? "I'm just working my way in, I like taking my time," Sheldon finally responded.

"Suuuure, you are," Chase teased him with a huge smile.

Sheldon watched Chase walk back over to the lifeguard stand and climb back up. Sheldon felt the pressure to go into the deep end with Chase watching. His brother and cousins waved him to swim across the line and into the pool's deep end. Sheldon nervously smiled and started moving that way. He was trying not to stare at Chase's perfect body but failing. *Sheldon, why are you looking at his body? It's just wrong.* Sheldon found a comfortable spot in the pool that came almost up to his neck as his family tossed the ball back and forth to one another.

When they decided to start jumping off the diving boards, Sheldon decided that was not for him and escaped to the bathroom.

On the way to the bathroom, he saw Chase switched out with his replacement. Chase entered the locker room behind him.

"Hey", he said to Sheldon and went to his locker to get his duffle bag. He started to leave, but he stopped to talk with Sheldon. "There is nothing wrong with being afraid of the pool," Chase encouraged. "If you like, I can help you."

Sheldon's mouth twitched, fighting a smile, "Really?"

"Yeah," Chase affirmed. "I can teach you how to swim… That's if you're interested."

Sheldon's mind started to race. *Alone with this guy in a pool might not be a good idea.* A girl called Chase's name from outside the locker room. "Hey, I gotta go to practice. I will talk to you later," Chase concluded before Sheldon had a chance to reply.

As Chase left the locker room, a petite blond wrapped her arms around Chase and kissed him. Sheldon walked out of the locker room, lost in thought, *practice? What kind of practice is he talking about?* Sheldon did not even notice the girl till they were already walking away holding hands.

Suddenly, Ninnie jumped out from behind a wall. "What are you doing?!"

Sheldon jumped and fell into the bushes. Ninnie died with laughter as she pulled him up. "Come back to the pool."

They walked back to the pool area, and Ninnie pointed to her sister, who was trying to mack on the lifeguard that replaced Chase. "Well, would you look at that. if her legs were matches, we would all be on fire." Ninnie remarked as she shook her head back and forth, "You know it has to be like the Grand Canyon in there, wide open, with as many visitors as she has had in and out of there." They both laughed. "Come on, let's cannonball into the pool."

Sheldon looked at her; he had no idea what she was talking about. "Come on, you must know how to do a cannonball?" Sheldon shook his head. "Okay, let me show you."

She took off running to the pool. As she jumped, she pulled her knees to her chest, and when she hit the water, a large splash went everywhere. It splashed Shawndrea in the face and drenched her. "Ninn, that was not funny!" Shawndrea cried out.

"Sorry, I just thought you could use a good cooling off," Ninnie replied with a smirk.

Shawndrea gave Ninnie a "go to hell" look and turned her attention back to the lifeguard.

Sheldon sat on the side of the pool with his feet dangled in the water. He began to think about how he had avoided dating girls. That could be what he needed: find a girlfriend and stop thinking about boys. Have sex with a girl and get married like everyone else. But who could he date? He saw his classmate, Stacy, sitting on a lounge chair by herself.

Sheldon noticed Stacy quietly reading a magazine and blending in with the crowd. That is who he should try to date, someone who is simple and does not draw much attention. She could help get his mind off Chase. Besides, Chase had a girlfriend, then so could he. Even though this logic was not sound, it made sense to Sheldon then. He went over to talk to Stacy, but she rolled onto her belly and looked like she was about to sleep. He turned to walk away, and as he did, he saw a new face.

The new girl was sitting on a lounge chair in the corner under an umbrella, reading a book. Sheldon walked over and asked the girl what she was reading. The girl was so into the book that she did not realize someone was speaking to her. "So, what are you reading?" Sheldon asked again as he straightened the back of a chair next to her and sat down.

The girl looked at Sheldon as he sat in a chair beside her, making himself comfortable. She stumbled to find the words. "I'm reading *Four Past Midnight*..." she replied hesitantly.

"*Stephen King's* new book!" Sheldon blurted out excitedly interrupting her. "I haven't got a copy yet. I just finished reading his book *The Dark Half*. He is such an amazing writer."

It was like a floodgate opened, and Sheldon rattled on and on about Stephen King. He even started to talk about some of his other favorite books and asked her if she had ever read *The Box Car Children* series. The girl just looked at him while he went on and on.

Sheldon kicked back in the chair and started talking to the stranger like they had known each other forever. The girl was a little taken aback by Sheldon's boldness, though she was impressed with how forward he was with a stranger. "I'm Sheldon, by the way."

He greeted her with his hand outstretched.

The girl hesitated momentarily, "Uh, I'm Ruby," She replied taking his hand with reservation.

Over at the lifeguard's chair Ninnie was still pushing Shawndrea's buttons. "I think he is here to save our lives, not to take a tour of your used merchandise." Ninnie quipped.

Before Shawndrea could respond, the lifeguard's girlfriend arrived at the pool area. She was talking to her friends, who were too happy to fill her in on what transpired. The girlfriend's name was Yesenia. She was yet another bouncing, big boob, bleached blonde. She immediately strutted over to where her boyfriend and Shawndrea were flirting with each other. She walked up to Shawndrea and shoved her into the pool. "I think you need to cool off a bit Little Miss Slutty Pants," Yesenia snarled when Shawndrea surfaced.

"Hey, Ninnie that's just what you said!" Jimmy shouted to Ninnie.

Ninnie looked at Sheldon and mouths the words, "Little Miss Slutty Pants?" She proceeded to say, "Uh, yea I did, Jimmy. Okay, boys, that is our cue to pack it up for the day. Get your stuff. We're headed home. I'm gonna get my sister before she does something crazy." Ninnie paused as she thought about what she just said. "Okay something crazier than normal."

Sheldon turned to his new friend. "Well, it was nice to meet you, Ruby. See you around."

They climbed into the van, and Ninnie turned to Shawndrea. "Boy, we haven't even started school here, and you have already made a best friend. Geez, isn't that swell?" Ninnie started the van and shook her head.

"Look, I do not need any of your crap right now. Besides, how was I to know the lifeguard had a girlfriend? He was flirting just as much as I was with him." Shawndrea defended herself.

"Yea, Shawndrea, we can't go anywhere without you causing a ruckus," Jimmy added with a mischievous chuckle.

"Et Tu, little brother?" Shawndrea gasped dramatically. "No loyalty these days, and Ninn, why didn't you let me kick that little bleach blond whore's ass?" Ninnie just ignored her and kept driving.

On the drive home, Sheldon could not stop thinking about what Chase had offered. Sheldon thought for sure he was going to be pissed and tell him not to come by his house again. It was as if Chase had forgotten all about the incident.

"What's next, guys?!" Shawndrea shouted. "What next adventure do you guys want to do now?"

"Ummm, no. You are grounded from making decisions for this group. You're in big trouble, missy," Ninnie commanded with authority in her voice. "I'm driving, and I say we are going home."

"Poo, you're seriously no fun," Shawndrea scoffed. "That's okay. I'm gonna meet up with him later anyway."

Ninnie's head flew around so fast. "Excuse me, I don't think so."

"Why, you're not the boss of me," Shawndrea retorted.

"Okay, let's see what Mom and Dad think about it," Ninnie snapped back.

"Fine, let's see what they think of the Hustler magazine under your mattress," Shawndrea hastily replied.

"You have been snooping in my room?!" Ninnie gasped and stammered a bit. "I… I was reading it for the stories; besides, it's Dad's copy anyway. I was only borrowing it."

"Wait, there's a hustler magazine in the house? Can I see?" Jimmy beamed.

"No!" Ninnie and Shawndrea both shouted.

Ninnie looked at Shawndrea. "You're really meeting up with this guy?"

"Yes." She replied.

Ninnie shook her head. "I give up, go, go and be a whore," Ninnie conceded, utterly exasperated and out of breath.

Ninnie pulled the van into their driveway before she even stopped the van Shawndrea opened the door and jumped out, yelling at Ninnie, "Fine, I will; at least I'm getting some; maybe if you got laid, you wouldn't act like you always have a stick up your ass."

Ninnie put the van in park. She sat there with her mouth open, trying to close it to say something but could not form the words. "Guys, do I act like I have a stick up my, you know what?" She pleaded for an answer.

"Yup, pretty much all the time," Jimmy answered with a giggle as he jumped out of the van.

Sheldon and his brother sat, afraid to say a word, and just looked at each other while Ninnie muttered to herself. "I guess we better get home. Thanks for taking us today," Sheldon offered as they left and headed toward their place.

§

A few weeks later, Sheldon had to work while his brother hung out with their grandmother at her house. He felt left out and would instead have gone with his brother. He was so busy at work he did not have time to think about it. The store was having a huge sale, and the place was packed. Now he realized why so many people were scheduled to work that day. It was like during the winter when the weather forecast called for a winter storm. Everyone rushed to the store to get bread and milk. The shelves would be bare in no time.

Today, there was a massive sale of meat, dairy, and vegetables. There were many times before Sheldon had envied the cashiers because they did not have to go out in the rain and the snow. However, he did not envy them today because it was a madhouse in the store, and some of the sale items would not scan correctly and had to be manually entered into the cash register. The cashiers had to keep overriding the prices. Plus, it was a beautiful day outside, and he enjoyed it, even for a moment.

Sheldon was carrying groceries for Mrs. O'Grady when he saw Chase walking across the parking lot toward the store. His heart started pounding and his palms got sweaty. When Chase got closer, he looked up, smiled, and nodded at Chase as he walked past. Sheldon walked back into the store, messing with his hair to ensure it was not too out of place. He went and started to bag the next customer's groceries. Sheldon's manager came over and told him to take his lunch break after he finished with the next customer.

Sheldon looked up and saw Chase standing in line with a bottle of soda. As Sheldon bagged the groceries, he could feel Chase watching him. Sheldon started feeling self-conscious as Sheldon placed the grocery items into the bags. At this point, Sheldon could effectively bag groceries with his eyes closed, but at that moment, he was off. Sheldon was so thrown off that he didn't even realize whose groceries he was bagging, which happened to be Ruby, the girl he met at the pool, and her Mom. He would have said something to her if he had not been distracted.

Sheldon helped the next customer carry her groceries to the car. As he headed back in, he saw Chase standing near the store's entrance. He smiled at Sheldon, and Sheldon smiled back. "How's it going?" Sheldon inquired.

"Good, just working on my dad's old car," Chase replied. "Do you get a break soon?"

"Yes," Sheldon answered nervously.

"Great, do you mind if I sit with you for a bit?" He asked.

"Sure, let me clock out for lunch and get my stuff," Sheldon said with a smile.

Sheldon came out to find Chase sitting at a table in the shade. Sheldon had gotten a sandwich from the deli and offered half of it to Chase, who politely declined. "So, what was it like growing up on a farm?" Chase inquired, looking at Sheldon.

Sheldon was taken aback. He had never been asked that question; he thought for a second and took a drink to wash down his food. "Humm, good question," Sheldon pondered for a click. "Well, it can be very difficult at times. We didn't really have a normal childhood growing up, and our dad was very hard on us. There was no getting up on Saturday mornings to watch cartoons. We had to get up early to care for the animals, whether it was raining, snowing, cold or sunny. The winters were horrible because the livestock's water would freeze, and you would have to break the ice so they could drink or get hot water to melt enough for them to drink. I could go on and on all day. Where are you originally from, and what brought you here?"

Chase had listened to Sheldon talk and was amazed at how different their lives were growing up. "We are originally from Santa Monica, California," Chase answered his question. "I grew up not far from the beach. My dad had done well in the construction business. I grew up with the sun almost always shining and plenty of beaches for surfing. One of my favorite places as a kid was the Santa Monica Pier. Still, as I grew older, I preferred the more secluded beaches, fewer tourists, and certain beaches are better for surfing.

My dad had a friend who lived here in Southern Illinois. He had wanted a change of scenery and to get out of the city. His business partner ended up stealing most of the business money. He was in charge of the finances of the business. He was putting most of the earnings into a separate bank account in his name. Once Dad realized this, his partner went to the bank, removed the rest of the business money, and took off. My dad decided that was a sign to make a change, and here we are. One day, I plan to return; I miss the sun and the great weather."

Sheldon hung onto every word he spoke. "I have always wanted to go to California for some reason," Sheldon confessed.

"You should definitely go. You will love it there," Chase encouraged him with smile. "I guess I had better let you get back to work."

Sheldon had utterly lost track of time. He enjoyed having someone to talk to. "Yeah, I guess I had better get back to it," Sheldon agreed, standing up. "I will talk to you later?"

"Yeah, see you later," Chase concurred as he got up from the table. "And thanks for talking to me."

Sheldon nodded and went back inside to clock back in and finish the rest of his shift.

That night, Sheldon was lying in bed listening to the radio. He was lost in his thoughts, thinking about being at the swimming pool. He chuckled out loud, thinking about Shawndrea being called "Little Miss Slutty Pants" and being shoved into the pool. He thought how fun it was to spend time together with his cousins. He smiled when he thought about Chase's eyes, how he smiled at him, and how the sun glistened off his sculpted pecs. Getting to know more about him and where he grew up was excellent. His eyes started to close when he heard *The Gatlin Brothers* singing *All the Gold*. Sheldon's eyes shot open, *that was freaking weird I was just thinking about this song.* He had a big smile and started to sing along to the radio as he drifted off to sleep.

Chapter Five

Ruby

Ruby turned on her stereo and looked at the boxes stacked in her room that still needed to be unpacked. *Why unpack them? We won't be here that long; we can't be. There is nothing here for us.* She pondered as she lightly kicked the boxes, and a smaller one fell to the floor. She bent down to pick it up. She decided to open it, and she looked inside. She smiled as she pulled out a small white bear. She placed the bear on the shelf next to her bed. The bear was the first and only thing she had put on the shelf.

She pulled out a hoodie and smelled it to see if it still smelled like him, and it did. She quickly tossed it on the bed and tried not to let her emotions get the best of her. If she started to cry, she might not stop. She pulled out a journal her best friend Jeremy gave her right before they left New York for Illinois. She opened it to a random page with a post-it note that said, *Never forget you're an extraordinary person.* As she read it, she had a watery-eyed smile.

The note gave her a huge smile, so she decided unpacking could wait another day. She jumped onto the bed and decided to write a letter to her best friend Jeremy back home.

June 11, 1990

Hey J,

This letter of boredom is coming from your best friend in the middle of fucking nowhere. I hope you still remember me! I miss you! I miss the city! Anyways, this place is so boring we are in the middle of a corn-field, literally. There is absolutely nothing to do here. I don't know how people keep from slitting their wrists here. There is no cinema, no arcade, not even a liquor store! There are plenty of Churches and gas stations, though. I really don't know what my dad was thinking about moving us here. Please, please, write to me and tell me what you're up to. Have you talked to Sage? I need to write her a letter as well. Have you seen Jake? I can't believe he didn't even come to say goodbye to me. What a jerk!

We have been here only a week, and I'm ready to return to New York. I do not see how I will ever call this place home. I did meet this strange guy at the pool yesterday. I was lying in the lounge chair reading Stephan King's new book. I was lost in the story when someone said, "Hey." I said "hey" back, thinking that was it, and continued reading. This guy proceeded to talk to me about Stephan King's previous book, The Dark Half, and how good it was and that it was his favorite book growing up. Then, he talked about another book about these kids living in a boxcar. I was like who is this guy and am I on the show Candid Camera. Who just walks up and starts to talk to strangers? That is what happens in this small town; they speak to everyone. They wave hello to everyone, and it's seriously the strangest thing. This guy said his name was Shane, Shelby, or something I can't remember. Seriously, I don't know how I'm going to survive here. Help!

Sorry for so many "!!!" but I just need to express myself, or I might explode. Maybe a good scream will help…. No, that didn't help. It just got the dog to start barking and my Mom asked if I saw another spider. Don't even get me started on the spiders here. God why are parents so lame. They only seem to ruin our lives. Anyway, gotta go have dinner with the faaaaamily and talk about our feelings.

You're Best Friend Forever,
Ruby

P.S. Also, if you see Jake, could you walk straight up and throat-punch him? That would be great. Thanks. Oh, and if you see Sage, give her a hug for me. I miss you so much!!

After dinner, Ruby came back upstairs to a bedroom that was still full of boxes. She flopped down on the bed and pulled the hoodie close. Ruby smelled the hoodie again as she curled up with it. Ruby started thinking about the good times with Jake as she fell fast asleep.

The following day, Ruby was awoken by the sounds of birds and nothing else. It was strangely quiet here; she was used to waking up to traffic, horns honking, and people talking. She kept thinking about how people live like this—where there seems to be no life. In a small town, everything moves at a slower pace. As her feet hit the floor, she noticed the house was very still, so she had to stop and think *about what day it* was.

She looked at her calendar on the wall and saw it was Tuesday. Being on summer break, she had her days running together. Tuesday meant both her parents would be at her Dad's office getting it ready for the Grand Opening. Her parents were Al and Sue Nash. Her Dad's name was Dr. Albert H. Nash, but everyone called him Al or Dr. Nash. He kept his medical practice in New York and will work there for part of the year.

Sue was a stay-at-home mom in New York, and Al was a general practitioner. Sue decided to help her husband get the practice up and running. Since she was new to town and did not have her Upper East Side gal pals to shop and have lunch with. Ruby figured her Dad would get tired of her Mom being up his butt and find some project that would keep her out of his hair. Ruby did not know what to do with herself, alone in a strange new house and town. She went downstairs, turned on MTV, and fell asleep on the couch. She was awakened by a sound and got up to see where the sound had come from. She looked out the front door and saw the mail carrier walking back down their walkway. She excitedly opened the door to get the mail, hoping she had gotten a letter from one of her friends back home.

Unfortunately, no letter came for her today. She could not help but feel like she was out of sight, out of mind for her friends back home. Frustrated, she went into the kitchen to find something to eat. She did not feel like making anything, so she popped some waffles into the toaster and changed the TV. She scrolled through the channels and came across the Golden Girls. She watched the hilarious older women cracking sex jokes and sharing cheesecake while she ate her waffles and laughed along with them. Somehow, watching this show made her feel better and at home.

She spent the next few weeks doing the same thing, lounging around the house the entire day in her pajamas. Her parents started worrying because it was not like her to sit around the house. She was usually outgoing, very social, and always on the go. They would constantly ask her if she was okay, and of course, she would say, "Yeah," and go back to whatever she was doing. One day, they asked, and she could not take it anymore. "What do you think; you ripped me away from all my friends and everything I ever knew, so yeah, it's taking a moment to adjust," She unloaded and went to her room, where she spent the rest of the night.

When she got up the following day, her Mom was in the kitchen reorganizing the cabinets. Her Mom started staying home and not going into the office. Ruby could not tell if it was to keep an eye on her or if her Dad had gotten tired of her always being around the office.

"Sweetie, I made a grocery list there on the counter. Is there anything you want to add?" her Mother asked. Ruby glanced at her sideways and wondered why she was being extra sweet.

Both women started to realize just how different their lives were now and how little they had hung out with each other in New York. They have done fewer mother-daughter things in the last few years and hung out with their friends. They had become attached to their friends and forgot how to communicate. She was about to leave the kitchen. "Would you like to run to the store with me?" Her Mom asked.

Ruby thought about it momentarily and decided she would go with her Mother. It's not like much else was happening, and getting out of the house would do her some good. "Sure, let me go get changed," she answered as she turned to get dressed.

Her Mother was surprised that Ruby had said yes. She figured she would blow her off.

They pulled into the grocery store parking lot. Ruby was surprised at how small the parking lot was and even more surprised at how small the store was inside. They were used to stores with large parking garages. Stores with aisle after aisle of international foods.

Sue immediately remarked that the end caps were full of Twinkies, Ho Ho's, or stack after stack cola. They went to the produce section to get some fresh fruits and vegetables. They are shocked at the cost of the fruits and vegetables. Her Mother picked out some good bananas. "You would think these items would be cheaper here, but it's much more expensive than in the city." Her Mom commented. "No wonder these people stock up on chips and soda. You can buy two bags of chips or two cases of soda for the price of one!"

Ruby rolled her eyes and kept pushing the shopping cart, looking for something exciting. She spotted a familiar face—Sheldon, the strange boy from the pool. Even though Ruby did not know Sheldon, he felt familiar somehow after the last few weeks of solitude apart from her parents. She started to call out his name and realized he worked there and was headed to the front of the store.

Her only request to get at the store was pizza rolls and waffles. They finished up their shopping and were in line to checkout. She thought about saying something to Sheldon, but he was focused on his job and did not even notice or remember her, so she didn't say anything. When they got home, she helped her Mom inside with the groceries and then ran to check the mail. She was thrilled and started jumping up and down when a letter was addressed to her, postmarked New York, New York, and the return address was Jeremy Butler.

Excited, she ran up to her room and ripped open the envelope. She jumped onto her bed, pulled out the letter, and began reading. She was so excited to get a letter from her best friend that she read it three times. She wanted to waste no time writing a letter in return because the sooner she wrote a letter, the sooner she would get one back. Before she could get started, her Mom called her name. "Sweetie, let's go for a drive and get some ice cream. What do you say?" Her Mom asked, opening her door.

Ruby started to say no, but with the look on her Mom's face, she couldn't. "Okay, Mom, but only if I can drive."

"Okie Dokey," Her Mom replied. Her Mom was happy her daughter agreed to go and spend more time with her.

"Okay," she looked at her Mom strangely. "This place is seriously starting to affect you."

After stopping and getting a frosty freeze, they took a little drive through the country. They were amazed at how much open space and how big everyone's yards were. As they drove by, people waved at them from their front porches and yards. "Now, you don't see that in the big city," Her Mom pointed out. There were fields full of cows, goats, and horses. When they got home, Ruby ran upstairs to write a letter to her friend.

June, 28 1990

Hey J,

I was so excited to get your letter today. You have no idea how happy I was. Oh my god did your Mom really ground you for sneaking a boy into your room? That is like so 1980's how lame is that? So, is this boy cute? Is he a good kisser? You have to tell me all about him. I haven't even seen one cute guy since we have gotten here. The guy next door is kinda cute. His name is Trey… I think. He has that football player look about him. You know I like them shaggy, scruffy, and a bit of a bad boy. But you never know. I may take one for the team and report back to you.

Oh, speaking of guys I ran into that strange boy from the pool. The one I was telling you about. He works at the grocery store here in town. Actually, I think it's the only store in this town can you believe that? I saw him when I went grocery shopping with my mom. (I know right! I wouldn't have believed it either, Mom and I grocery shopping together, who would have thought.) Anyway, he was bagging our groceries; I don't think he recognized me. He seems nice and all, but I have yet to get a read of what he is all about. You know me I like a good challenge.

My Mom and I actually went together for some ice cream and a drive through the country. I believe this has been the most time we have spent together since I was ten. People are weird here, as you drive past them on the road they wave at you. If they are in their yard they wave at you too, it's the strangest thing. In the city you don't even say, "Hi" to your neighbors. Oh, and get this, our neighbors actually brought over a pie, not a store-bought pie either this shit was homemade. Man, it was so good too, way better than anything you get at the store. I put some vanilla ice cream on it, and it was amazing. Oh, speaking of heaven you would so be in love with the neighbor boy Trey. He is mowing their yard as I write this, with his shirt off and definitely has a body that even I might want to eat pie off of. Shit, I just drooled onto the paper. HA!

Sorry, got a little distracted watching him mowing the yard. I hope to call you soon. I need to hear your voice! Talk to you soon.

You're Best Friend Forever,
Ruby

§

Ruby was awoken by the sound of snaps and pops outside her window. She moaned as he rolled over. She could not believe it was already the Fourth of July; time was flying too fast. She was not looking forward to starting school in a few months. "Don't think about it," She commanded out loud to herself. She threw back the covers, got out of bed, and went downstairs to see what her parents were doing that day.

Her parents had not been speaking to each other. It was like they were two strangers living together. Her Dad had taken to sleeping in the guest room. She thought it would only last a few days or weeks, but it has continued for over a month. Her Dad was reading the paper at the table, and her Mother was washing the dishes from breakfast, which she must have missed.

"Good morning," Her Mother greeted her. "I made you a plate, and it's in the microwave."

"Good morning, sweetie," Her Dad replied as he looked up from the paper. How did you sleep?"

"Actually, very well, thanks," Ruby said, getting the plate from the microwave and taking a bite of bacon as she sat at the counter. Ruby enjoyed this family time, which felt nice and made it feel like they were a real family again. "So, what are you two doing today?" Ruby queried her parents.

There was a long pause, "Well… I'm going to hang out with my friend Sharron and take her shopping," Her Mom answered with an undertone. Her husband just left her for a younger woman…" Her Mom paused, glaring at the back of her husband's head, still buried his face in the paper.

"Dad...?"

He shuffled the paper, trying to fold it like it had come. "Well, Sweetie, I'm going into the office for a bit to get some paperwork done." He kissed her forehead as he left the kitchen. "I will see you tonight."

Her Mom, appearing annoyed, grabbed her purse and headed for the door. 'I will be home later to make supper," Her Mom announced as she opened the door. "Oh, and sweetie, if you go out, make sure to lock the door, I saw one of those strange men lurking around the house the other day."

"Uh… that was the guy from the gas company," Ruby replied with a half chuckle. "He was installing a new meter."

Her Mom was already out the door before she finished her sentence. Her Dad left shortly after that. She could not help but wonder what was happening to her family? Moving here was supposed to bring them closer, but they could not be further apart. She decided she wanted some beef jerky and a Dr. Pepper. She dressed and put on her shoes to go to the grocery store. Walking to the store, she wondered what her friend Jeremy was doing and if he would go with his new boyfriend to see the fireworks tonight. She could not help but wonder about Jake and whether he had seen anyone yet. They had a big fight right before she left New York. She wanted to ask Jeremy in her following letter if Jake was seeing someone, but she was afraid to hear what the response might be.

Her neighbors smiled and waved at her, but she still felt weird about the friendly neighbor thing. However, she smiled and waved back at them, which felt nice. She turned on her Walkman, listening to Devo, when someone ran past her, making her heart feel like it had stopped for a second. She was not expecting that to happen. The guy stopped and turned, still jogging in place, and smiled at her. It was her neighbor Trey, who was running without his shirt on. The sweat was running down his muscular chest and arms.

He turned back around and continued on his way. She continued walking. What *was that all about? And did he have to run with his shirt off? We get it. You have a nice body.* "Fuck! I'm sexually frustrated," She shouted out loud, forgetting she had her headphones on, and yelled louder than she intended. Sweet white-haired Mrs. Clemens sat on her porch in her rocking chair and waved at Ruby. Ruby laughed and waved back; *I don't think she heard what I said.*

The next thing she knew, Trey ran past her again. He turned and started running backward. "Don't worry, she didn't hear what you said. Maybe you should yell louder. Hey, nothing wrong with a little sexual frustration. We all experience it from time to time." Trey teased with a smirk smile.

He was so busy trying to be cool that he did not see that the sidewalk was uneven. He did not step up high enough, causing his right foot to catch the sidewalk where it had separated, and he started to fall. Trey tried to counterbalance himself with his left foot, but it was futile. He did a twist and rolled into the ditch. Ruby looked around to see if anyone else had witnessed what had just happened, but there was no one. Mrs. Clemens had already gone inside; Ruby saw the screen door slamming shut. She looked down at him, trying not to laugh, asking him, "You, okay?" She reached out with her hand to help him up.

"Yeah, I'm good. I've got it, thanks."

She could tell he was embarrassed as he pulled himself up, trying to act as if nothing had happened. He limped briefly, and Ruby could see blood running down his leg. Suddenly, Mrs. Clemens was standing beside her, handing her a first aid kit. "Honey, I think he is going to need this," Mrs. Clemens cringed as she handed Ruby the kit, trying not to look. "Sorry, but I don't do well at the sight of blood."

"Blood?" Trey questioned, looking pale.

"Yes, blood," Ruby answered half smiling. "Now sit down here on this step, and let me look at it."

She opened the first aid kit and took out the antiseptic wipes. "This might sting a little," she warned as she opened it. The cut was just below his left knee, which must have taken some of the impact when he fell. She put her hand around his calf, and as she did, she looked into his eyes, a deep shade of green. Something inside of her tingled, which took her by surprise. She started to clean up the cut, which appeared to be very minor. "How did you get around the block so fast?" She asked him as she got the Band-Aid ready.

"Well, I'm really fast and… I cut through the alley," Trey admitted holding back a smile. "I cut through the alley and someone's yard just to run past you again. Plus, I have to be fast in my position on the team, and… you walk kinda slow."

She slapped his leg as she put the band-aid on and got up. He howled in pain while laughing. Ruby thought he almost had me with those beautiful green eyes. "I do not walk slow," Ruby scoffed as she stood up.

"Is everything okay now?" Mrs. Clemens called out looking around Ruby.

They had both forgotten she was even there. "Yes," Ruby replied. "Unfortunately, he will live. Thank you for the first aid kit."

Ruby handed the first aid kit back to Mrs. Clemens. "You two make a cute couple," Mrs. Clemens cooed as she returned to her house.

There were a couple of awkward glances and smiles at each other. Then Trey spoke up first and reached out his hand. "I'm Trey, by the way. I don't think we have officially met."

She put her hand into his hand and tried not to stare too long into those green eyes. "I'm Ruby."

She let go of his hand and turned to continue her walk to the store but turned back. "What sport do you play?"

"Football I'm the Wide Receiver. Do you follow football?"

"That doesn't surprise me," She remarked with a smile. "And no, I don't."

She turned and kept walking without looking back. When she finally got to the store, she had a smile on her face she could not hide. She grabbed her beef jerky and a Dr. Pepper and entered the checkout line. She saw they had Hubba Bubba Bubble Tape; she had not seen it in a long time, so she grabbed a roll.

She was on cloud nine and had not noticed anyone else in the store. She was in her own world. "Oh, wow, Bubble Tape," Sheldon teased. "So do you want this bagged?"

Sheldon had watched her come in and was waiting for the right moment to say something. "Oh, no, I'm good," Ruby said, surprised that he was talking to her. "How have you been?" she asked, realizing he was laughing at her choice of gum. "Hey, don't be making fun of my bubble tape."

They both laughed as Sheldon handed her her gum. "Have a good one," Sheldon said with a smile.

"You too," she replied, practically dancing out of the store.

Sheldon looked at her inquisitively, chuckled, and went back to work.

Ruby walked home with a bounce in her step. Something inside her felt glad they had moved to Illinois, even though she missed her friends. Ruby started to feel as though everything was going to be okay. She was in such a good mood that she kept walking past their house and to the park. At the park, they were setting up for the fireworks and festivities for that night. She liked the park so much that she decided she would return later for the fireworks, even if it was by herself.

When she got home, the house was quiet, and she took a quick nap. Then, she would get up and write a letter to her friend. Ruby slept longer than she had meant to and did not wake up until the smell of something cooking woke her. She stretched as she went down to see what her Mom was cooking and what her parents had planned for tonight. She found her Mom in the kitchen as she snatched a baby carrot off the counter.

"Where's dad?" She asked. "Isn't he going to be home for dinner?"

"Your guess is as good as mine," Her Mom replied curtly, and Ruby was taken back a bit. "He spends so much time at that damn office. I'm beginning to think he is fucking his receptionist."

"Moooom," Ruby gasped as she about choked on the carrot she was eating. "Don't say that about daddy."

"What? Have you seen her?" her Mom shrieked as she furiously chopped vegetables for the salad and waved the knife around while she talked. "She is young, beautiful, and blonde. Did I mention young?"

"Well, I highly doubt that, Mom. Dad loves you," Ruby reassured her as she munched on another carrot. "Plus, you're way prettier than her."

"Thanks for saying that sweetie. Anyway, the pot roast should be done in twenty if you're hungry," Her Mom attempted to change the subject.

"Okay, I'm gonna shower and get ready to go watch the fireworks in a bit. You wanna come?" Ruby offered.

"No thanks sweetie I'm going to go over to Susan's," Her Mom replied. "Make sure you eat something before you go."

Ruby got ready and went down to the park. She found what she thought was a comfy spot next to a tree to watch the fireworks. She had just sat down when she heard. "Hey, you have any of the bubble tape left?" Someone asked as she turned to see Sheldon standing there.

"Hey, you wanna sit with me and watch the show?" Ruby asked, moving to make room.

"Sure, it will be nice to sit with someone," Sheldon admitted. "This is actually the first time I have come to watch the fireworks. We usually sit at home on our porch and crane our necks to see them way off in the distance, but I didn't want to miss it this year."

They sat talking and laughing. Ruby shared stories about New York, and Sheldon spoke about growing up on a farm and living in a small town. They were both laughing when they heard someone call out Ruby's name. They both turned to see Trey standing there with a huge grin. Ruby turned a dark shade of red. "Hi, Trey," Ruby smiled. "What are you doing here?" She realized that was a dumb question.

Before he could respond, someone shouted, "Trey!" It was Chase. "We are sitting over on the other side of the park."

Chase walked over to see who Trey was talking to. He spotted Sheldon and smiled. "Hey there, you two are welcome to come over and sit with us," Chase offered, gesturing with his hands to come with them.

Ruby and Sheldon looked at each other. "Thank you, but I think we are going to stay here," Ruby spoke confident in her response.

"Okay, but if you change your mind, you're more than welcome to come over," Trey offered as they left.

When the two guys walked off, Ruby and Sheldon leaned into each other and giggled. "Wow he was so into you," Sheldon pointed out with a cheesy grin.

"Yea, whatever," Ruby half laughed thinking for a moment. "His friend was totally checking you out."

There was an awkward silence for a moment and Ruby picked up a small tree branch and started poking the ground. "I always say stupid stuff when cute boys come around," Ruby broke the silence. "Asking him what he was doing here like it was not obvious.

"Trust me I do the same thing," Sheldon concurred. "It's like my brain decides to stop working properly."

You know my best friend back in New York, he is gay," Ruby threw it out there to see if she could get Sheldon to open up some more. "We always have such a great time hanging out together, because it doesn't matter if someone is gay."

There was another long silence. Finally, Ruby nudged Sheldon's shoulder with her shoulder. "Say something." Ruby urged him to break the awkwardness.

Sheldon shifted uncomfortably. He changed his posture, knowing it would not make this conversation more straightforward. "I don't know what to say," Sheldon finally said as he nervously picked up a small twig and started breaking it into pieces. I have never talked to anyone about it for fear of what people would say or think."

"I know you don't really know me yet," She acknowledged as she touched his shoulder. "Buuuut, you can talk to me about anything. In fact, I will go first. I think my Dad is cheating on my Mother," She blurted out.

Sheldon's jaw dropped. That was not what he was expecting her to say. "I don't even know what to say," he expressed at a loss for words. How do you know?"

"It's kind of obvious, spending more and more time at work, new cologne, and dressing younger," Ruby replied matter-of-factly. "Also, the fact my Mom thinks he is screwing his receptionist. I thought moving here would bring us closer together and at first it seemed that way, but things have gone wrong fast."

"I'm sorry to hear that," Sheldon offered as he put his arm around her shoulder. "You can tell me anything as well." They smiled at each other as the fireworks started.

July, 19 1990

Dear J,

The last few weeks have been kinda hectic here and I'm sorry for my delayed response, don't think I have forgotten about you. The fourth of July fireworks here are nothing compared to ours back home. Though the real fireworks here were not in sky, remember that guy Trey I was telling you about? Yea, he was there and very flirty, but me being me I didn't know what to say as usual. So, those fireworks weren't as awesome as they could have been if you know what I mean. Then again who knows, he might be the player type. Though, I'm hoping he is not. I will keep you posted on that subject.

I miss going to the movies with you. Tell me you didn't go see Ghost without me. You know if I was there Jake would have dragged me to watch Robocop 2. Man, I wish you were here to go see The Exorcist III with me next month that movie looks like it's going to be scary. Who am I going to hang onto during the scary parts? Who's going to scream with me? I think I might ask Sheldon to go. Sorry about going all over the place I just have so much to tell you.

Sheldon has turned out to be a pretty cool guy, but I think he plays for your team. We haven't actually talked about it yet but when you know you know, you know? However, here being gay is definitely not something you want to be. The redneck guys here seem to be dumb as a box of sardines, dumber than ole Travis McGee if you can believe that. I'm dreading starting school next month but hey I will know at least one person.

Sheldon was telling me about living on a farm and what that was like. Only makes me glad I grew-up in city. Man, when I have kids, I will definitely not subject them to this kind of life, or do what my parents did to me. Sheldon was telling me that in the fall he wants to take me to go teepeeing. Heck I'm not even sure I'm spelling it right. Get this you buy a bunch of toilet paper and go to someone's house and cover their trees, bushes and whatever is in there yard with toilet paper. I think he is joking who does that?

Well, I have to cut this short Mom is yelling at me to go shopping with her. She wants to take me to get clothes, shoes, and supplies for school, this should be interesting. Next time I write I will tell you about what is going on with Mom, Dad, and this guy Trey.

You're Best Friend Forever,
Ruby

Ruby started to visit Sheldon at work. They sat and talked during his lunch break. They would get lost in each other stories. Ruby told Sheldon how she met Trey and bandaged his bloody knee. They both were quiet for a moment. Ruby was lost in thought about Trey, and Sheldon was thinking how he had not seen Chase in weeks and wondered what he was up to. "He has a girlfriend," Sheldon finally spoke.

At first, Ruby was slightly panicked and thought he was talking about Trey. Sheldon continued, "I saw her when she picked him up at the pool. She looked like a cheerleader. She must be from another school because I have never seen her before."

"Well, I don't care," Ruby remarked after catching onto who Sheldon was talking about. "With how he looked at you, there isn't a doubt about what he really wants." They were quiet for a beat. "I can't believe school starts in less than two days."

"You're going to do well," Sheldon encouraged her. "Hey, you already know two people."

"Two people?" Ruby questioned.

"Yea, Treeeeey and me."

She punched him in the arm, and they both laughed.

"I better get back to work," Sheldon said. I will see you on Monday and relax. It's going to be a great year; in fact, I'm predicting the best year ever."

"Yea Yea," Ruby jested as she started to head home. "See ya Monday!"

§

It was the night before school started. Ruby tried to relax and fall asleep, but she had no luck. She heard something hit her window. It sounded like a tree branch tapping against the window, but no trees were near her window. She got up to see what was going on. She looked down and saw Trey throwing what appeared to be mulch at her window. She opened the window. "What are you doing?" Ruby whispered loudly. "Are you crazy?"

"I wanted to know if you would like a ride to school tomorrow."

Ruby stepped back from the window out of sight and did a little dance. "Ruby Jean, what is going on with you? He is just a boy. Pull yourself together." She composed herself again and looked out the window. "I guess that would be cool, seeing how we are both going to the same place."

"Cool, I will pick you... I mean, meet you out front of your house around 7:45."

"Sounds good," Ruby replied as she shut her window.

Ruby climbed back into bed even more excited, looking forward to starting school. She had a tough time falling asleep that night.

Chapter Six

Swimming Lessons

Sheldon pulled into the school parking lot, blasting Patty Love-less's *Timber, I'm Falling Love.* He was excited to start his junior year and felt more confident about this school year than last year. Sheldon had a new friend, Ruby, and will see more of Chase. However, Chase was a grade below, so Sheldon would not get to see him as much as he would like. Even a glance into those beautiful eyes would make his day complete.

Sheldon got out of his blue '63 Chevy Nova convertible. As he looked back, admiring his ride, a brand-new Lincoln Continental pulled into the parking lot. Something caught his eye; the passenger looked familiar. He realized it was Ruby and walked over to greet her. When the driver got out of the car, he was surprised to see it was Trey. Sheldon had a smirk on his face as Ruby turned to face him. She mouthed, "Don't even start," as she smiled.

All three stopped and stared as a cherry-red 67 Mustang convertible pulled into the parking lot. "Whose car is that?" Ruby asked Sheldon.

"I have no idea," Sheldon admitted with curiosity. He became a little excited as he watched it go by. "But that is a sweet ride."

The car went to park at the far end of the parking lot, away from the vehicles and did not want to get the door dinged. Everyone waited to see who got out of the car as if whoever it was someone famous. As the driver stepped out of the car, he tossed his bangs to the side, turned, and made eye contact with Sheldon. "Oh my god, that's Chase," Ruby gasped as she elbowed Sheldon's arm and smiled at him. "Who would have thought?"

"He worked on that car all summer," Trey interjected, turning back to see the looks on their faces. "I haven't seen or heard from him the last few weeks. I think he was practically sleeping in the car. I will catch you later. I'm going to say hi to him."

"Look at that butt. It just doesn't quit," Ruby whispered as Trey walked away.

Chase and Trey walked toward the entrance of the school. Chase turned to wave at Ruby and Sheldon, and they waved back. Ruby looked at Sheldon, smiled, and raised her eyebrows.

Ruby could not stop staring at Trey. "Come on, wipe the drool off your face, and let's get our first day over with," Sheldon teased as he playful pulled Ruby by the arm and dragged her towards the school. "Are you two seeing each other, or what?" Sheldon asked as they were walking towards the school building.

"No, he just offered me a ride," Ruby replied, laughing, knowing that, by the look on Sheldon's face, he was not buying it. "Seriously, he asked me last night if I wanted a ride, and I thought, why the heck not?"

"Mmmhhhmmm," Sheldon looked at her suspiciously from the corner of his eye as Ruby nodded. He opened the door, and they both laughed. "Do you have your class schedule? What is your first class?"

"Hey, wait for me!" Ninnie yelled after them as the door was about to close. "Thank goodness I caught up with you; I didn't want to get lost."

"Well, I think it would be hard to get lost in a school this size," Sheldon laughed.

"I guess you're right," Ninnie said, looking down the hall. "I don't think I have ever gone to a school this small."

"Neither have I," Ruby added, looking around in disbelief. "I'm used to much bigger schools in New York."

"The high school consists of two long halls. There are other classes outside, like shop class and so forth, but I don't think those will be classes either of you will be attending."

"What's your first class?" Sheldon asked. "I have Algebra II."

"Me too," Ninnie chimed in. "But I'm starting to question my decision-making on that class because it is too early in the morning to think that much."

"I have chemistry," Ruby groaned. "I want to go with you two instead. We should have planned this out better."

"Okay, you win," Ninnie conceded as she realized there were worse classes at the beginning of the day. They made their way to their lockers.

"Yeah, don't get lost, ladies," Trey joked as he passed them. "I have chemistry too. I will show you the way if you don't mind walking with me."

Ruby turned to face Sheldon and Ninnie with her back to Trey and mouthed, *"Oh my god, "smiling* a huge smile and batting her eyelashes. When she turned back around, she put on a serious face. "Okay, I guess since we are both going to the same place," Ruby played coolly.

"Well, that was not obvious at all," Ninnie coughed out, trying to be funny. "But who is that hot guy that keeps looking over here?"

Sheldon looked to see Chase talking to someone, but he kept looking over at them. Sheldon turned back quickly. "Oh, that is just Chase. You think he is hot, huh?" Sheldon commented as he tried to downplay the fact Chase was nearby.

"Yeah, but he isn't my type. Poor guy won't know what hit him. I will have to break his little heart." Ninnie tossed her hair back, trying to look sexy, but it was completely awkward. Sheldon tried to contain his laughter.

"I'm sure he will survive," Sheldon laughed, unable to hold it in any longer. He had a knot in his stomach, hoping he was looking at him, not her. Now come on, or we will be late."

§

It was the last period and time for Sheldon to head to work. He felt lucky that he got to work for his final class of the day while everyone else was in class. Sheldon was getting books out of his locker. He did not realize someone was standing right behind his locker door. He jumped as Chase popped his head around the side of the door.

"Hi," Chase was standing there with a massive smile.

Sheldon was not expecting anyone; he did not even hear him walk up. The halls were empty, and everyone was already in class. "Hi," Sheldon replied. He could feel his cheeks turning red.

Chase had his face pressed against the open locker door with his cute dimple smile. "Soooo… What do you think of my car?" Chase asked him.

"It seems okay from what I have seen," Sheldon responded while shoving books into his backpack, trying to play it cool, but inside, he was screaming kiss me. "I haven't ridden in it yet, so I can't really tell you," Sheldon hinted with a smirk.

"You headed to work?" Chase inquired, trying hard to talk to Sheldon. "Maybe I could give you a ride in it sometime."

Sheldon threw his backpack over his shoulder and nervously shifted it around to make it more comfortable. "Yeah, I am," Sheldon shyly answered as he turned to head out. I like getting a paycheck because it helps pay for the expenses of my car. Who knew having a car was so expensive with taxes, registration, gas, and not to mention the insurance?"

Sheldon could tell he was rambling because he was nervous, so he shut up. "Do you mind if I walk out with you?" Chase asked, eager for Sheldon to say yes. Sheldon nodded, and as they walked, Chase mentioned swim lessons again. They got to the door, and Chase grabbed Sheldon's arm to stop him and get his full attention.

He looked deep into Sheldon's eyes, "Hey, don't be ashamed that you don't know how to swim. No one has to know I'm teaching you if… you don't want to. I think it's a shame you have never learned how. Tuesdays are your day off, right?"

Sheldon looked at him, surprised he knew that. He tried to hold his excitement inside as he nodded yes. "Perfect," Chase cheered. We can meet at the pool after school every Tuesday, and I can teach you, deal?"

Sheldon could not help but smile, looking into those gorgeous blue eyes and that smile. "Deal," Sheldon replied.

Chase pounds his two fists together. "Awesome! You're not going to regret it," Chase exclaimed.

Sheldon laughs at the sight of Chase awkwardly fist-bumping himself. "Did you just fist-bump yourself?"

"Maybe…" Chase chuckled and smiled that dimpled smile again.

When Sheldon turned to leave, he gave Chase a curious look. Chase responded with an eyebrow raise and bit his bottom lip. Sheldon headed to work. As he drove, he could not help but wonder how Chase skipped classes so much. Also, how did he know I was heading to work or that I had Tuesdays off?

§

Tuesday after school, Sheldon arrived at the swimming pool. He was surprised by the size and that it was an Olympic pool with lanes. He wondered why he had never been to the school's pool before. Chase was already in the pool doing laps. Sheldon went into the locker room to get changed. He came out to the pool area, unsure what he would do today. Though deep down inside, he secretly was hoping those sexy lips would at some point be touching his.

Chase moved through the water smoothly and effortlessly. As his head came out of the water, he shook his head and wiped the water out of his eyes. Chase spotted Sheldon and waved him over. "Today, we are going to start in the shallow end of the pool," Chase explained as he waved him into the water. I want to begin with breathing exercises to help you get more comfortable with the water. How does that sound?"

"Sounds good to me. You're the expert," Sheldon affirmed, nodding his head confidently, but he was nervous as hell.

"Good, now let's start with putting your face in the water and breathing out through your nose and mouth," Chase instructed. He bent over to demonstrate, almost putting his face in the water. "Let the air come out of your nose and your mouth. Let me show you." Chase demonstrated for Sheldon.

Sheldon could not help but admire the beauty of his body. He watched Chase's rib cage move as he demonstrated breathing underwater. Chase returned to the surface, flinging his hair back, and wiped the water from his face. The water was running down his pecks and his six-pack. *Focus on what he is saying*, Sheldon told himself.

"Okay, now you try it," Chase requested. He could see Sheldon was a bit nervous, and he almost put his hand on Sheldon's shoulder but caught himself. He leaned forward to look Sheldon squarely in the face. "Relax, it's okay. You can do this."

While still holding onto the side of the pool, Sheldon put his face into the water but did not stay under long. Sheldon came out of the water and started to wipe the water away quickly because he felt claustrophobic. "Trust me, you're not going to drown, and besides, I'm very good at CPR." Chase half chuckled. "Remember, I'm a lifeguard. It's okay. Let's try this again. Watch me." He demonstrated it again for Sheldon. "Let's try something a little different instead of hanging onto the side of the pool by resting your hands on your knees," Chase showed him as he urged him to try again. Sheldon did as he was instructed. "This way, you will feel like you have more control." Sheldon tried it again, and this time, he did much better. He relaxed and focused on controlling his breathing like Chase had shown him. "Very nice. See, I knew you could do it," Chase praised Sheldon as he patted him on the shoulder.

"Today, we will work on some basic aquatic skills," Chase explained. "I want to start with floating, which is important in building confidence. You can use this technique when you panic in the water to help you relax."

He showed him how to do a jellyfish float, a tuck float, a front float, and a back float. Sheldon did not think this would be as serious as an actual class. "Next, let's try treading water," Chase requested. Sheldon had relaxed so much that he did not realize how far into the deep end of the pool they had drifted and panicked for a moment. "It's okay. I got you," Chase reassured him as he saw Sheldon panicking. He put his arm around him and pulled him to the side of the pool. "We can start next to the side of the pool if you feel more comfortable. Okay, try holding onto the side of the pool and treading water."

Every time Chase touched Sheldon, he relaxed and felt at home. An amazing feeling always came over Sheldon whenever he felt Chase beside him. While treading water, Chase showed him how to scissor kick and breast kick. Sheldon was surprised at how much exercise he was getting from treading water. "Okay, I can tell you're getting a little tired, so we will tread for five minutes more and call it a day," Chase instructed while treading water with him.

"We have done a lot for your first day. I like to swim a lot. It helps me to stay in shape. Swimming is a great cardio and strengthens my muscles without overexerting myself."

Sheldon was in awe of how easily Chase could tread water while he instructed him. Sheldon thought Chase was adorable talking and treading water. He would occasionally have to spit out water while talking. "What are you smiling at?" Chase asked as he took his hand and flung water at Sheldon. "I'm gonna do some more laps. If you want to stay, you can see the techniques I showed you today. It will help you understand how it all works together. But you can head out whenever you're ready if you have somewhere to be." He smiled as he turned and started doing his laps.

Before Sheldon got out of the pool, he could not help but watch how smooth Chase's strokes were and how fast he was moving. Sheldon decided it was time to stop drooling and get going. He went to the ladder and started to get out of the pool. "Hey, you did a great job today," Chase acknowledged as he stopped swimming momentarily, watching Sheldon getting out of the pool. Sheldon pulled at his shorts, which molded to his semi-erection. Sheldon blushed with embarrassment. He did not know Chase was watching. "I will see you tomorrow," Chased called out, then continued doing his laps.

That night, Sheldon's legs were sore from treading water. He decided to take a hot bath to relax. He was soaking in the tub, thinking about the past few months. It was nice to have a new friend and his cousin Ninnie going to the same school, and it did not hurt to have a cute boy to look at in just a pair of swim trunks. He was so relaxed he drifted off to sleep. He was awaken by someone knocking on the door. "You okay in there," his Mother asked. "You have been in there quite a while."

"Yeah, I'm okay," Sheldon replied. "I fell asleep."

By then, the water was ice cold. Sheldon proceeded to rinse off and get out of the tub. As he dried off, he could barely move. Afterward, he headed straight to bed.

The next day at school, Sheldon slowly sat down at the lunch table while Ruby and Ninnie watched him with quizzical expressions.

"Are you okay," Ruby finally asked.

"Yeah, and we aren't buying this whole. I just woke up sore crap you gave us this morning," Ninnie added. "Spill! What did you get into?"

"Okay, I started taking swim lessons with Chase," Sheldon mumbled, waiting for the teasing to start.

"I knew something was up," Ninnie smirked as she looked at Ruby.

"And how's that going?" Ruby asked. Ninnie and Ruby were on the edge of their seats, waiting for something juicy.

"It's going well. Chase wore me out the first day," Sheldon admitted as he shifted in his seat, trying to get comfortable.

"Oooh, I bet he did," Ninnie remarked as she playfully elbowed Ruby.

"It's not like that. Chase is actually teaching me techniques," Sheldon countered, trying not to smile, adding to the fire. "Not… That I wouldn't mind other things, too."

"Well, that sounds just plain boring," Ninnie scoffed, cleaning up her stuff from lunch. "I have something I have to go tend to."

"Tend too?" Ruby questioned with high curiosity. "We just sat down to lunch. You make it sound like you have to feed the hogs or something like that. Right, Sheldon, isn't that how you say it?"

They all laughed. "No, seriously, where are you going?" Sheldon asked her as Ninnie abruptly left the cafeteria.

"Wow, she totally ignored the questions," Ruby added as they continued to finish their lunch, with Sheldon talking about the stuff Chase had him doing and how great it felt when he touched him.

The following Tuesday, Chase and Sheldon met for another swim lesson. Chase had Sheldon start with the same routine, working on his breathing underwater. Sheldon was getting comfortable with having his face in the water. Chase had him tread water for a few minutes. "We are going to end the day with some basic strokes," Chase instructed." I will show you two basic swimming strokes. The front crawl and the back crawl. Let's start in the shallow end of the pool."

Chase started demonstrating the front crawl. Sheldon was impressed by how little water splashed as Chase moved through the water. Sheldon had watched him repeatedly. Chase showed him the movements and how to cup his hand. Sheldon emulated the movements while standing still in the pool and watching Chase swim the length of the pool.

"Okay, you ready to give it a try?" Chase asked as he finished his lap and stood up.

Sheldon proceeded to attempt the same movements that Chase showed him. He did three strokes and then stood up trying to catch his breath. He turned to see Chase dying of laughter.

"Water was flying everywhere," Chase chuckled as he doubled over laughing. "You had arms and legs going in all directions and splashing water like a floundering fish." Chase pulled himself together, trying to be more serious. "You need to relax and realize you're not fighting the water. Remember what I told you. Relax and make smooth strokes, and don't forget to breathe. I bet your heart is racing," he said as he put his hand on Sheldon's chest, which sent a tingle throughout Sheldon's body.

He was not expecting that, and it caught him off guard. "See your heart is racing. You need to relax and breathe normally." With one hand still on Sheldon's chest, he took his other hand, grabbed Sheldon's hand, and put it on his chest as he demonstrated breathing in and out. "You ready to try it again?" He questioned, breaking the moment as he pulled his hand away once Chase realized he was leaning in to kiss Sheldon. Not before Sheldon notice Chase's heart had started pounding harder too. "Okay, let's do this again."

Sheldon tried it again. This time, he was thinking about what Chase had taught him and focused on relaxing. Sheldon did much better on his second attempt. His only problem was he forgot to breathe and would have to stop after a few strokes. "Wow, that is much better," Chase cheered as he clapped. "You're going to get this stroke down; I believe in you. Just remember to breathe. Eventually, your strokes will get smoother, and there won't be as much splashing. Try a few more times. Try to make it to the end and do the backstroke on your return trip, and we will call it a day," Chase explained with a smile. "Remember, if you stop in the deep part of the pool, do not panic. Just tread water, catch your breath, and try again."

Sheldon was impressed with himself. He was far from perfect, but he did it just the same. He stopped in the middle of the deep end and began to panic. He could hear Chase saying, "Relax and begin treading water till you have caught your breath and continue." When he reached the end, he grabbed the side of the pool and held on for a moment to catch his breath. He laid his head back in the water, looked up at the ceiling, and laughed momentarily. He was actually doing it after years of being afraid of the water. He was AC-TUALLY doing it. He stayed floating on his back with his head in the water, trying to catch his breath, plus the water felt good on his head. Chase came and stood over him. Sheldon admired the view of Chase in his speedos with his nice bulging package.

"Okay you ready to try the back crawl down," Chase interrupted his daydreaming about his package. "Just remember, if you have to stop for some reason, don't panic."

Sheldon started doing the back crawl and was surprised at how much easier it was than the front crawl. Granted, he kept splashing water everywhere, but that only made him try harder to smooth out his strokes. Before Sheldon knew it, he had made his way to the end of the pool and was looking up at Chase, who was standing over him smiling, and there was that damn package sticking out in front of him. Chase's mouth was moving, but Sheldon's head was still underwater. He was enjoying the view. When he pulled his head up, he could hear Chase.

"Damn, you went all the way without stopping," Chase cheered with pride as he applauded. "Good Job! I'm going to do a few laps before calling it a day. I will see you next week."

"Thank you," Sheldon replied while he got out of the pool. "I will see you next week."

But Chase could not hear him. He was already doing his laps. Sheldon changed and headed home.

The next day, at lunch, Ruby and Ninnie discussed fashion and the current trends while Sheldon daydreamed again.

"Hey, Earth to Sheldon," Ruby called out. "What is going on with you lately? You seem tired all the time and lost in thought."

They both had stopped talking to each other and now staring at Sheldon. "What?" Sheldon asked.

"Wait, she is right," Ninnie chimed in. "Usually, we can't get a word in edgewise. What is going on with you?"

"Nothing. I think maybe swim lessons are making me tired," Sheldon explained as he pushed his food around.

"Mmmhhhmmm," Ninnie quipped. "Are you sure swimming

lessons are the only thing wearing you out?"

Ruby was leaning in, waiting for his answer. "That is all that is happening," Sheldon laughed, but he was still not ready to talk to them about his feelings. "Trust me, that is all that is happening," he stated again with a chuckle at their persistence.

"Humm, okay if you say so," Ninnie teased as she finished her salad quickly. "Gotta go. Mrs. Torkelson gets mad if you're not at your typewriter ready to type when the bell rings, the old goat."

Ruby was still looking at Sheldon with questioning eyes. "Nothing is happening," Sheldon said dreamily. "Not that I haven't thought about it with how he looks in his speedos."

"Hey, come back to earth," Ruby snapped her fingers and laughed. "Come on, or we will be late for class."

The following week Chase showed Sheldon how to do the butterfly, breaststroke, elementary backstroke, and the sidestroke. Each Tuesday Chase would have Sheldon warm up with a few laps of the previous strokes he had learned before showing him something new. After a few lessons, Sheldon became less nervous about being around Chase. During his warmups, Sheldon started to feel confident. He decided to ask Chase how he missed so many classes without getting into trouble. Chase chuckled. "I guess that's one of the perks of being the quarterback."

Sheldon stopped what he was doing and looked at him. "Wait, you're the quarterback?"

"Yeah, and you would know that if you ever came to a game."

"How do you know I never come to a game?" Sheldon stammered.

"Trust me I know," Chase reassured him with a smirk. "Now quit being a little bitch and do another warmup lap," He teased while pushing Sheldon playfully in the water. "Today, we're going to learn how to dive."

Sheldon finished his laps and leaned on the side of the pool to catch his breath. Chase was sitting with his legs crossed, waiting for Sheldon to finish. "So do you miss California?" Sheldon asked.

"Yes, very much so," Chase replied. "I will probably move back there one day. I often wonder what my friends are up too. I could write them but time flies by so fast."

"What are you friend's names?" Sheldon inquired as he tried to get Chase to share more about himself.

"Glenn Ford and Camille Salazar," Chase stated, looking at him curiously. "I will tell you about them sometime, but right now let's try some diving."

Sheldon did not like the idea of jumping headfirst into the water; it just did not seem natural to him. "Let's do a few off the side of the pool before doing the diving board," Chase requested as he immediately dove into the pool.

Chase demonstrated a few dives and made it seem easy. "Now you try a basic dive," Chase requested.

Sheldon stood at the edge of the pool and kept leaning in like he was going to dive, but the fear of the water was winning, and letting go was hard. Finally, Sheldon dove into the pool. He dove awkwardly and hit the water at an angle, splashing water everywhere.

"That wasn't that bad," Sheldon observed as he came back up. "I got some water in my ear, but it wasn't that bad."

"Not bad at all," Chase remarked as he tried to encourage Sheldon. "That is why it's important to press your arms to your ears as you enter the water it helps keep water from rushing into your ears."

They both took turns diving before stopping for the day. "Do you work tomorrow?" Chase asked.

"Yes, only a couple of hours so not too bad," Sheldon replied.

"Nice, well don't work too hard," Chase said as he dove back into the pool to do some laps.

Sheldon watched him for a second before heading out. He never knew what to say to Chase to get him to share more intimate details.

Saturday as Sheldon was leaving work, he found Chase leaning against his car. "What are you doing here?" Sheldon asked him with a smile on his face.

"I told you I was going to take you for a ride in my car so you can see how nice it is" Chase replied. "Now get in, or do you have somewhere better to be?"

"Shut up," Sheldon fired back. "I hope you're a better driver than you did during driver's Ed."

"Please, I'm the best there ever was," Chase protested with a cocky attitude. "Now buckle up."

They drove out of town into the country with the music blaring and the top down. It was nice to smell the fresh air and wind blowing through their hair. Sheldon puts his hand out to feel the wind blowing on it until a bug hits his arm, causing him to scream like a girl; they both laugh. Sheldon was the happiest in that moment than he had been in a long time. It was nice sitting next to Chase in his car. They drove without a care in the world. If he could freeze time, he would have. They both laughed and sang along to the radio. When they finished driving Chase dropped Sheldon off to his car. Sheldon went to open the car door, but it would not open. Chase leaned over coming remarkably close to Sheldon.

"You have to push as you pull the door handle," Chase explained, slightly embarrassed as he opened the door. "I'm working on getting that fixed." He paused for a moment looking deep into Sheldon's eyes. Their faces were the closest they had ever been.

Sheldon's heart started pounding so loud he thought Chase could hear it. He felt like Chase was about to kiss him, but the moment passed. "I will see you Monday," Chase whispered as he looked at Sheldon with that cute, innocent look.

"Yeah, see you Monday," Sheldon choked out, not wanting to get out of the car, but he did anyway. His body moved like it had a mind of its own. "Thanks for taking me for a ride."

"Anytime. Have a good night," Chase smiled, waiting for Sheldon to get into his car and start it up before he drove off. "What a gentleman," Sheldon said aloud and headed home.

Chapter Seven

A Long-Wet Kiss

Ruby danced around her room with a hairbrush and sang along with Pat Benatar's *Love is a Battlefield*. She kicked empty boxes towards the door as she danced around the room. She finally decided to unpack the last of her stuff and was celebrating. Ruby decided to get rid of Jake's old letters. She could not part with his hoodie, which was boxed up and shoved in her closet. She decided to write a letter to Jeremy before she got busy again. Ruby grabbed her notebook and jumped onto the bed.

October, 20th 1990

Dear J,

Sorry, I haven't written lately. I have been busy adjusting to the new school and new friends. I'm surprised because I didn't think I would meet any cool people here, but I have made a really awesome group of friends. Though, no one could ever replace or compare to you. I can't believe Halloween is a little over a week away. I miss going to the movies with you. I loved it when we would watch a good scary movie and scream our heads off. I still haven't gotten to see The Exorcist III, so I should ask Sheldon and Ninnie if they want to see it together to celebrate Halloween.

I wanted to go with Trey, but he has been kind of distant. He asked me to ride with him to school a couple of times, but that was it. As good-looking as he is, I'm sure he has a girlfriend or two. Plus, I don't know why I even care; he isn't my type. Though there is something about those eyes, those lips. Sorry, I drifted off there for a moment. Ha-Ha. Enough about me, what about you? In your last letter, you didn't tell me about your new boyfriend what is up with that?

I feel like my life has been all over the place much like this letter, but that is kind of how the past few months have been. It's like everything has been upside down. My parents are acting strange and barely talking to one another. Moving here was supposed to bring us closer, but in fact, it seems to have only pushed them further apart. Anyway, on the bright side, they are letting me do pretty much whatever I want without question.

I guess I should wrap this up and take my empty boxes to the trash. Yes, I finally finished unpacking. I have settled into the fact that we are living here now, at least for a little while. Ugh, I have a paper to write for English Lit that I have been procrastinating on. I need to get started on that, too. I promise I will write to you again soon.

You're Friend Always,
Ruby

A couple of days later, Ruby and Sheldon were in the library working on their paper for English Lit. They both decided to skip lunch to finish their paper due the next day. The library and cafeteria were next to one another and separated by massive floor-to-ceiling glass walls. Everyone could see what was happening in either room. At that moment, the seniors and juniors were having lunch when Ruby whispered, "Isn't that your cousin all up in that girl's face?"

Sheldon looked to where she was pointing and said, "Yes, it is, but what is she doing with that Susy Q in her hand?"

At that exact moment, Shawndrea shoved the Susy Q chocolate snack cake right into Yesinia's face, and the whole cafeteria roared. "Oh man, your cousin has some balls," Ruby admired. "I love it! She shoved it right in her face, and look, it's all in her hair and everything."

Yesinia's boyfriend was at the jock's table, and one of his friends commented, "Dude, these girls are totally fighting over you. Shit, you have it going on, my man." They started high-fiving each other.

Yesenia had been spreading rumors all over the school that Shawndrea was a whore and would fuck anyone's man. Shawndrea was at the vending machine getting something out of it when she heard

Yesinia talking shit about her when something in her snapped. She had enough of Yesinia bad-mouthing her and took matters into her own hands. Yesinia got up from the table, wiping the chocolate cake and the white cream from her eyes.

You could tell she did not see that coming. Yesinia's friends just sat at the table for a second in shock, and then they all jumped up from the table, grabbed their things, and backed away. Suddenly, a circle formed around the two girls. "Ooh bitch, you don't know what you just did," Yesenia smarted off with a pissed-off look on her face as Shawndrea turned to leave. Shawndrea had a proud look as Yesinia grabbed the back of her head with a handful of hair and jerked her backward.

The two girls attacked each other like two wild animals on Animal Planet. Each girl had their hand entangled in the other girl's hair, trying to pull each other to the ground and trying to be the one on top of the other girl. Ruby looked at Sheldon. "Holy shit, this is better than any fight I saw in New York," Ruby commented, not taking her eyes off the fight.

The crowd around the girls started cheering them on by chanting, "Fight! Fight! Fight!"

"Scratch the little whore's eyes out!" Someone from the crowd yelled.

"They are cheering like it's a football game," Ruby remarked as she stood on her chair to watch.

The lunchroom doors flew open, and two male teachers entered the room. They started to push their way through the crowd. Each one grabbed a girl and tried to pull them apart, but the two girls were latched onto each other so tight. They were going at each other so intensely that they shoved one of the teachers backward, causing him to lose his balance. When he stepped back to balance himself, he tripped over a chair and landed on his back with his legs in the air, flopping around like a bug. Everyone burst into laughter, which only pissed the teacher off even more. When he stood back up, he started yelling at the crowd surrounding the two girls, "Go on about your business. There is nothing to see here."

They finally got the two girls pulled apart, and each girl had a hand full of the other girl's hair. Yesinia had blood running down her face from a cut to her eyebrow. She tried to kick her legs towards Shawndrea, but the teacher pulled her back and firmed his grip on her. Shawndrea was breathing heavily, and her hair looked like a wild woman. They took the two girls out of the lunchroom. Neither girl was seen the rest of the day.

"That was intense; you think it was all over a man?" Ruby inquired, looking at Sheldon, raising her eyebrows.

Sheldon chuckled, "Funny what a guy will make you do sometimes," Sheldon commented. He thought about Chase and the things he would do for him or… to him. "I bet it had to be more to the story for Shawn to go and try and kick her butt."

"Yea, it is funny what guys make us do," Ruby agreed, smiling at Sheldon. "Speaking of men, how are your swimming lessons coming along?" She asked teasingly, watching his reaction.

"They are going well," Sheldon replied with a huge smile, trying not to look her in the eye. "Hey, did you know Chase is a football player?"

"Yes, everyone knows that. Where have you been?" Ruby asked, looking at him, unsure if he was joking or serious. "Plus, he isn't just a football player. He is the quarterback. Speaking of football players, Trey is on the team too."

"Hum, I didn't know that either," Sheldon pondered, lost in thought. *How did he not know this about Chase? Had he been that self-involved?* "Well, you know me and sports."

"You should come with me to a football game sometime," Ruby requested. "It's no wonder you don't have a lot of friends, being that you're not very social and live in the middle of a field. Hey, do you think you could do me a favor?"

"Uh, sure, what is it exactly?" Sheldon asked, looking at her from the corner of his eye.

"Do you think that maybe you could ask Chase if Trey is seeing anyone?" Ruby asked, kind of shy and innocent, with her arms stretched out on the table and her hands crossed in a twisted manner.

"Wow, we are definitely in high school. Let me see what I can't find out for you," Sheldon smirked, raising his eyebrows. "Detective Majors is on the case. I will ask him when I see him later today. Right now, we better get to class."

"Thank you," Ruby replied, gathering her stuff together and getting ready to head to class. "Oh, now I'm nervous. Maybe you shouldn't ask."

"Ruby quit being a pussy," Sheldon commanded her as they were leaving the library. "It will be okay either way."

"Well damn, look at you being all hard and shit," Ruby remarked, half laughing as they walked down the hall. "You're really coming out of your shell, and I like it. See you later."

"See you later, Ruby," Sheldon waved as he headed to class.

§

Later that afternoon, Sheldon walked into the pool area, and as usual, Chase was already doing laps. *No wonder he is in such great shape. He is always moving.* Sheldon stopped to watch before going to change into his swim trunks. He came out, and Chase was toweling off his face as the water dripped down his muscular, well-tanned body. He must have been in the sun a lot with his shirt off because he did not have a farmer's tan. Sheldon caught himself staring and quickly looked away as Chase turned towards him.

"Now, let's start with some warmup laps," Chase instructed as he walked with Sheldon to the pool's shallow end. He turned away to reach into his speedos and adjust himself like a guy typically does.

Sheldon tried to pretend he did not just see that or that he was semi-erect. "Sorry, I just bought this new swimwear," Chase quickly acknowledged, then cleared his throat, looking to see if Sheldon approved. "After warming up, we will begin to practice some of the newer strokes I have taught you."

Sheldon did as instructed. When he finished, he found Chase sitting on the pool's edge with his feet dangling in the water. He was watching Sheldon intensely, and Sheldon could feel it. "What?" Sheldon inquired Chase with a half-smile, "Did I do something wrong with my strokes?"

"No, sorry, I was just thinking," Chase replied dismissively. "Now, let's work on perfecting your breaststroke."

"I wanted to ask you something," Sheldon asked, pulling himself to the side of the pool next to Chase.

"What do you want to know?" Chase replied with an inquisitive look on his face.

"Is Trey seeing someone, and what does he like to do for fun?" Sheldon asked awkwardly, and as soon as it was out of his mouth, he knew it was strange to ask out of the blue about another guy.

"Yes, he is single, and he likes to do things that normal guys like to do," Chase replied, a little annoyed. "Why are you asking?"

Sheldon had yet to think this through thoroughly. "No reason. I was just curious," Sheldon replied, stating the first thing he could think of. He did not want to push the subject further, and he could tell it bothered Chase, though he wasn't quite sure why. *What do "normal" guys do?* Sheldon pondered for a moment.

"Good, now let's get to it," Chase snapped, pulling Sheldon out of his thoughts. He no longer had a smile. Chase sat on the pool's edge at the shallow end, watching Sheldon lost in thought. Suddenly, he saw that Sheldon was not slowing down and looked like he would crash into the wall. Chase jumped into the pool to stop him. He got between Sheldon and the wall. Sheldon came up half-shocked. He was not expecting to run into anything, let alone Chase.

"What were you thinking?" Chase asked sternly.

"I… I… don't know. I was focusing on my form, and I didn't realize how close I was to the wall," Sheldon replied, a little taken back at how upset Chase seemed over the situation. "I would have stopped."

"Well, it didn't appear that way to me," Chase countered with a concerned look.

Suddenly, something snapped inside of Chase. Sheldon could see it clearly on his face. Chase stepped closer to Sheldon. He put his hand on Sheldon's hip and pulled their bodies together. He placed his other hand in Sheldon's hair at the base of his neck and pulled Sheldon in for a passionate kiss. The surprise kiss threw Sheldon off literally. He lost his balance from being pulled closer, which caused them both to go under.

At first, Sheldon began to panic for a second. Being in Chase's arms, their bodies pressed against one another, helped Sheldon let go for once and become lost in the moment. Having Chase's tongue in his mouth seemed foreign, yet it felt like it belonged there. He could not tell if he was doing it right, but that did not matter.

He only knew he never wanted the moment to end. The feeling was one of the greatest feelings he had ever felt. Nothing and no one else in the world mattered at that moment. Only the two of them shared this experience.

When they broke the surface, so did the moment. Chase looked at him with his hand still on Sheldon's face. Sheldon could see pain in his eyes and an innocent expression. "I'm sorry I shouldn't have," Chase confessed with one hand on Sheldon's shoulder. He turned to leave. "I can't, I have to go."

Chase climbed out of the pool and ran to the locker room. Sheldon was left standing there in the pool in shock. For him, it was like all the pieces of the puzzle had just fit together, and he wanted to savor their experience together. By the time Sheldon got out of the pool and went to the locker room, Chase had only left a water trail. He did not even stop to change his clothes. He grabbed his stuff and ran. Sheldon was confused about what just happened. He got changed and left. On the drive home, he had almost convinced himself that it had not happened.

The next day, at lunch, Ruby could tell something was troubling Sheldon even though he was attempting to hide it. "What is up with you today?" Ruby asked as she was eating her salad without dressing.

"Nothing, just a lot going on," Sheldon replied, looking at her. "I still do not know how you eat a salad without dressing."

"I don't know how anyone eats salad with dressing. It seems unnatural to me," Ruby remarked, poking at her food, then she laid her fork down. "Now quit trying to change the subject and spill what is it?

"You know I have been taking swim lessons with Chase, and they've been strictly instructional and serious?" Sheldon asked.

"Mmmhhhmm," Ruby replied as she took a drink of water and looked at him intensely, waiting for what he would say next.

"Well..." Sheldon paused as he hesitated on what to say. "He kissed me," He finally blurted out.

"What?!" Ruby quietly exclaimed. "He did what?"

"Yes, now he is not talking to me," Sheldon replied. "I have not seen or heard from him since."

"Yup, suspend for two weeks," Ninnie interrupted as she placed her stuff on the lunch table. "Little Miss Hot Pants got a two-week free get-out-of-jail card."

She looked at the two of them, sensing something was off with them. "Ooookay, you two, what good stuff did I miss?" Ninnie asked, eyeballing them both.

Ruby shifted a little in her chair as she and Sheldon exchanged looks. "Weeell... I kissed someone," Sheldon drawled out shyly, "and... it was fucking amazing."

"Shut the fuck up!" Ninnie shouted so loudly that people around them looked. "Who? Tell me! Tell me!" Ninnie commanded in an attempt to whisper.

"I can't tell *you* here," Sheldon whispered. He knew when he told her she shouldn't be near other people. "I will tell you later."

"Uhhuhh, you're going to spill now, Mister," Ninnie demanded as she dragged him into the hall. "I can't wait for news like this. Are you crazy? Who was it?" Ninnie asked as soon as they were in the hall and checked to ensure no one was around.

Ruby could hear Ninnie yelling, "What?!" loudly from outside the cafeteria, but no one else seemed to take notice. Ruby tried not to laugh at Ninnie as they returned to the cafeteria.

Ninnie looked a bit shocked, and it was hard to shock her. She took a few moments to compose herself. It looked like Ninnie was about to say something. "Now Chase is not talking to him and has completely shut down," Ruby exclaimed with frustration as if it were happening to her.

"Maybe he just needs time to process what happened," Ninnie surmised, stammering and stuttering. "Kind of like me. Are you sure he kissed you? Cause... I thought for sure he was into me."

"Yes, Ninnie, this is something you know whether it happened or didn't happen," Ruby answered for Sheldon.

Sheldon watched the two of them go back and forth, answering each other's questions and leaving him out even though it was his story. He could not believe this was happening; it was like watching a tennis match. Despite the girls talking, they still managed to finish their food. Sheldon, however, did not eat, which was highly unusual for him. "I just want to forget it happened," Sheldon finally interjected, getting up from the table. "Okay? Can we not talk about it anymore?"

They all got up from the table and threw away their garbage. One could see the wheels turning in Ninnie's head. She did not like awkward situations and always felt like she had to fix things. "I know what we can do tonight to let our hair down and have some real fun," Ninnie mentioned as they headed out of the cafeteria and to their next class.

"Ninnie, I don't think Sheldon is in the mood to get his toenails done," Ruby teased, making fun of Ninnie's lack of a wild side.

"Hey! I can get just as crazy as everyone else," Ninnie defended herself. "I... I... I think we should go Teepeeing," she blurted out. As the words came out of her mouth, she felt as if someone else was uttering them.

Even Sheldon stopped in his tracks and turned to face Ninnie. "Okay, where is Ninnie? What have you done with her?" Sheldon asked as he grabbed her shoulders and examined her eyes for traces of something foreign inside her. "Do you even know how to teepee?"

"You guys keep talking about teepeeing," Ruby stated, standing beside them. "You have to take me, but I definitely do not want to go cow-tipping.

They both looked at her weirdly, "Cow tipping? No one does that here. Freak," Ninnie teased as she playfully nudged her.

Just then, the bell rang, and all three of them were late for their next class. "This conversation isn't over, Ninnie," Sheldon demanded as he pointed at her and took off for his next class.

"Eeeehhhh," Ninnie moaned. "What is becoming of me? I'm late for class, and now you want me to trash someone's yard!?" Ninnie commented as she realized she was now standing alone in the hallway. "And great, now I'm talking to myself. You two are a bad influence!" she yelled after them.

§

October 31ˢᵗ 1990

Hey J,

Oh my god, I had to write this down before I forgot. Tonight was one of the funniest nights ever. I finally found out what Teepeeing was all about. Heck, I'm still not sure how it's even spelled, but who cares? We had a blast.

Now, I know why Sheldon loves this time of year. With the leaves changing colors and falling, pumpkins everywhere you go. It feels like there is this sense of newness, or freshness in the air.

Anyway, let me tell you how this amazing night started. First, Sheldon took Ninnie and me to the grocery store to get supplies, including a lot of toilet paper and snacks. Did I mention a lot of toilet paper? We each grabbed two of the most extensive packages of toilet paper we could find. As we were standing in the checkout line, I began to freak out. I was worried about what people would think about us buying so much toilet paper. Of course, Sheldon knew everyone there, and they teased us. They knew exactly what we were up to. Sheldon's manager came out of the office and took one look. She said you better not go to my house with that toilet paper, Mr. Majors.

The checkout girl looked at me and must have seen how anxious I was because she said this is your first time, huh. Don't worry about it. You will have fun. We paid for our supplies and left the store.

As we headed out of town, we stopped for hot chocolate, and I ran into Trey. He was standing next to the car, and he saw it loaded down with toilet paper. At first, I was so embarrassed, and I could feel my face turning red. He looked into the car and said wow, you either have a serious problem, or you're about to have some fun. It's nice to see the big city girl starting to fit in around here. He smiled and winked at me. Then he turned and walked away.

I barely got two words out of my mouth, and why I still don't know much about him or if he is even single, which reminds me that Sheldon never reported back. I guess he got distracted by being kissed and all! God, I love to watch Trey walk. He looks so fine in his blue jeans. Okay, sorry, I got off course. Now, back to the topic. So, as we got close to the house where we intended to litter their yard with toilet paper, Sheldon shut the car lights off as he was driving down this deserted road, and we stopped down the road from a farmhouse. Ninnie didn't realize where they had gone at first, but when she did, she was ecstatic. As it turns out, we were going to teepee Yesenia's house, the girl that gave Shawndrea hell. Sheldon said the family must stick together.

So, there we were, dressed in all black but with white toilet paper in hand, looking like ninjas. I started to think it was not such a good idea. I felt completely exposed in the open as we crept to someone's house. Shel-

don told me they were probably in town, so we would be okay. These people had giant trees and bushes in their yard, so I knew it was about to get ugly.

Sheldon showed me how to pull some of the paper loose, and then he threw the roll into the air. When the roll came down, it hit branches and left trails of paper throughout the huge tree. Each time the roll came out of the tree, it left a long sheet of paper blowing in the wind. Seeing that got me so excited that I started lobbing rolls in the air like a mad woman. I don't know what came over me.

Ninnie was off wrapping the bushes. She wasn't good at throwing the roll into the tree and said fuck it. She started decorating the bushes. I went through all my toilet paper and began on Ninnie's when we saw headlights coming down the road. I froze like what they call a Deer in headlights. Yes, that is an actual saying. I just froze. I felt like the jig was up. Sheldon grabbed me and said we have to go now. Ninnie threw the last roll at the house, and it went over the house, leaving a long trail. She was surprised yet irritated at how far the roll flew. It took adrenaline to give her the strength to throw it that far. We jumped in the car and took off just before the car got close enough to see us. We were out of breath from running and laughing at the same time. I don't think I have ever had so much fun. Man, this has to be one of the longest letters I have ever written. I guess you can see how excited I am. I think you would love Sheldon and Ninnie. You would fit right in here. Oh, I almost forgot we have a four-day weekend. Friday is parent-teacher conferences, and then Monday is the start of hunting season, so we get Monday off, too.

I am starting to like this small-town life. Anyway, since it's the long weekend, they are going camping, and I'm going with them if you can believe it. Can you imagine me camping? That's never happened. I'm riding with Ninnie and her family. Sheldon told me Ninnie's Mom can be quite scary at times. I will have to tell you all about it once I get back.

I truly hope you're happy, and I can't wait to see you again soon. I hope we come to visit during the holidays, but with the way my parents are acting, I don't know anymore. That will be for another letter, another time. Talk to you again soon.

Your Friend Always,
Love, Ruby

P.S. Happy Halloween!!!

Chapter Eight

Camping

Early Friday morning, Sheldon gathered his camping gear. He was only half awake, and the sun was not fully up yet. There was dew on the ground and a light fog in the air. He and his family started to load the Suburban with their camping gear. His Mom, Mandy, backed the suburban up and attached the horse trailer. They loaded the trailer with the horses and the riding equipment. Then, they headed into town to meet Aunty Letty. As Mandy pulled into the town square, she saw Aunt Letty, her kids, and Ruby already parked. Mandy pulled up next to them.

"Hey, Mandy, I bought some donuts if you and the boys want to grab one before we hit the road." Letty offered as she was standing next to their van with a cup of coffee, eating a donut, and smoking a cigarette. "They are fresh, just made. Come on and get one before Jimmy devours them all." She waved them over and laughed with her unique boisterous laugh. Sheldon could see they had their van loaded up and were ready to go. They all grabbed a donut and hit the road.

Everyone was in great spirits as they headed out of town. In the Suburban, everyone was singing along to the radio, and in the van, the girls were laughing while Shawndrea recounted the Susy Q incident. Aunty Letty was trying not to laugh. "And that there, missy, is why you're still grounded," Aunty Letty remarked, not taking her eyes off the road. She took a drag off her cigarette. Aunt Letty always took driving seriously with both hands on the wheel at two and ten, but she always had a cigarette clutched between her fingers.

Every year, they went camping at the Garden of the Gods in southern Illinois, about an hour and a half south of where they lived. Fall in southern Illinois was a beautiful time of the year. Though the leaves were dying, they made a colorful landscape. The trees were full of vibrant colors, leaving one in awe. Fall was the perfect time of the year to go camping.

When they got to the campsite, they looked for a suitable place to camp. Sheldon's Mom, Mandy, spotted her longtime friend Wendy, who already had her camp set up and a fire going. "Well, we have arrived, boys," Their Mom sang out as she parked the suburban and horse trailer next to Wendy's camp. Letty and her kids can park next to us. There should be enough room for their van and horse trailer."

"Wow, you don't waste any time," Mandy commented as she exited the vehicle and walked up to Wendy, seated by the fire. "What time did you get here?"

"You know I do not waste any time. I have been here since yesterday," Wendy replied, greeting Mandy and the boys. "It's been quiet for the most part. Last night, there was a little drunken scuffle with the Marshal Brothers, but the Park Ranger already kicked them out."

"It's so good to see you," Mandy stated as she hugged Wendy. "It's been too long. We need to get together more often than once a year."

"Let's get this party started," Shawndrea shouted as they walked up. "Where are the hot boys?"

"Get your butt back to the van and get the damn tents out. We are not here for boys," Aunt Letty ordered Shawndrea, pointing towards the van. "We aren't here five minutes, and you're already on my damn nerves," She muttered as she lit a cigarette. "As soon as you get that shit set up, get me a beer."

Mandy introduced Letty to Wendy. They sat beside the campfire and chatted while the kids set up the tents. Sheldon and Mandy would sleep in the Suburban. The boys would sleep in one tent, Ninnie in another, and Ruby in another. Aunt Letty and Shawndrea would sleep in the van.

The following day, Sheldon woke up disoriented, unsure of where he was. Before we even opened his eyes, he could hear muffled voices. He quickly remembered they were camping, and he was in the back of the Suburban. It was early Saturday morning, and voices came from outside the vehicle. The sun was not even quite up yet. His Mom's sleeping bag was already empty. He threw back his sleeping bag and found his shoes and jacket. He scooted towards the rear door to get out of the vehicle. He slipped on his shoes and climbed out of the Suburban. He could see the dew on the ground and felt a slight chill in the air.

He headed to see what everyone was up to and to use the porta-potties. It was chilly outside, and the dew made it feel even colder. The smell of the forest in the morning was amazing. One could not help but draw in a couple of deep breaths. The air was so fresh, aside from the campfire smoke.

Wendy and Mandy were already sitting by the campfire, having coffee and laughing. Sheldon noticed the way Wendy was looking at his Mom. Has *she always looked that way at his Mom, or is he only now noticing?* Suddenly, someone poked him in the ribs from behind. He jumped as he turned to see Ninnie and Ruby standing there. "I still can't believe we convinced you to come," He remarked as he looked at Ruby with a slight smile. "How did you two sleep last night?"

"This one snores like a bear in hibernation," Ruby tried to imitate Ninnie snoring, causing Sheldon to laugh while Ninnie gave her a "bitch please" look.

"Psssh, whatever," Ninnie scoffed and shrugged off her statement as if she did not know what Ruby was talking about. "This one here tossed and flopped all night long. You would think she was fighting someone in her sleep."

"I can say this has already been an interesting experience," Ruby remarked with both eyebrows raised as she pulled her jacket tighter. "I didn't realize how cold it was going to be. I'm glad I listened to you about bringing a jacket." They started walking towards the bathrooms as they all thought the same thing.

"What an interesting family you two have," Ruby commented as she turned to look at Ninnie and Sheldon. "You guys are a nonstop laugh fest, and I love it. It's different than my family dynamics."

"Glad we can be of service," Ninnie teased as she bowed her head towards Ruby. "Surprise, surprise, there is already a line for the women's bathroom." The girls waited in line while Sheldon was glad to be a guy. He went and took care of business. When he came out, Ninnie and Ruby stared at Wendy and Mandy. "What I'm more interested in is the fact that your Mom's friend Wendy hasn't stopped staring at her like a piece of meat since we got here," Ninnie continued, not missing a beat as she motioned with her head towards where Mandy and Wendy were sitting.

"Yeah, I noticed that too," Ruby agreed as she entered the women's bathroom. "I was going to ask what is up with that."

Sheldon and Ninnie waited for Ruby to finish in the ladies' room before returning to the camp. "You know I have no idea what is going on there," Sheldon responded as he watched his Mom and Wendy. I don't think Mom even notices it, but she does seem to enjoy whatever "IT" is. Where is your Mom?" Sheldon asked, looking at Ninnie.

"Oh lord, are you kidding me? The royal Highness herself does not roll out of bed before Ten O'clock," Ninnie scoffed. "And her sidekick Shawndrea is right there with her. Jimmy is off with Levin," Ninnie added, shaking her head. "They think they can go hunting with just a stick."

"Mom and Wendy will want to go riding by eight-thirty at the latest," Sheldon stated, looking at Ninnie. "Should we go wake them?"

"If you value your life, I wouldn't," Ninnie warned with a profoundly severe look. "You think I'm kidding?" She chuckled without humor.

Ruby and Sheldon laughed. "Well, maybe we could wake them up without them knowing it was us?" Ruby asked. She could see their questioning, so she continued. "We could throw rocks at the van, make loud bird noises, maybe rock the van a little, and yell earthquake?"

"Girl, I like where your head is at. You like living dangerously, don't you?" Ninnie remarked, looking at Ruby with her head half-cocked. "But I love it! You will fit right in with this family."

The three of them walked over to the van nearest the woods and about five feet from the forest's growth. They gathered a couple of small stones and twigs. They each hid behind a tree. They took turns lobbing the objects at the van and making bird noises. Sheldon made bird sounds that resembled a bird being murdered.

Ruby and Ninnie were trying to keep from laughing. Ninnie waved her hands at him to get him to stop.

Suddenly, the van door flew open, and they hid behind the trees. Aunt Letty popped her head out and yelled, "Jimmy! I'm going to kick your goddamn ass if you don't stop right now!"

The three of them were bent over as they tried to laugh as quietly as possible. They made bird noises as they ran away from the scene of the crime. They came to a clearing and stopped running. "Oh my god, that was too funny," Ninnie burst out laughing as she bent over, trying to catch her breath from running. "Jimmy got the blame even though he wasn't there."

When they returned from the woods, they hurried to the campfire and sat beside Wendy and Mandy. Sheldon tried to look innocent as he sat down next to his Mom. "We have been here the whole time," he whispered as he leaned over the arm of his chair to tell his Mom.

"Okay," She replied, looking at them curiously.

"That goddamn brat," Aunt Letty grumpily muttered as she walked up to the campfire. Her hair was flat on one side, with a cigarette hanging from her mouth. "Let me have this chair." She demanded, looking at Sheldon.

Sheldon got up, and she plopped down. She lit a cigarette with the one that was just in her mouth. "Get me a cup of coffee, will ya?" She instructed, looking at Ninnie. "Be useful for more than just sitting there and keeping that chair warm.

They were all looking at her, waiting to see what she would say or do next. She coughed a little as she rubbed her neck. "Now I remember why I stopped camping. Sleeping in that damn van is hard on my neck."

"I'm going to go get the horses ready," Wendy stated, looking uncomfortable as she got up from her chair. "Are you coming, Mandy?"

"Right behind you," She replied. She stood up and smiled at the kids. "We will be heading out in half an hour."

Aunt Letty mouths the words, *Are you coming, Mandy?* "What the fuck is up with your Mom and that Dike?" Aunt Letty bluntly asked Sheldon once Mandy and Wendy were out of earshot. She was exhaling smoke out her mouth while she talked. "She has been up your Mom's ass since we got here."

"Mooooom!" Ninnie exclaimed as she handed her a cup of coffee and sat back down.

"What?!" She retorted. "Well… It's true. Am I not right, Rudy?"

Ruby looked like a deer in headlights, and her mouth fell open, unsure if she was supposed to answer. She wondered how she got pulled into the debate.

"Mom, her name is Ruby," Ninnie snapped at her Mom. "Aaand that is just plain rude. If Dad were here, he would tell you the same thing. We are going to go and get the horses ready. They are heading out soon, and I want to be ready."

The three left Letty sitting there sipping her coffee and muttering to herself. "What did I do? Besides, your dad isn't here, is he? That's right, I'm divorcing his ass," She chuckled with a sinister smoker's laugh followed by a smoker's cough. "Nin, get my horse ready too!" She yelled out after her.

"I told you two we were awaking a sleeping monster," Ninnie reminded them as they walked over to the horse trailers to get out the saddles and bridles to saddle up the horses. "And where are Jimmy and Levin? I am not saddling their horses up for them."

They started to prepare the horses. After finishing their horses, Mandy and Wendy walked over to help and offered to prepare the other horses.

"Are you okay?" Sheldon asked Ruby, who had no idea what to do and looked worried. "You will be fine. It's like riding a bike."

"Uh yeah, if the bike is five feet off the ground," Ruby countered, looking nauseous. "That is a long way down if I fall off. Maybe I should wait here till you get back."

"Oh no, little missy, you're going to get your little butt on that horse and ride with us," Aunt Letty demanded as she walked up behind them. "This here is Blackjack. He is the nicest of the bunch and will take good care of you."

Ruby was afraid to even say no to Aunty Letty at this point. "This was more like six feet off the ground," she muttered as she walked over to the horse and tried to climb up. It was like trying to watch a drunken person step up onto a curb. "You guys had better not be laughing at me," Ruby snapped at Sheldon and Ninnie as she tried to put her foot in the stirrup. "This is not as easy as Mandy and Wendy made it look."

"Get over there and help her, Sheldon," Aunty Letty ordered Sheldon and shoved him in Ruby's direction. "Where are your manners, and where are those boys? She started to yell Jimmy and Levin's names so loudly there was no way the whole camp could not have heard it."

The boys ran out of the woods just as everyone got on their horses. Once everyone was ready, they started heading for trail marker number one. A slim older man in his mid-to early fifties with dirty blonde hair rode up on a beautiful palomino horse. He rode his horse right up to Mandy, who happened to be in the front of the line, with Wendy second and Aunt Letty third.

When he got up to Mandy, he started talking to her. Sheldon could not hear what he said clearly, but he sure heard Aunt Letty. So Sheldon pulled his horse between Aunt Letty and Wendy. "Who is this bozzo?" Aunt Letty asked, looking him up and down.

"That is one of the park rangers," Wendy replied, looking annoyed. "His name is Ted. He has been eyeballing Mandy since she got here."

Both Aunt Letty and Sheldon looked at each other with a smirk. Mandy turned her horse around to explain who the guy was and what he was telling her. "This is Ted. He is one of the Park Rangers. Due to recent storms, many trees have been knocked down and blocking the trails. His orders were to lead anyone going down the main trail personally."

"Sounds like a lot of horse shit if you ask me," Aunt Letty protested with a snort. "He sees a bunch of women, thinks we are helpless, and that he can get lucky with one of us. I may have been born at night, but it wasn't last night."

Mandy shook her head at Aunt Letty and rolled her eyes. "Come on, everyone," Mandy called out as she turned her horse around and fell behind the Park Ranger.

"I can't believe this crap," Wendy fumed as she glared at the back of the Park Ranger's head. If her eyes were lasers, his head would have exploded. "I don't need any man showing me the way."

As they rode down the trail, Sheldon admired the beauty,

peacefulness, and fresh air. At times, it was so quiet that all you could hear were the horses occasionally snapping a twig under the weight of their hooves. They took minor detours around downed trees. The problem with the detour paths was that they were still working to clear the branches and bushes, and they had to duck under low-lying branches. Sheldon would look back at Ruby, checking how she was doing. Just as he turned around, a branch smacked him square in the face. "Look out! Ninnie shouted with a giggle.

"Thanks, but a little late on the heads up there, Ninnie," Sheldon said, turning around to warn Ruby while rubbing his forehead. "Watch out for the branch."

Suddenly, there was a commotion from the front of the pack, and they all had to stop. Mandy's horse had gotten stung by something and started to buck, almost throwing Mandy off before bolting through the woods. The Park Ranger took off on his horse to catch Mandy. He was able to get his horse in front of Mandy's horse. "Well, isn't he just the Hero," Wendy snorted, highly irritated. "Mandy's an expert rider and she can get her horse under her control by herself. You okay, Mandy?!" Wendy yelled as Mandy rode back to the trail.

"Yeah," Mandy laughed as she and the Park Ranger returned to the trail. "She just got a little spooked from the bee sting. She will be fine," she added, patting the horse's neck.

The rest of the ride was relaxing and peaceful. Ted stuck to Mandy like glue, which rubbed Wendy the wrong way. If smoke could truly come out of someone's ears, it would be Wendy's right about now. Ted was taking up all of Mandy's attention.

That night, Sheldon, Ninnie, and Ruby sat around the campfire while everyone else was off doing their own thing. The adults went to watch a live band and to dance. The boys were off into who knows what. The three talked about what they planned to do for their future. Ruby was talking about going back east and attending Brown University to study psychology. She decided she wanted to be a family psychologist.

Ninnie talked about heading out to California and working for a resort, eventually opening her hotel or resort one day. Sheldon was thinking about what he wanted to do. "Honestly, I have no idea; I guess I haven't really thought about it. I want to do something creative. I think. I definitely know, I do not want to be a farmer or a factory worker like my parents."

"You better think about it soon," Ninnie stated, looking at him, surprised by his response. "Because next year is senior year, and then we are done. Oh my god, done," Ninnie realized with a shocked look as it fully registered. "Man, saying that out loud makes me truly realize it's going to really happen. I have been so ready to finish high school, but now it seems like it's happening so fast. I need to get my shit together, too, and start looking at which schools have programs for hotel management. Sheldon, I'm surprised you don't know what you want to do after high school. There are not many options here for us."

"That is true," Sheldon agreed with a thoughtful look. "Let's not dwell on that now. Oh, I asked Mom if she realized Wendy was in love with her, and she called me crazy. I pointed out all the signs, and she said I was being ridiculous."

"Denial," Ninnie said, and they all laughed. That lady has it bad for her, like her pants are on fire, and Aunt Mandy is the water that can put out the flames."

"Oh my god, speaking of hot pants," Sheldon interjected as he suddenly realized he had forgotten something. "We were supposed to go check on Shawndrea to ensure she is okay or not getting into trouble."

Shawndrea decided to drink with a few guys at their camp. Sheldon didn't think it was a good idea, but Shawndrea insisted she would be okay and didn't need a chaperone. She told him they could check on her after an hour to ensure she was alright. It was a way out in case she wasn't feeling it with any of the guys.

"I'm not going. Shawn made her bed so she could lie in it." Ninnie remarked, annoyed as all hell. "I'm gonna sit here by this fire and enjoy the peace and quiet without her loudmouth being here ruining it."

"I will go with you," Ruby offered. "Sorry, Ninnie, this should be interesting, and I don't want to miss out."

Sheldon and Ruby made their way in the direction Shawndrea said the camp was. It would have been impossible to see their way without the moonlight because it was so dark. As they walked down the path, the darkness started making it harder and harder to see. The path went in different directions. "Uh, maybe we should have brought a flashlight," Ruby's voice quivered as she looked around, afraid something would jump out of the bushes at them. She held on tighter to Sheldon's arm.

"I was just thinking the same thing," Sheldon agreed. "I think it's straight ahead."

"What was that noise?"Ruby asked, slightly panicked. "Did you hear that?"

"It was a frog, but... Stop," Sheldon explained as he saw the moon reflecting before them. He stopped them just before they walked into a pond. "That was close. This trail is misleading."

The trail was deceiving; it led straight to the pond's edge and veered right. If you were not careful, you could walk right into the pond. The two slowly started making their way around the edge of the pond. "I do not want to know what could be lurking in that water," Ruby confessed, looking at the water with disgust. "It looks like a monster from any scary movie could come out of it at any moment."

They could see campfires in all directions as they reached the other side of the pond. Campers were scattered everywhere. "How will we find Shawndrea in all these camps?" Ruby asked, looking in both directions. "There are a lot more camps on this side than where we are."

"I have no idea. Wait, do you hear that?" Sheldon asked, listening as they came out of the trail around the pond. "I would know what laugh anywhere. Ninnie calls it "The Shawndrea Mating Call," and it's unmistakable."

"I think it's coming from that direction," Ruby pointed to their right. "Yeah, that is definitely her."

They heard guys cheering, whooping, and hollering as they approached the camp. Shawndrea was up dancing around the fire. She was clearly drunk and flirting with all the guys. She was giving each guy a lap dance. "Hey, Shawndrea, your Mom asked us to find you," Sheldon called out in his most masculine voice. "She said we have an early day tomorrow and need to call it a night,"

"Heeeeey everyone, this here is my cousin Sheldon," Shawndrea slurred as she stumbled over to Sheldon and Ruby. She was almost falling into the fire. "They have come to join the party. Come on and sit down, guys."

The guys looked him up and down as they sized up his skinny stature. Sheldon looked at Ruby, who had an "oh shit" look on her face. "We really should be going," Sheldon stated as he locked arms with Shawndrea. "We have an early day tomorrow."

"Now, now, you two just got here. Have a drink," Shawndrea advised as she spilled beer all over them. "Don't be a party pooper like Miss Ninnie Poo Poo." She laughed too loudly at her own joke. The guys looked at her and did not laugh. They only had one thing on their mind.

"Maybe you should just leave her here. We will take good care of her," One of the rednecks ordered as he turned to look at Ruby. "And little Missy, you can join in too."

"That's okay. Her Momma is waiting for her," Sheldon claimed as Shawndrea started to sway back and forth. Sheldon and Ruby got on either side of her, put their arms around her, and began to walk her out. "See you guys."

"Oh, I think I'm gonna be sick, guys," Shawndrea warned as she started to sound nauseous. "Stop spinning me around. I think I'm gonna puke."

"Get her out of here. We don't want to clean up puke," One of the other rednecks shouted.

They had taken only a few steps when she broke free from them, ran over to a tree, and held onto it as she threw up. She straightened back up and wiped her mouth. "I think I'm feeling better, guys. Let's go back to the party," Shawndrea insisted as she staggered back towards the guys.

They resumed their previous positions on either side of her and started to walk back to their camp. "What all did you drink?" Ruby asked as she cringed at Shawndrea's breath.

"We started out with some Jack and Coke. I think we did some Jaeger shots, too," Shawndrea slurred her words. "Not much, really," she claimed as she burped loudly. "Oh wow, excuse me. Oh, hey, our camp is right over there; we are going the wrong way," she pointed as she started to drag them towards the pond.

"Oh no, no, we almost went swimming once tonight!" Sheldon exclaimed as they tried to steer her away from there. "We need to go around the pond."

"Where I don't see a pond," Shawndrea remarked, craning her neck, trying to find the pond. She proceeds to drag them toward the pond again. She was about a foot taller than them and could swing them around relatively easily.

"Trust me, there is a pond there," Ruby added as they steered her to the correct path. "I do not want to find out what lurks in the water, personally."

They all laughed on their way back, but Shawndrea's drunk laughter was louder than theirs, causing the frogs to jump into the pond and the animals to scurry into hiding. "Could you imagine trying to explain that one to Aunt Letty?" Sheldon chuckled, looking around at Ruby. "We have to get her back and in bed before Aunt Letty sees her like this. She is still in trouble for the whole Suzy Q incident."

"That bitch had it coming," Shawndrea loudly stated as she slurred her words again. "I would do it again if I could. I think I'm going to be sick again."

"We are almost there…" Sheldon said, but it was too late; she had lost it in the middle of the trail. Well, I hope no one steps in that," he said as Shawndrea wiped her mouth.

As they walked up to their campsite, Sheldon could hear Aunt Letty. "Shit, what are we going to do?" Sheldon muttered more to himself than Ruby, and Shawndrea was out of it.

Ruby stepped on a twig as it snapped. Ninnie whipped her head to see them and stopped her Mom from turning around to see what made that noise. "Oh, Mom, I think something bit me on the back of my neck. Will you look?" Ninnie asked as she waved the three of them on.

They got Shawndrea to the van and inside. They put a bucket next to her head just in case. They made their way back around to the campfire as they heard Aunt Letty laughing. She was telling Ninnie a story. "Oh, hey Sheldon, just in time; I told Ninnie about Wendy having the hots for your Mom. The look on Mandy's face when you asked her about it was priceless," Aunt Letty choked out the last part as she was coughing and laughing.

When he asked his Mom about it, Sheldon didn't realize anyone was around.

"The sad part was when that guy Ted took your Mom out on the dance floor tonight, Wendy bolted out of there like her ass was on fire," Aunt Letty recounted with a fucked up, drunken sad face. "Poor Wendy, but man, it was a sight and nothing like free entertainment."

They could see she had a few drinks in her. "That explains why I heard something bang near Wendy's trailer shortly after you two left." Ninnie detailed. "But I sure the heck wasn't going to go investigate alone. Besides, someone had to tend to the fire so it wouldn't go out. Hey, I've seen those horror movies where the beautiful always die first," She was trying to justify her actions and hoping her Mom did not ask where the two of them went as she poked the fire, causing the ashes to blow toward her Mom.

"God Damn it, Ninnie, why the hell did you do that for?" Aunt Letty snapped at her and fanned the ambers away from her face. She leaned back, avoiding the ambers, just as her chair made a popping noise. All you could hear across the quiet side of the campground was, "Oh shit," and the snapping sound of the chair breaking as she toppled backward. With her legs in the air, she cried out, "Help me the fuck up!" Aunt Letty hollered, half laughing but half pissed off.

"I guess I thought you weren't getting enough smoke in your lungs," Ninnie sarcastically quipped while she laughed and helped her Mom up off the ground.

Ruby and Sheldon both tried to contain their laughter.

"Oh shit, I'm gonna feel that tomorrow," Aunt Letty moaned, trying to rub her back and dust herself off. "That chair was a piece of shit anyways," She stated as she threw it into the fire, sending a bunch more embers into the air.

"Wait! You can't just throw it into the fire!" Ninnie shouted as it looked like she would go in after it and thought twice.

"Ah fuck it, we will worry about it tomorrow. Now smart asses, off to bed, all of you. It's late, and we have an early day tomorrow," She ordered them all to bed. "Hey, speaking of trouble, have you seen Shawndrea?"

"Oh, yeah, she went to bed about thirty minutes ago right after

Levin and Jimmy," Ninnie claimed, unsure whether she would believe that story.

"Yeah, I think she ate something that didn't agree with her stomach," Sheldon added. That way, she wouldn't question the bucket next to her head.

"Don't wait up for your Mom," Aunt Letty chuckled to Sheldon as he headed to the Suburban. "I imagine she will be tied up with the Ranger all night… if she is lucky," Aunt Letty mumbled as she put a cigarette in her mouth and lit it. "Lucky bitch," she muttered to herself.

Sunday came and went. Things were still awkward between Mandy and Wendy, but everyone else enjoyed themselves. They spent their last night sitting around the campfire, telling ghost stories. Ninnie disappeared for a while, and Sheldon kept waiting for her to come and scare them. Ninnie returned later, stating she had napped, and that the day had worn her out. Sheldon and Ruby looked at each other, not buying her story.

They collected aluminum cans for recycling on Monday morning, the last day of camping. They broke up into pairs. Mandy and Wendy paired up. Then Levin and Jimmy took off together. Letty and Shawndrea went in another direction. Lastly, Sheldon, Ruby, and Ninnie went off together. "You would be surprised how much money you can get if you collect enough cans," Sheldon said, throwing the cans into Ninnie's bag. She gave him a "you got to be kidding me" look. "Okay, yes, it's lame and a bit dorky, and it's great for the environment, too."

They almost had their bag full when Mandy climbed out of the pond's brush area. Her hair was a mess, and she looked frazzled. "Don't even start with me, Sheldon," his Mom snapped at him, passing by in a huff. She knew he had something witty to say by the look on his face. "Let's pack up. We're heading home."

"Mandy, wait up," Wendy called after her as she climbed out of the brush. "I'm sorry."

Sheldon, Ninnie, and Ruby looked at each other with shocked faces. They followed the two of them back to their camp. "I can't talk to you right now, Wendy," Mandy huffed as she gathered their stuff. "I just want to get my stuff, my kids, and head home."

"But give me a chance to explain," Wendy pleaded to Mandy with sad puppy dog eyes.

"No need to explain," Mandy stopped, not wanting to hear anymore. "You're not yourself today. Let's forget this ever happened."

"Can someone tell me what the hell is going on?" Aunt Letty inquired as she approached them. "I can hear yelling..." She stopped talking after looking at Mandy's face and hair, which was all out of sorts. "Okay, kids, nothing to see here. Let's get our stuff packed up." Aunt Letty shuffled the kids back to camp.

Jimmy convinced his Aunt Mandy to let him ride with her and the boys. He and Levin had bonded on this trip and liked hanging out together. Sheldon decided to ride back with Aunt Letty and the girls. Sheldon, Ninnie, and Ruby were in the back, discussing and laughing about the past few days' events. "Ugh, I do not want to go home and be around my parents. They are driving me up the wall," Ruby grumbled as she laid her head back on the seat and looked out the window, saddened.

"Well, look on the bright side. You will get to see Trey tomorrow," Sheldon teased her. "And just think he is super single."

"Hold up, single?" Ruby questioned as she whipped her head around and sat up straight. "How do you know he is single?"

"Chase told me right before his mouth attacked mine," Sheldon stated as he realized he had forgotten his mission. "I guess I forgot to mention that part."

"You think?" Ruby shrieked sarcastically. "How could you leave out that critical piece of information?"

"I don't know. Maybe it had something to do with the fact I had someone's tongue down my throat for the first time," Sheldon replied.

They all started laughing.

"Go, Shell," Shawndrea proudly cheers from the front seat. "I trained you well, huh."

"Hell yea, go get 'em, Sheldon," Aunt Letty shouted as she lit a cigarette. "Hell, that's more action than even I have seen in a long time. Fuck, I need to get laid," She mumbled with a cigarette hanging out her mouth.

"Not as much as Shawndrea," Ninnie murmured so only they could hear.

The three of them busted out in laughter as Aunt Letty turned on the radio. "Oh, this is the shit right here, yea boy!" Aunt Letty shouted as she held a cigarette. She reached to turn up the radio. They laughed and started to sing along to Tom Petty's *Free Falling*. "Hell yeah, turn it up!" Ninnie shouted as they all sang along. The ride home was full of song and laughter…

Chapter Nine

Where There's Smoke

It was Tuesday morning after the great camping weekend. Sheldon walked up to Ruby as she opened her locker door. "How are you feeling after a weekend with my crazy family?" Sheldon asked with a smile. He was surprisingly in a good mood.

"You know, I had a lot more fun camping than I imagined," Ruby admitted. She smiled as she closed her locker. "Sometimes it's not always about where you are but who you are there with. Some people can make anything fun, and laughter is the best medicine."

"I'm sorry I forgot to tell you about Trey."

"Don't worry about Trey. I don't think he is really that into me anyways, or he would have already made his move."

"I guess we will have to see 'cause don't look now, but here he comes," Sheldon smiled as he turned to head to class. "I will see you at lunch," He threw over his shoulder.

"Hey, how was your weekend?" Trey asked, smiling as he walked up to her. "I didn't see you all weekend."

"I went camping with Sheldon and his family," Ruby replied, surprised that he had noticed she had not been home. So, yeah, it was an enjoyable weekend. How about you? How was your weekend?" She noticed she was babbling again.

"It was okay, nothing spectacular. The coach had us practicing and working out every free moment. He wants us ready for the big game in a couple of weeks, which is why I have been so preoccupied," he replied, smiling at her. But this weekend, he is letting us have a little break, and I was wondering if maybe you wanted to do something this weekend?

"Sure, that would be nice," She tried to play it cool like it was no big deal, but inside, she was jumping and screaming joyfully.

"Awesome. I will let you know the details later. I have to get to class now," Trey smiled, started to walk away, and then looked over his shoulder. "Since we live so close to each other, I'm sure I will see you," he said.

She started doing a little happy dance when he was out of sight. *Yes! Yes! Yes! Why are you so excited? Calm down, Ruby. He is just a boy, but a cute one, though.*

Ruby couldn't wait till lunch to share her news with Sheldon. She turned down the hall to her class and saw Sheldon's brother Levin talking to some girl. Ruby could see that the girl was crying, and he was trying to console her. She did not know it then, but the girl Levin was consoling was Laramie's girlfriend. Suddenly, a teacher rounded the corner and asked them what they were doing outside class. Ruby was already late for class and knew she would get written up, but being late was worth getting asked out by Trey. She hurried past the teacher and went into the class.

She was relieved to see the teacher had not arrived yet. Ruby rushed to her seat and sat down as the door opened. The teacher from the hall came inside, and her heart jumped. Oh shit, is he *coming in to give me a detention for being in the halls?* She sat with her head resting on her arm and doodling on her notebook like she had been there the whole time.

She tried hiding her face by pulling her hair to hide behind. "Hi everyone, I'm Ben Stevens, aka Mr. Stevens. The Principal sent me to tell you that a substitute will be arriving momentarily," Mr. Stevens stated as he looked around the classroom.

Students started to whisper about who this guy was. "What happened to Dr. Spangler?" a fellow student named Tommy asked, looking at the young teacher.

Mr. Stevens cleared his throat and aligned his posture. "They rushed Dr. Spangler to the hospital, and that is all I can say now," he explained confidently and sternly. He was pleased with how authoritative he sounded on the matter.

"Ms. Nash, can I see you in the hall, please?" Mr. Stevens asked seriously. "Everyone, please remain in your seats. I will be back to check on you."

Ruby was silently freaking out. *Why am I being called out in the hall, and how did he know my name?*

Ruby's heart started pounding in her throat as the classroom door closed. "Now, Ruby, just because an instructor isn't here doesn't mean you can roam the halls," He stressed as he hovered over her like a dad lecturing his daughter. "I know your Mother wouldn't be happy to hear about this. I'm only saying this because if another teacher had caught you roaming the halls, you would have been written up or given detention."

"But..." Ruby started to defend her actions but paused as a thought hit her. "Wait... How do you know my Mother?"

"That's not important right now," He retorted as he steams rolled through. "What is important is that you stay out of trouble because your Mom is having a rough time. She doesn't need any more stress."

"Wait a minute. How do you know my Mother?" She insisted.

"Like I said, that isn't important right now," he said, trying to steer the conversation back to her. "One day, you will understand."

"Do not talk to me like I'm a little girl," She snapped, getting in his face. "I want..."

"Hey, I'm not your enemy here," He defended himself as he cut her off. "I-I..."

He was interrupted from finishing his sentence when a loud noise erupted from the classroom. It sounded like glass breaking and girls screaming. Then, fire alarms started sounding. Mr. Stevens opened the classroom door to investigate.

Tommy Adler was sitting in the back of the biology room when Mr. Stevens went into the hall with Ruby. Tommy thought turning on the gas for the entire classroom was a good idea. The science teacher, Dr. Spangler, was often drunk and habitually leaving his office unlocked. Tommy entered the office and turned on the gas for the classroom.

Then, he proceeded to do a little science experiment. Something went wrong. The beaker exploded, and fire started shooting in every direction. That was when Mr. Stevens walked in to investigate why the girls were screaming. Then the fire alarms went off. He rushed into the office and shut off the gas. "Everyone, out of the classroom now!" He ordered as he pointed towards the door. "Please do so in a single file order and head straight out of the building. Ruby, please lead everyone out."

Ruby was impressed by how quickly this guy acted during an intense situation. "Everyone except you, Tommy," he stood glaring at Tommy. "Wait right here till everyone is out. I do not want you out of my sight for a minute. Were you involved in this alone?" he asked Tommy as they left the smoke-filled classroom and headed for the exit.

"Yes, but…" Tommy was answering when he was cut off by the Principal walking up.

"What happened here?" The school Principal asked, "Is everyone okay?"

"Yes, and everyone is headed outside," Mr. Stevens replied, holding the doors open for the last students to exit the building. "But you need to ask your son what happened."

Principle Adler looked at his son with disbelief. Growing up, his son was never a problem. He got good grades, always listened, and never gave them any issues. Since the divorce, he had been acting out. "You and I will talk after I make sure everyone is okay," he said, looking at his son, and went to check on all the students.

Sheldon and Ninnie found Ruby, who explained the recent events and how Tommy had started the fire. Ninnie looked concerned as she watched Tommy talking with his dad. "That is crazy," Sheldon remarked. "Luckily, no one was hurt. Also, who is this new guy?"

"That's what I was going to ask you. The new guy says his name is Ben Stevens, and he is a new teacher, and that's not all…" Ruby whispered as she paused to look around to ensure no one could hear what she was about to say. "I think he is sleeping with my Mom."

Ruby now had Ninnie's full attention as her head wiped around. "Whaaat?" Ninnie gasped in shock. Ninnie had a look on her face that said, "Did you just say what I think you said?".

"He did not come out and say it, but his tone and words said everything. He seemed to know me and my Mom's situation,"

Ruby explained as the teachers started ushering the students back into the school. "I will find out more when I talk to my Mom tonight. I will tell you more at lunch."

The three of them went their separate ways. Before letting the kids back into the school, the staff had ensured the fire was completely out and the smoke had cleared. Going back in, one could barely tell anything had even happened. Their first-period class was over, and it was 15 minutes into the second period. Tommy followed his dad to his office.

Principle Adler closed the door and calmly walked around to sit at his desk. Tommy was trying to measure just how pissed his dad was. "Son, I don't understand these recent acts of defiance," His dad stated, leaning forward in his chair to look his son in the eye. "I'm going to have to suspend you for two weeks. I expect you to do community service, too. Is this because your Mother and I are getting a divorce?

"No, it's not about you and Mom divorcing," Tommy answered, shifting in his chair before unloading everything bothering him. "Sometimes it feels like someone controls everything we do. We aren't children anymore, yet they treat us that way. We do not have the freedom to do what we want and when. They don't give us the freedom to do what we want when we want. They time and plan everything, ensuring it never veers off course. Sometimes, it just makes me want to scream. I know what I did was wrong, and I'm ready for punishment. But you have to know how I feel."

"I had no idea, son," his dad said, looking at him with pride. "Honestly, I'm impressed by your words and understand you're getting to the point where you want to branch out independently. Trust me, you will have the opportunity to do that very soon. However, you can't keep up this pattern of disruptive behavior. Next time something bugs you, tell me about it. Even if you don't think I want to hear it, tell me anyway. Is that a deal?"

"Yes, I understand," Tommy agreed as he left.

"You will have suspension for two weeks," his dad requested as he stood up. I have no choice but to set an example. Otherwise, people will think I'm going soft on you. I will see you at home."

Ninnie was sitting in class when she caught herself looking over at where Tommy normally sat. He usually sat there staring off into space. Something about him had caught Ninnie's eye on the first day of school. She wasn't sure if it was the way he would brush his straight blond hair out of his face, the sadness in his eyes, or that sometimes when everyone else was laughing at something funny, a smile would creep so subtly at the corners of his mouth. She knew today it was because he was a bad boy, which got her juices going. Something inside her wanted to kiss him, rip his shirt off, bite his nipples, and kiss him again. She was getting wet thinking about it. She was pulled out of her daydream when someone called her name.

"Ms. Myer, would you please rejoin the rest of the class and share why studying history is important?"

"Umm, because…" Ninnie was racking her brain, trying to remember what a previous history teacher explained. "Because if we study and understand past events, we are more equipped to handle current and future situations. Essentially, it helps us evolve into higher life forms."

"Outstanding, Ms. Myer," The history teacher commended. He was impressed with her answer. "Anyone else cares to add to that…"

Ninnie drifted out again, thinking about when she wrote Tommy a note. Something inside her said to write him a note and tell him she was a good listener if he ever needed someone to talk to. Another voice said that was lame, cheesy, and dumb. What are we, third graders?

The other voice won over. Ninnie had scribbled a simple note that if he needed someone to talk to, he would meet her by the gym after lunch, and she signed it, Ninnie. She dropped it on his desk, walked out, and headed to lunch.

§

At lunch, all everyone could talk about was the fire. The story had changed from a simple truth to a significant story. Stories ranged from Tommy smoking a cigarette to him building a bomb. That his dad was shipping him off to a military school, and so on. Ruby told her friends what happened and the mysterious teacher who knew her and her Mom. "I will let you know what I find out from my Mom tomorrow," Ruby told them as they were leaving lunch.

Ninnie and Sheldon usually walked together to their next class in the same school area, but Ninnie started heading towards the gym. "Where are you going? Class is this way," Sheldon inquired.

"Ummm… I have something to take care of first," Ninnie replied as she kept walking.

"Oookay, I guess I will see you tomorrow," Sheldon concluded as he headed to class.

After class, Sheldon went to his locker as usual before leaving for work. Laramie walked by, calling Sheldon his usual names like fagot and queer. "What? Now you're too good to look at me?" Laramie asked as he walked past. "Then fuck you, fagot!" He turned around to yell as he kept walking.

Sheldon was over his immaturity, which put him in a bad mood. *I don't understand what he gets out of calling me that.* Sheldon walked down the hall heading out of the building when Sheldon saw Chase talking to the coach. He didn't want to run into or see him, especially in his current mood. Sheldon might say something he would regret, so he turned and went the long way to get out of the building. Sheldon decided while walking to his car to shake it off and not let it affect his time at work.

§

The next day at lunch, Ruby filled them in with what little information she could get from her Mother. "She basically told me that he was the son of one of the women she had recently become friends with," Ruby explained as she ate her salad. "One night, after her friend passed out from drinking too many glasses of wine, her son sat listening to her problems. That was all that supposedly happened. When I pressed the matter, she told me it was none of my business and that when she was ready to discuss it further, she would." She paused to sigh. "I don't know what I'm going to do if my parents separate," Ruby confessed as she pushed back her lunch.

"I don't know if that means one or both of them will move back to New York," Ruby continued. "I just know things are not cool at home. The tension is so thick you can cut it with a knife. Neither of them wants to move out and expects the other one to leave. At least I have going out this weekend with Trey to look forward to."

"Yeah, when my parents split, it was very ugly, but it got better once my dad moved out," Ninnie said, trying to provide some comfort in knowing it's not the end of the world. "Honestly, they both seem much happier now."

"Yeah, I have to agree with Ninnie. It can be tough at first. My parents have been divorced for over two years now," Sheldon added. "Trust me, it gets much better. Hold up, did you say you're going out with Trey this weekend?! Ninnie, you see how she tried to slip that one by us?"

"I noticed that," Ninnie agreed in a drawn-out voice, leaning forward. "Now spill."

"Yesterday, he asked me if I would like to hang out this weekend," Ruby replied, trying to downplay her excitement. "It's no big deal."

Sheldon and Ninnie looked at each other and then back at her with a sideways stare, knowing this was a big deal. "Just like that, no big deal, huh?" Sheldon questioned, looking at her. A guy you have talked about since school started and even gotten a few rides from asks you out, and it's no big deal?"

"Yeah, I'm not buying it either," Ninnie confirmed, looking at Sheldon.

"Look, guys, I don't want to make a big deal of it yet," Ruby pleaded as she nervously tore up a paper napkin. "I mean, what if we hang out and there is nothing there, nothing more than a physical attraction? What if we have nothing in common but to stare into each other's eyes and listen to the crickets outside? Those eyes that you can get lost in and those lips…."

"Okay, we have lost her," Ninnie chortled to Sheldon. "Earth to lover girl"

They all laughed as Ruby looked at them like she had not just been daydreaming about Trey.

"Mom has decided to move back to California next summer and has asked me to go with her," Ninnie mentioned randomly.

Sheldon and Ruby both look at her with blank stares on their faces.

"Wait! What? Moving and leaving us here alone?" Sheldon shrieked as he tried to wrap his mind around what she just said. "As in the summer after we graduate?"

"I told her maybe, and that's a big maybe, so keep your shorts on," Ninnie demanded with a laugh. I'm thinking of maybe moving out there after I graduate college anyway. Besides, I told you this while we were camping."

The table was silent for a moment. "I guess you did mention it, but at that time, it seemed like a long way off in the distance, but hearing you say it now, it seems like tomorrow," Sheldon explained, half sulking.

"You know how well Mom and I get along. I couldn't torture myself like that while still in high school," Ninnie admitted as she looked at the two of them. "But seriously, what's here in this small town for us? Let's not think about it now. We need to get to class."

They got up from the table and threw their trash away. "I will see you later," Ninnie said quickly, immediately heading in the other direction.

"Where is she going?" Ruby asked with a furrowed brow. "She flew out of here like her pants were on fire, or a bear was after her."

"Honestly, I don't know," Sheldon replied, looking in the direction Ninnie just went. "She did that yesterday, too. In fact, she has done that quite a bit lately. Anyway, we better get to class."

Rushing to class, Sheldon turned the corner and ran right into Chase. Chase grabbed both of Sheldon's arms to keep Sheldon from going backward. "I'm sorry. I should have paid attention to where I was going," Sheldon apologized, having a tough time looking Chase in the eye.

"I'm sorry too," was all Chase could get out. Sheldon could tell he wanted to say more but had to get to class. *That was like running into a wall of muscle.* He thought to himself as he walked into class, just as the bell sounded. *Those eyes are something I could look at forever.* He was mentally smacking himself. *Focus, Sheldon. You have to improve your grades to do something with your life.*

Ninnie's conversation with them at the campsite and lunch today sparked something in Sheldon. He realized he was going through the motions of school to finish, not caring about his grades. There is life after high school, and if he wanted to go to college, he needed to start caring and figure out what he wanted. It just clicked what Susan had been telling him all along. *Why hadn't he put it together before? Why am I just getting it now? What was Chase about to say to him? Stop, you're doing it again.*

Sheldon pulled out his notebook and started taking notes like the other straight-A students did in class. Sheldon did not see Chase the rest of the week, which was unusual because he saw him almost every day at some point. He usually saw him around the time he went to work. Not seeing Chase was for the best because Sheldon had a new goal to focus on.

Chapter Ten

The Football Game

The sound of the car hummed along the highway. Cornfield after cornfield, small family farm after small family farm, flew by the car window. Mariah Carey's *Vision of Love* blared from the car speakers. While driving home in her blue Chevy Cavalier, Susan sang along to the radio. Susan was excited to be heading back. She had some news to share with Sheldon and wanted to do it in person. The drive home was over four hours, so she entertained herself by singing along to the radio.

Susan had gone to college at Illinois State University. After graduation, she decided to stay and work in Bloomington, Illinois. Partly because Susan didn't want to leave her corporate job and the guy, she had been dating for the last three years. Suan felt at home in Bloomington. It was big enough to keep her entertained, and Chicago was only a short car ride away. Her trips home became more sporadic. Susan recently told Sheldon that she would not return to her childhood home if it were not for him. Susan had promised Sheldon she would come and spend more time with him.

Sheldon drove home from work as he got closer. He saw Susan's car in the driveway, and all the stress from that day at school and work melted away. This time, it had been months since he saw her last.

Susan met Sheldon in the driveway and asked if they could go for a drive and catch up. Susan wanted to tell Sheldon her news before she told anyone else, and she was a little nervous about what she had to say to him. They got in the car without a planned destination to drive and catch up.

"How's Mom doing since the separation?" Susan asked.

"She seems to be doing well," Sheldon answered, wondering if that was what she wanted to talk to him about.

"How are you doing?" she inquired. Not waiting for an answer, she kept talking. "I can see you're doing well; you seem much happier. Are you dating someone?" Susan could see Sheldon suddenly getting uncomfortable. As he shifted in his seat, his demeanor changed, and she decided to change the subject.

"So, you remember the guy I have been dating, John?" She asked as she stopped and put the car in park. She didn't wait for Sheldon to reply when she blurted out, "He asked me to marry him!"

Sheldon was initially shocked by her news because he thought she would press the subject of him dating someone. "Holy shit!" He exclaimed as he hugged her. "I'm so happy for you!"

"I'm glad you said that because I want you to be a part of my wedding," She cheered as she hugged him again. "I want you to be the one to walk me down the aisle."

"Wait, what about dad?" Sheldon asked, shocked.

"Who?" Susan joked as they both laughed. "Soooo?"

"Fuck yea, of course, I would be honored," Sheldon replied excitedly. "Have you set a date yet? What is Mom going to say? Are you sure this guy is the one?"

"Whoa... Whoa... I think you're more excited about this than I am," she mused. We are planning a spring or fall wedding, depending on schedules, but as soon as I know, I will let you know, aaaaaand I expect you to bring a date. That isn't a request. It's an order. I love you, and I want you to be happy," she commented as she smiled and hugged him again.

"I love you too, sis," he replied.

"By the way, I saw Tammy Lowry in town. She told me about the football game and plans to attend it tonight. She asked if we could join her. Do you want to go watch the game with me?" Susan asked while putting the car back into drive. Tammy said she would love to see you, too."

"Oh, wow, I forgot you knew Tammy," Sheldon realized as he rolled down the window to feel the wind on his face. "Yea, I will go with you."

Susan had gone to school with Tammy's sister, Sheri. She would sleep over at their place, do each other's hair, and include Tammy. "Hey, you want to get some ice cream and cruise around?" she asked, hoping he would say yes.

"That sounds like a good idea to me," Sheldon agreed as he put his hand out the window. "Anything else you want to do while in town? We could go see a movie or whatever you old people do these days," Sheldon teased with a smirk.

"Old?!Old?! I will show you old," Susan scoffed with a half-smile and a half-shocked look. "I don't know if I like this new side of you. You're getting quite a mouth on you, and what's with the cussing?" She questioned with a laugh. And speaking of old, if I remember correctly, you always ended up with the old maid card."

"That's because you always cheated," Sheldon stated as he egged her on. "You wanna go see Grammy while you're here?"

"Yes, I do," She replied as she nudged him. "Nice, try changing the subject. Cheated! I never cheated. It was just intellect and strategy."

They both laughed as they ordered their ice cream. Susan had to pull the car over at one point because she had gotten such a head rush from drinking her slushy freeze too fast. "I guess at some point we should visit Dad," Susan said hesitantly. "But we are going to drag Levin with us. There is no sense in us suffering alone."

"Man, do we have to, too?" Sheldon asked, like a little kid stomping his feet, and then he laughed. "I was just thinking how great this day was going."

Well, he is your father," Susan remarked with a serious look. "Despite everything that has happened, we still have to respect him as a parent."

"My father!" Sheldon exclaimed with a furrowed brow. "He's your father too."

Suddenly, Susan got another brain freeze from her ice cream slushy. "Ow, ow, that hurts!" Susan shouted as she put her hand to her head, causing them both to laugh. "Do you think Mom would like to come to the football game with us?" she asked, still in pain.

"I seriously doubt it," Sheldon replied, still laughing. "If it does not involve horses, or if it's dealing with large crowds, forget about it."

"What should I wear tonight?" Sheldon asked, slightly panicked. "I have never been to a football game before."

"Just wear what you would normally wear," Susan replied with a chuckle as she pulled into their driveway. "But dress warm because it will be cold."

Susan shut the car off, and they sat in the driveway momentarily as they finished their treat. "I guess I should go in and talk to Mom about the wedding," Susan remarked as she started to open the car door. "Can you just do it for me?" she joked.

"Uh… Good luck with that," Sheldon quipped as he exited the car. "If you need backup, I will be in my room," He laughed as he shut the car door.

"Hey, be ready to go by six," she called after him. "The game starts at seven, but I want to get there early."

Sheldon headed to his room, and Susan went to talk to their Mom, who was playing solitaire on the kitchen table. Susan told their Mom about the wedding plans, hoping she would give her input or advice, but Mandy was half-listening as she focused on her card game. She wanted to know if she thought her plans, were a good idea. As usual, Mandy was indifferent and had no input or any ideas. Their Mom acted as if she would not even be there. Susan was getting frustrated and decided to change the subject before she got upset and said something she might regret. "Sheldon and I are going to the football game tonight. Would you like to come?"

"Oh no, you go ahead," Mandy dismissed, still not paying much attention, and barely looking up from her card game. "I don't want to miss my shows."

Susan got up quietly and calmly and walked outside. Susan started walking down the road, and when she was far enough away from the house, she screamed. Susan let out all of her frustrations with her Mom. She promised herself she would never treat her children like their parents did. That was one of the remarkable things about being out in the middle of nowhere. You could be as loud as you wanted. *No one would ever hear the gunshot if I just took her out one day. Okay, Susan, get yourself together.* She pulled herself together and continued walking, enjoying the peacefulness of it all as if nothing had happened. When she returned to the house, she checked in to see what Sheldon was up to, but he was sleeping. She let him rest for a few more minutes, but he looked too peaceful to wake yet.

Sheldon woke from his nap to find Susan watching TV with their Mother. She was dressed and ready to go. "Let me go get ready really quick," Sheldon told Susan. "It won't take me long."

"No worries," Susan replied calmly. Sheldon looked at her, thinking it was weird how calm she was.

Sheldon threw on a pair of jeans and a T-shirt and grabbed his hoodie. As they headed for the car, Sheldon noticed how surprisingly calm Susan was. "Did you ask Mom if she wanted to go?" Sheldon asked as they got into the car and headed to the game.

"Yes, and you were right," Susan said as she started the car. I love her to death, but it's a wonder we turned out as "normal" as we did with such dysfunctional parents."

They both laughed. "So, what did Mom say about the wedding?" Sheldon asked.

"The usual indifferent OH's and Uhuh's she didn't say much," Susan replied, a little hurt. "I asked her if she was coming, and she said, and I will quote, 'We will see,' which always means no."

The car was silent the rest of the ride into town. They pulled into the school parking lot and parked. "Let's shake off the bad juju," Susan recommended as she shook herself. "Okay, let's go make our happiness and not let others define our happiness."

"Sounds like a plan to me," Sheldon agreed as he exited the car. "Let's do this!"

Sheldon spotted Chase's car parked in its usual spot, and Sheldon's heart jumped for a second. "That's the spirit!" Susan shouted happily. "Let's do this."

Sheldon thought he had not talked to Chase since the kiss. Maybe he would not even notice he was there. "Let's go," Susan said, pulling Sheldon out of his thoughts. "What are you looking at?" Susan asked, turning around. "Ya, ya, that's a nice red car. Let's find Tammy; I want to talk to her before the game starts. Besides, I didn't think you were that into cars anyway."

"I'm not," He said as he smiled at her. "I'm coming. How long has it been since you have talked to Tammy?"

"That's a good question. It's been a long time. I think it was freshman year of college," Susan pondered as they walked down to the field. "I tried keeping in touch after the funeral, but life happens. School and work got in the way. Time gets away from you."

Sheldon was walking along like he knew where he was going. "Where are you going?" Susan asked as she stopped.

"I want to sit on this side of the field," Sheldon replied.

"That's the away team's side," Susan pointed to the other side. "The home team sits there, but you can sit over there. I prefer to sit on the home team's side."

Sheldon had yet to learn that the teams sat opposite, but it made sense. Only a short time after they took their seats, Ruby showed up. "Hey, I didn't think you came to the games," Ruby called out as she climbed the stairs.

Sheldon laughed. "I usually don't, but I'm here with my sister Susan," he replied, introducing the two. Susan, this is my friend Ruby."

"Well, it's nice to meet the infamous Ruby finally," Susan chimed as she smiled and shook Ruby's hand. "I was beginning to think he made you up."

"Now that sounds like something he would do," Ruby teased. "He does like to tell crazy stories all the time."

"Oookay, I'm going to go get a hot dog and some popcorn," Sheldon stated as he got up to change the subject. "Do either of you want anything?"

"No, but thank you, I'm good," Ruby replied.

"I'm good too, thanks," Susan added.

"I will be right back," Sheldon said as he turned to walk down the stairs.

"Sheldon sure likes his food," Ruby commented with a laugh.

"Yes, he does," Susan agreed, nodding her head. "He would probably eat no matter what was happening."

As soon as he left, Susan cleared her throat. "So, has he mentioned that he is interested in anyone?" Susan asked while watching Sheldon walk to the concession stand. Susan could feel Ruby looking at her and debating on how to respond.

"Weeeeell, there is this one guy, and they kissed," Ruby answered hesitantly, not knowing if she knew he was gay.

"Whaaaa??!!" She exclaimed. "Man, I wish he would tell me things.

Okay, so who is it?"

"I can tell you he will be here tonight," Ruby replied, relieved she hadn't said anything that the sister had not already surmised. "He hasn't talked to you about him being gay, huh?"

"I suspected, heck, we all did," Susan replied, looking a little teary-eyed. "But no one really talks about it, and every time I approach the subject, he shuts down completely."

"Honestly, I think I'm the first person he has told," Ruby remarked. "I don't think he has fully come to terms with it himself, and when the guy kissed him, I think that was the first time he had kissed a guy or anyone."

"I can't even begin to imagine, but good for him," Susan commented. "Maybe he will open up soon."

"Give him some time," Ruby offered with a slightly sad face. "I think he will, especially after the guy ran out after they kissed, and they haven't spoken since."

"Soooo, are we talking about Sheldon's boy toy?" Ninnie interjected as she popped her head between them from out of nowhere.

"Shit Ninnie!" Susan exclaimed as she turned around to look at her with eyes as big as quarters. "You scared the shit out of us. Wait, she knows about Sheldon?"

"I think we are the only two," Ruby pointed out. "This one would make a great detective; she is like a dog with a bone," Ruby quipped as she pointed her head at Ninnie. "She thought Chase was hanging around us because he wanted to get down her pants when, in fact, it was Sheldon's."

They all laughed. "Wait, I knew before you did?" Ninnie asked, looking at Susan. "Aaaalright," she cheered while doing a happy dance. "I'm finally not the last to find something out."

"Where is Shawndrea?" Susan asked Ninnie.

"Oh, you mean Little Miss Hot Pants," Ninnie joked in her usual Ninnie style. "Getting suspended from school has brought both our parents down on her and grounded her indefinitely, including all school functions. Since our parents have decided to get a divorce, we are suffering because now they want to be strict parents, but what they don't know is that she still sneaks out and gets it on with boys as often as she can."

"Wait! What? Suspended for what?" Susan exclaimed, half laughing.

"Ruby, you didn't tell her?" Ninnie questioned as she nudged Ruby.

Ninnie loves to tell a good story and was extremely dramatic, retelling the tale and how it started at the pool.

"Wait, I remember her getting shoved into the pool," Ruby reminisced. "We had just moved here, and that was the first day I met Sheldon. I had forgotten all about that being your sister. I knew then this wasn't your normal town in the middle of a cornfield."

"My parents are quite the opposite now that they are divorcing," Ruby added. "My dad is dating his twenty-one-year-old assistant, and my Mom always goes shopping or hangs out with the ladies. They don't seem to care what I'm doing."

"Wow, I have missed out on some excitement," Susan remarked. "I can't imagine what it's like to live with divorcing parents," Susan added. "Though I can tell you that I see a huge improvement in Sheldon since our parents separated. He has cool friends now and more freedom in life. It was hard initially and pulled in two different directions, but it gets much better."

"Look who I found," Sheldon announced as he stepped to the left and revealed Tammy. "Tammy, this is my friend Ruby and my cousin Ninnie."

Susan and Tammy sat together, catching up and laughing as the game began. As they watched the game, Ninnie and Ruby explained to Sheldon how the game worked. "Wow, these guys look good in their uniforms, and look at their butts," Sheldon commented, forgetting he was in public. "No wonder Shawndrea always comes to watch these games. Which one is Trey?"

Sheldon knew Ruby would know right away. "He is number twenty-three," she said, pointing to the field. Sheldon laughed at her. "Whaat? Why are you laughing?" Ruby asked. "Chase is number eight."

"Wow, I didn't realize how much taller Trey was than Chase," Sheldon pointed out as he watched them. "I don't like guys taller than me."

"Oh, not me I like looking up at them as they are about to kiss you and..." Ruby confessed as she trailed off.

Both Ninnie and Sheldon were looking at her now. "And?" Ninnie asked. "You can't just leave us hanging like that."

"I don't know what you're talking about," Ruby teased as the crowd cheered.

They all turned and stood up to watch Chase dodge the other team's attempts to block him as he ran like lightning down the field and scored a touchdown. They all cheered, and then it was halftime.

"Is it already over?" Sheldon asked. "That was intense."

"No, it's halftime. The teams take a little break before they start the second half of the game," Ninnie explained with a half laugh. "Oh, shit, what is he doing?" Ninnie remarked, looking at the field.

Sheldon looked to see Chase running up the steps. Everyone's eyes were on Chase as they followed his ascent up the bleachers.

Chase had seen Sheldon sitting in the stands as he was leaving the field for halftime and, without thinking, ran up to where he was sitting in the audience. "You finally came," Chase cheered with his cute smile as he kneeled before Sheldon. "Can I talk to you after the game?"

"Yes," Sheldon replied shyly. Chase's jester completely took him back.

While Chase talked to Sheldon, Susan leaned behind Ninnie and poked Ruby. "You didn't tell me he was the quarterback," Susan whispered to Ruby. "Or that he was someone I would consider leaving my fiancé for.... Well, that's if he was of legal age, of course."

Ruby and Ninnie both died of laughter with Susan.

"I'm sorry for interrupting," Chase apologized as he looked at Susan, Ninnie, and Ruby. "I will see you in a bit," Chase concluded as he looked back at Sheldon, but the coach was yelling at Chase before Sheldon could respond.

After watching him leave, Sheldon sat back, and the reality of what had just happened set in. When Chase came around him, it was like no one else existed except for the two of them. Suddenly, he could feel many eyes on him and was afraid to look around, so he just stared forward. "Are you okay?" Ruby asked as she leaned over and nudged him with her shoulder.

"Yeah," Sheldon choked out as he looked at her. "I was not expecting that." A smile emerged on his face, and he glanced over at Susan.

Susan smiled, raising her eyebrows up and down with approval. She gave him the thumbs up. Sheldon had a smile he could not hide as he turned his attention back to the game, shaking his head at the dorky thumbs-up she gave him.

After the game, Chase ran up to Sheldon like he was on cloud nine. "Do you mind waiting while I shower and change?" he asked Sheldon. "I don't want to be sweaty and smelly when we talk."

"Do you mind?" Sheldon asked, looking at Susan.

"Not at all," Susan replied with a mischievous smile.

"Thank you," Chase expressed to Susan. "Or I could drive you home. I don't mind."

"Sure," Susan and Sheldon both said at the same time.

"That will give me more time to spend with Tammy," Susan happily stated as she winked at Sheldon.

"Cool, I will see you in a bit," Chase told Sheldon. "It was nice meeting you," Chase nodded to Susan.

They all watched him walk away, staring at that tight muscular butt through his football uniform. "Ooookay," Ninnie cooed, "I'm going home and taking a cold shower."

"I'm going to go and wait for Trey," Ruby pointed towards the school. She got up and walked away, and Ninnie followed her.

"I guess I will see you at home, little brother," Susan smiled as she hugged Sheldon. "And yes, do something I would do, and I want to hear all the details later."

Sheldon waited for Chase outside of the locker room. He couldn't help but feel how this was like a dream. *What does he want to talk to me about?*

When Chase came out, he looked adorable, with wet hair and in a t-shirt and jeans. "Thank you for waiting for me." Chase greeted him as they started to walk to his car. "I have been thinking about what I would say to you the next time I worked up the courage, but I realized there was no perfect moment or words. Sometimes, we must make the moments ourselves and grab life." Sheldon thought he would kiss him then, but someone came out of the gym and interrupted.

They both got in the car and started driving. "Which way do you live?" Chase asked as he reached the highway.

"Turn left," Sheldon instructed, not knowing what he would say next.

"You see, growing up in California, being gay wasn't as big of a deal as it is here in Small Town, USA," Chase explained as he glanced over to see Sheldon's reaction. "I have dated both girls and guys, but I prefer guys. However, I told myself when I got here I would only date girls because being gay here is such a big issue. But I met you and I couldn't help myself. Do you realize how hard it is to be in your presence and not want to kiss, touch, and hold you? During swim lessons, it took everything I had in me not to touch you or kiss you. I would do extra laps and cold showers after you would leave to get myself under control. But when you started asking about Trey, I got jealous and lost control. For that, I'm sorry. I'm sorry I put you in this position."

Sheldon was speechless. He didn't realize that was what Chase had been thinking this whole time. Chase looked over to see Sheldon's face and get a read on what he might be thinking. "Don't leave me hanging here after pouring myself out like that," Chase pleaded, putting his hand on Sheldon's leg.

Sheldon put his hand on top of Chase's and smiled. "I had no idea you felt like that about me," Sheldon admitted as he looked at Chase. "I thought you were going to tell me the kiss can't happen again because you're not gay. Oh, turn here; this is our road."

Chase pulled onto the gravel road and stopped the car. As he put the car into park, he leaned over and put his hand behind Sheldon's head. Chase pulled Sheldon towards him for a kiss. A kiss so intense they were both out of breath. "I was afraid you were going to tell me the same thing. It would have crushed me because I haven't felt like this before," Chase admitted. "I don't want to stop kissing you and I want to hold you all night."

"But what about the girl I saw you with at the pool?" Sheldon asks but afraid of the answer.

"Oh, Tiffany, she was just a friend that I was trying to date," Chase replied with his hand on the stirring wheel, looking sexy as fuck. "But we both knew we just weren't into each other. Plus, I kept talking about you, which was a mood-killer for her. We mutually decided that we were better off as friends."

They kissed until a car pulled onto the road and stopped to ensure they were okay. Chase told them they were waiting for someone and sent the person on their way. They laughed because they were embarrassed, but they started to kiss and forgot all about it. "I guess I should get you home," Chase kissed Sheldon one more time before he drove the car and headed down the road. "We can talk more about this later. I just had to share my feelings with you, and I didn't know how."

"I'm happy you did," Sheldon expressed with a big smile. "Take the next right. Our house is right there," Sheldon pointed across the field.

"Wow, you guys really do live out here in the middle of nowhere," Chase remarked as he pulled into their driveway and parked. "Now I know where you live, and I can stalk you too," Chase teased with his dimple smile as he kissed Sheldon. "I will see you very soon; I will wait till you make it inside."

"Thank you," Sheldon kissed Chase one last time before leaving the car. "See you soon.

When Sheldon opened the back door, his brother Levin greeted him. "Uh, where is Susan, and was that Chase De Longpre's car?" Levin asked, looking at him with curious eyes.

"Oh well, she wanted to hang with a friend, so Chase offered me a ride home," Sheldon answered as he started to head to his bedroom, leaving Levin with many questions.

Sheldon entered his room, closed his door, and got ready for bed. He climbed into bed so excited that he did not fall asleep immediately. He lay there thinking about the day's events and how great it felt to feel Chase's hands touch him, his lips pressed against his. The smell of Chase lingered with him. Before he knew it, he had drifted to sleep and dreamed of Chase.

Chapter Eleven

Wildest Dreams

The next morning, Sheldon awoke to the smell of bacon and Susan humming in the kitchen. Aside from being hungry, his first thought was that he hoped last night with Chase was not one of his wildest dreams but a reality. Sheldon stretched as he got out of bed, with a huge smile that he kept trying to hide. Sheldon was glad Susan was home. She had a way of making the place feel like home.

Sheldon walked into the kitchen, scratching his head and yawning. "So, I see someone decided to get up," Susan teased as she stirred her coffee. "Must have been quite a night for you too. Levin has been questioning me all morning. He is like a dog with a bone. I can see by the smile on your face that things went well last night."

While eating breakfast, Sheldon filled her in on everything that had happened, including how they first met, their driver's Ed together, and how he got caught driving past Chase's house.

"Wait, you stalked him at his house?" Susan asked with a smirk on her face. "Wow, now that took some guts, crazy, but gutsy. Man, that first kiss in the pool sounded intense and made me jealous. My first kiss wasn't as hot or exciting as yours. Mine was in third grade. No, wait, make that the fifth grade and it was on the playground by the jungle gym. It was Little Mikey Wilson. His ball came rolling at my feet. I bent over and picked it up. I refused to give it back to him. So, he kissed me to distract me as he stole the ball back. I remember being so grossed out at the time," Susan reminisced as she sipped her coffee. "Where were we?"

Sheldon laughed as he continued telling her stories about their cousin's escapades. She died laughing about Shawndrea getting shoved into the pool. He told her about wanting to get more serious about school and thinking about going to college. This news made her the happiest of any part of the stories. She had always wanted the best for Sheldon and believed in him even when he did not believe in himself.

"I'm looking forward to Thanksgiving and seeing all the family," Susan stated as she got up to wash her coffee cup.

"How was your time with Tammy last night?" Sheldon asked as he cleaned his plate.

"It was nice seeing her again. I hadn't seen her since the funeral," Susan explained somberly. "She took her sister's death really hard. I cannot even begin to imagine. She told me they never found out who killed her either or what she was doing at that truck stop. I guess some things in life are left a mystery. Tammy has three boys now and lives in Atlanta with her husband. She was teaching volleyball at a school in Georgia but took time off to raise their kids. It makes me realize how short life is and how much I want a family of my own one day."

"Here comes Levin and Mom," Sheldon remarked.

Susan flipped open a bridle magazine and pretended they had been discussing her wedding plans. "So, I'm thinking a traditional gown with a vale and a short train," Susan explained as she changed the subject and winked at Sheldon.

Their Mom came and stood at the end of the table as Sheldon and Susan turned to look at her. "So, you two were out late last night, huh?" she remarked with a smile as she looked from Susan to Sheldon.

"Not too late," Sheldon replied, half smiling back at her.

"Why is everyone smiling? What happened last night?" Levin asked, completely confused as to what was going on.

"Nothing, son. Keep moving along and quit being nosey," Their Mom instructed. She waited for Levin to leave the room. "A Mother knows all."

She had been watching from her bedroom window when she

saw lights on her wall, which meant someone was driving down their road. She watched the car pull into the driveway. "I do not sleep till all my children are home and accounted for," she remarked, turning and looking at Susan. "No matter how old they get," she continued as she left the room.

Sheldon and Susan looked at each other with questions in their eyes. "Does she know?" Susan mouthed to him.

"No," He whispered, "I'm not ready to go there yet."

"Let me know if you need any help," Susan offered as she got up from the table, giving him a half hug. "I'm going to get ready; I'm meeting Tammy in town.

§

The next few weeks were uneventful. Sheldon spent his time hanging out with Susan. They did some early Christmas shopping for the family. Thanksgiving dinner was entertaining, with Ninnie and Ruby all telling different stories around the table: about Tommy almost burning down the school, their teepeeing escapes, and fitting in at a new school. Shawndrea kept trying to interject a story of her own, but it always had a weird ending or ended in sex.

Sheldon wondered if Chase was enjoying his time with his family. Saturday came, and Susan had to head home. She wanted to get back and settle in for the work week ahead. Sheldon was always sad to see Susan leave, but he knew she had a life to return to. Sheldon lay in bed Sunday night, thinking about Susan's wedding and what Chase was up to as he drifted off to sleep.

§

Monday morning, Sheldon was up and ready to go. He had not been this excited to get to school in forever. Sheldon arrived at school a little early. Sheldon hoped to see Chase before early morning practice, but it was too late. Sheldon opened his locker, and a note fell out. He looked around before opening it.

I can't wait to taste those lips again,
Lips that are the sweetest that have ever been,
I can't stop myself from thinking about them.
Since the moment, your lips touched mine
I became yours, heart, and soul.

Sheldon looked around to see if anyone noticed the huge smile he had on his face as he read it again. *How cheesy is the poem, but I love it.* Sheldon pulled out his notepad and quickly drafted a poem in response.

I was lost in my own problems.
You were lost in a strange new place.
I clearly remember the day we met.
You have a face I just can't forget.
My lips await.
Their sweet fate

"Ugh, I'm not good at writing this stuff," Sheldon grumbled as he wadded up the paper to throw away, but he changed his mind. He walked over to Chase's locker and slid the note inside. As Sheldon started to walk down the hall, lost in thought, he had a massive smile. Sheldon brought the paper to his face. Even the note smelled like him. *What is it about him that drives me crazy?*

Sheldon saw Ninnie coming down the hall and was trying to hide his smile, but it was nearly impossible. "Good morning," He greeted her. "How's it going?" He said, a little too chipper.

She could see his huge smile. "Oh my god, Ruby told you, didn't she?" Ninnie inquired as she went past him to her locker. "After, I asked her not to tell anyone."

"What are you talking about?" Sheldon asked with a half chuckle. "I don't have a clue what you're talking about."

"So, you're not smiling because of what happened to me after the game?" Ninnie queried as she opened her locker.

"No, but now I'm curious," Sheldon stated while Ninnie pulled stuff out of her bag. "What happened?"

"Well… No, I can't tell you it's too embarrassing to think about, let alone say it out loud," Ninnie confessed as she turned red and closed her locker door. "I - I just can't… Have you seen Ruby yet?"

"No, I haven't," Sheldon replied, looking at her and waiting to hear what happened.

"Okay, Ruby and I were chilling by the van after the football game. We were waiting for Trey to come out. I didn't want to leave her there alone. We were discussing being spontaneous and living on the edge. After seeing Chase come up to you at the game, I suddenly felt inspired to be spontaneous. Ruby was saying I couldn't be spontaneous because I never do anything unplanned," She paused for a beat. "And… And… And…" She stammered like a stuck record. She could not breathe.

"It's okay breeeath," Sheldon reassured her as he put his arm around her. "What did you do that has you so freaked out?"

"She dared me to kiss the next person to walk by," She confessed, not wanting to tell the next part. "So, I just walked right up and kissed someone on the lips."

"Okay, kissing someone is normal, but wait. Who did you kiss?" Sheldon questioned, knowing there were not a lot of cute boys to kiss. Ninnie wasn't responding. "Oh no, who did you kiss?" Sheldon asked, becoming nervous about whom she was going to say.

"Oh no, is right," She nearly screamed the words. "I kissed one of the Rogers twins."

"Wait, what?!" Sheldon exclaimed, looking at her as if he could not quite comprehend what she had said. "One of the Rogers twins? The Rogers Twins?" Sheldon repeated twice, trying to wrap his mind around the idea. "Was it Alana or Alicia?

"I don't know," Ninnie stated with her hands to her face. "I have no clue because they both look so much alike in the dark. I heard her say not bad, but I no longer swing that way. Who even says that?"

"Can you imagine if Shawndrea finds out you will never live this down," Sheldon remarked as he tried hard not to laugh, "This is a whole other level of fucked-up-ness.

"Ding ding ding, we have a winner, is what Shawndrea would say," Ninnie joked as she tried to make light of the situation. "Now you see why I don't want anyone knowing. Besides, I like guys but do not know what came over me. I want to forget the whole thing.

I was just wrapped up in our team winning the game, the romantic jester of Chase, and I just needed to do something spontaneous. I'm always the good girl and needed to be *baaad* for a change. Also, I don't think Alana or Alicia would be my type if I were into women. They are too preppy. To top it all off, Tommy Adler saw the whole thing."

"Oh man, Shawndrea has been trying to be best buds with him lately," Sheldon pointed out.

"Don't even get me started with Shawndrea trying to flirt with Tommy," Ninnie fumed. "Anyway, I walked up, gave her a huge kiss, and then I just walked away and didn't even look back. Poor thang, she didn't even see me coming either. That is when Ruby saw Tommy standing there with his mouth hanging open. Shit, what am I gonna do?" Ninnie asked, panicked.

"Maybe everyone involved will forget, and nothing will come of it," Sheldon answered, hopeful as he tried to reassure her. "Here comes Ruby now."

Ruby greeted the two of them, and Tommy walked by with a huge smile as he looked at Ninnie. "Oh god, he is going to say something," Ninnie moaned.

"Maybe not, but we better get to class," Ruby remarked. "If I'm late one more time, I will get written up or given dentition."

"We will see you at lunch, Ruby," Sheldon called after, and he and Ninnie walked to class together. He nudged her with his shoulder. "It's gonna be okay, Cuz."

Sheldon finally saw Chase walking down the hall as they walked to class. His hair was wet from just showering. He smiled at Sheldon as he passed by, and his heart started pounding just looking at him.

"Damn, he is good-looking when wet," Ninnie commented. "Now come on, or we are going to be late."

Ninnie dragged him towards class. Sheldon turned again to see Chase look back at him, smiling.

§

Later that day, Sheldon was getting his stuff out of his locker when someone whispered in his ear. "You're a good writer," He turned to see Chase standing behind him. "Have you ever thought about writing a story or a song?" Sheldon nervously chuckled.

"Thanks, but I'm not as good as you," Sheldon shyly admitted as he put his hands in his pocket. "I really enjoyed kissing you. I was trying to get here early enough to catch you before football practice."

"Football is over, silly. That was the last game of the season," Chase teased, half laughing at Sheldon's innocence about sports. "Kissing you was a great way to celebrate winning regionals. Anyway, I was here early to practice with my band."

"Oh," Sheldon remarked shyly. "A band, huh? Man, is there nothing you cannot do? It was nice getting your note first thing this morning."

"You're too funny," Chase responded as he bumped his shoulder into Sheldon's and smiled. "Come on, I will walk you out,"

They started to walk down the hall when Laramie turned the corner. "Majors," Laramie stated cockily and sarcastically as he passed by. "I'm not done with you yet, punk."

"What is his deal?" Chase questioned as he turned to look at Laramie.

"Who knows with him," Sheldon responded, but he could see Chase was not going to let go that easily. "He is just someone that used to harass me a lot."

"I'm going to keep a close eye on him," Chase stated as he turned to ensure Laramie was continuing and not coming up behind them. "Let's go in here," Chase suggested as he led Sheldon into the gym.

As soon as they were inside the gym, Chase pushed Sheldon up against the wall. He put his hand behind Sheldon's neck and started to kiss him very roughly. He was biting his lips till both lips were wet as they fervently brushed one another. Their tongues intertwined as if they were meant to be together. Sheldon turned Chase around, pushed him up against the wall, and started to kiss his neck. He made his way up his neck, kissed his chin, and nibbled his bottom lip. Sheldon took a deep breath, breathing him in and kissing him. They kissed for quite a while, both breathing heavily, trying to catch their breath, unable to come up for air.

They lost track of time till they heard something bang inside the gym. It was dark, so neither of them could see anything. They headed for the gym exit, and as they opened the door, daylight filled that part of the gym as they walked outside. They walked out with both of their hair a mess, and they had to straighten themselves up. Chase held Sheldon's hand and did not want to let go but did for fear of being seen.

"I'm sorry. I hope I don't make you late," Chase apologized as he smiled at Sheldon, looked around, and gave him one more kiss. I will see you later."

"No worries," Sheldon retorted as he bit his lip. "It was well worth it. I will see you later."

Sheldon turned and headed to his car. When he opened the car door, he turned back to see Chase standing there and waved. Chase waved back. Sheldon had a huge smile while he drove to work.

§

Sheldon came out after work to find Chase waiting in the parking lot. He was leaning against Sheldon's car with his arms crossed, making his biceps bulge bigger than usual. Chase wore a white tank top, making his olive sun-kissed skin look perfect. He wore a pair of snug basketball shorts across his package. His calves looked muscular from all the swimming and running in football. "I wanted to talk to you about a few things," Chase said in a deep, sexy voice.

They got inside Sheldon's car. "Okay. Sheldon replied curiously. "Let's not sit here in case someone sees us," Sheldon recommended as he looked around.

"Good idea," Chase agreed as he thought for a second. "How about we drive to the park?"

What they did not know was that Laramie had already spotted them. Sitting in his truck drinking a beer, he watched them enter Sheldon's car. "Fucking faggots," Laramie muttered as he drank his beer.

"I'm thinking we are on the same page about keeping this private between us," Chase stated as he put his hand on Sheldon's leg. Sheldon put his hand on top of Chase's.

Sheldon looked over and smiled as he looked back at where he was driving as Chase grabbed his hand. "Yes, it's going to be a challenge, but I think so," Sheldon affirmed as Chase kissed his hand.

"It's not that I don't want to, but you know how people are here," Chase confessed as Sheldon kissed his hand. "Maybe we can go to the movies one of these weekends."

"That sounds perfect," Sheldon responded, glancing over at Chase and then back to the road as he continued to kiss Chase's hand.

They were almost to the park when Chase requested that he pull over.

Sheldon barely got the car in park when Chase started to kiss him. They unbuckled their seat belts to maneuver in the car better. The only thing they needed was each other and their connection. Nothing else mattered then, but the two lost in one another. Sheldon's hand ran up Chase's leg, and he could feel the hair on Chase's leg and the warmth coming from his body. He enjoyed being able to touch him. They continued kissing. Sheldon moved his hand further up Chase's leg while his other handheld onto Chase's. As he was reaching for Chase's face, he accidentally brushed his arm against Chase's hard-on, which was sticking up. "Wow, you're so big and excited," Sheldon commented, biting his lip before leaning back to kiss Chase again.

"Just being around, you, I can't help myself," Chase confessed with that cute, dimple smile. He kissed Sheldon again.

They pause for a second. "I need to tell you something," Chase stated. "Despite what you might think, I'm still a virgin. I know I have an attitude of acting 'experienced.' Honestly, I haven't gone all the way with anyone. Yeah, I have messed around, and I know what I want. I just haven't had sex yet."

"Well, thank you for telling me," Sheldon said. He was shocked but somehow relieved. "I haven't either."

They both chuckled and started to kiss again. They kissed until their lips were sore and the windows fogged up. Sheldon drove the car and headed to drop Chase off at his place. Sheldon parked in front of Chase's house. They could not stop kissing. Before Chase exited the car, he snuck one more kiss and gave Sheldon a wink as he shut the door.

Sheldon waited till Chase walked up to his door, and then he drove home.

The next day was a typical day for Sheldon. He was feeling good and genuinely happy for once in his life. Sheldon was getting his homework out of his locker so he could head to work when his locker door slammed shut unexpectedly. There stood Laramie, staring straight into his eyes. Not the person he was expecting to see. "So, faggot, you think your mister big shot now that you're dating the quarterback," He hissed as he shoved Sheldon up against the lockers. "Don't play like you're not because everyone knows it's not like it's a big secret."

"Go away, Laramie, and leave me alone," Sheldon demanded as he tried to walk away. "It's none of your business."

"What did you say, you fucking queer?" Laramie asked, grabbing Sheldon's arm. "None of my fucking business?" Laramie questioned as he pulled Sheldon backward and shoved him against the lockers again.

Sheldon thought someone would have heard them and come running out, but no one did. "You like this, don't you," Laramie insisted as he got very close to Sheldon's face, and he pressed his whole body up against Sheldon, keeping him pinned up against the lockers. "Admit it, you used to look me up and down and wanted some of this."

"Maybe before, but now your personality makes you ugly," Sheldon gibed as he started to get mad and tried to pull away.

"What did you say fucking faggot," Laramie questioned as he became enraged and punched the locker next to Sheldon's head. "I think you're a fucking liar," Laramie snapped as he started kissing Sheldon.

Sheldon had had enough. He pushed Laramie back far enough to bring his leg up and kneed Laramie in the crouch as hard as he could. Laramie bent over as Sheldon kicked him in the ass, and Laramie fell to the floor, cussing. "You're going to pay for that, you fucking queer," Laramie shouted as he was still on the floor writhing in pain with his hands between his legs.

"In your wildest dreams, Miller," Sheldon stated as he turned to take off before Laramie could get to his feet. He moved quickly to the exit and headed to work. Sheldon heard someone calling his name but was afraid to turn to see who it was calling after him. Finally, he turned, relieved to see Chase running down the hall after him.

"Hey, sorry I'm late," Chase apologized as he walked up to Sheldon to hug and kiss him. I'm glad I caught you before you left," Chase stated as he looked into Sheldon's eyes, smiling and pushing a piece of hair behind Sheldon's ears. "Is everything okay?" he asked, concerned; he could tell something was wrong.

"Nothing, it was just a rough day," Sheldon responded with a forced smile. "I will see you later."

"Most definitely, I will meet you at our usual time and place," He affirmed as he looked around and gave Sheldon another kiss. He smacked Sheldon on the butt as Sheldon turned to leave. "I will see you later, sexy."

Sheldon chuckled and smiled as he walked out. Somehow, Chase made him forget everything troubling him and made his day sunny.

Ruby walked over to Sheldon's locker the following day to tell him good morning. He jumped back, looking startled, thinking it was Laramie. "Are you okay?" Ruby asked. You look terrible."

"I didn't sleep well last night," Sheldon replied as he turned to head to class. "I can't really talk about it."

"Hey, you can tell me," Ruby offered as she grabbed his arm to get his full attention. "I'm here and a great listener when you're ready to talk."

"Thanks, but I'm gonna be late for class," Sheldon said as he hurried off.

Ruby had a concerned look on her face, watching him walk away as Ninnie walked over. "What's going on? You look like someone just told you they were all out of pizza rolls at the store," Ninnie joked with a chuckle.

"Nothing, good morning," Ruby replied as she turned and smiled at Ninnie, not wanting her to know about her concern for Sheldon. "How's everything?"

They chatted as they walked together down the hall heading to class.

§

At lunch, Sheldon sat beside Ruby, who was picking at her food. "So, I talked to Trey, and we are considering going to the movies next weekend. I thought it would be cool if you and Chase came along kind of a double date," Ruby suggested with a smile as she looked at Sheldon. "Okay, what is going on with you? You're not your usual chipper self."

"Something happened yesterday, and I don't know what to do," Sheldon confessed, trying to look at Ruby. "I can't tell Chase, that is for sure."

"What happened?" Ruby asked, even more concerned now.

Sheldon told her about Laramie coming to his locker and calling him faggot. He paused, then said, "Out of the blue, he kissed me."

"Oh my god!" Ruby gasped. "He kissed you?"

"Yes!" Sheldon exclaimed. "Out of the blue,"

"Are you okay?"

"Yeah, I'm okay, thanks, but I don't think I should tell Chase."

"What did you do?" Ruby asked, sitting forward like watching an episode of *One Life to Live*.

"I kneed him hard in the nuts," Sheldon explained with a half chuckle. "Then I kicked him in the ass when he bent over in pain."

"Good Job!" Ruby cheered and was quiet for a moment while what happened sank in. "Oh shit, yea, you can't tell Chase he will go crazy, but you can't tell him either. Oh, this is a tough one."

"What's a tough one?" Ninnie inquired as she put her salad down on the table. Sheldon and Ruby looked at each other. "Oh, come on, guys, you always have the good juicy stories, and I'm always the last to know. Wait, it's not about me, is it?"

"No," Ruby replied as she looked at Sheldon. He nodded his head, giving her permission to tell her what happened. She proceeded to recount the events.

"Where is the cock sucker? I will kick his ass!" Ninnie exclaimed as she stood up from the table.

"No, wait," Sheldon requested as he reached over and pulled her back into her chair. "You can't say anything about this to anyone."

"That's bullshit," Ninnie declared as she sat back down. "His punk ass needs kicked."

"I agree," Ruby affirmed as she tried to calm Ninnie down.

"But Sheldon did a surprisingly excellent job of that. He kneed him in the balls and kicked him in the ass while he bent over in pain."

"Hell Yeah! That is how you take care of business," Ninnie jeered.

They all laughed. "Hopefully, this thing will blow over, and it will be like nothing happened," Sheldon said. "I just want to focus on the good stuff. "I will talk to Chase about going to the movies," he said, looking at Ruby.

"Movies?" Ninnie asked, looking confused and hurt. "You didn't invite me to see a movie?"

"You want to come?" Sheldon asked. "Maybe you can see if Alicia or Alana is free."

"You little asshole you," Ninnie said as she leaned over and grabbed some peas from Sheldon's tray and threw them at him. "That was totally uncalled for."

"Heck, why not both," Ruby added as she laughed.

"You too!" Ninnie exclaimed at Ruby and flung a pea at her. "There is no loyalty with you two anymore."

Ninnie flung another one at Sheldon for laughing at her. They all laughed when a pea flew into Sheldon's mouth as he was about to say something else. "That'll teach you," Ninnie remarked with a smirk. "Go ahead, say something else smart."

"I guess you're right, though. I haven't even been asked out on a date in like forever. My astounding beauty must intimate them all," Ninnie boosted as she flicked her hair back.

"That must be it," Ruby quipped as she held up one of her books, bracing for any peas hurled at her.

"You two are about the most ungrateful bitches I have ever met," Ninnie stated as she raised her nose at the two of them. "I grace you with my presence each day and this is how you repay me? Just think I could be sitting with those amazing people over there," she pointed at a table where a few nerdy, awkward-looking guys were seated, and one was picking his nose. "Well, maybe not that table, but you get the point."

They all laughed out loud again. "We better get to our next class," Sheldon remarked as he gathered his lunch trash.

"You're welcome to come to the movies with us," Ruby offered Ninnie as they walked out of the cafeteria. "You might feel like a fifth wheel, though."

"Thanks, maybe next time," Ninnie replied as they walked through the cafeteria doors, and they closed behind them. She started heading in the opposite direction. "Besides, I have plans of my own."

Ruby and Sheldon wondered what Ms. Ninnie had up her sleeve and what she had been hiding.

§

Sheldon opened his locker Friday morning to find another note, which meant Chase would be late practicing with his band. It was easier for them to practice at school, and they could be as loud as they wanted in the sound booth. He opened the note and read the poem.

Life is full of surprises.
Surprises like you make a life.
A life worth building, a life worth living.
You make my heartbeat with joy.
A heart that beats for you

After reading such a beautiful and inspiring note, Sheldon couldn't help but let everything negative go and be happy again. He wasn't going to let someone else make him feel bad. In return, Sheldon scribbled a poem.

Life is a journey,
And in life we must choose a path
The paths we choose shapes us.
Shapes us into who we will become.
That path is you.
I choose you.

Sheldon hurried over to Chase's locker before anyone could see what he was doing. He kissed the letter before shoving it into the locker. They had decided to go to the movies with Ruby and Trey.

So, he went about his day excited he would be going on an official date with Chase that night. His wildest dreams were about to come true.

Chapter Twelve

Date Night

It was an unusually warm Saturday afternoon for December as Sheldon, Chase, Ruby, and Trey headed to Evansville, Indiana. They had planned to go Friday night, but those plans fell through. However, going on Saturday meant they would have more time to enjoy themselves in the city.

Since it was an hour away, they didn't make it to Evansville often. They wanted to go somewhere no one would recognize them, where they could be themselves and no one cared. Trey decided to take his parents' Lincoln Town car; it was more comfortable. They headed out, and Trey admitted feeling awkward about seeing Chase and Sheldon together.

"You two aren't going to start going at it, are you?" Trey asked. He immediately knew it was a dumb question, but the words were already out of his mouth.

"They are just like everyone else. They aren't going to go "at it" as you so intellectually phrased it," Ruby remarked as she shook her head at Trey. "Maybe they will hold hands and snuggle if they feel like it."

Sheldon and Chase smiled at each other, both thinking if they only knew. "I don't know about you, Sheldon, but I think we should start making out every chance we get," Chase teased as he put his arm around Sheldon. He smirked and winked at Trey.

"Okay, smartasses, I get it," Trey said, looking in the review mirror. "I'm sorry it was a dumb thing to say."

"You seriously need to get in the world a little more. That small town is frying your brain," Ruby instructed him. "When two people love each other, it shouldn't really matter."

"I know I just never saw anything like that before except what you see in porn," Trey stated.

"Wait, you have seen gay porn?" Chase questioned, astonished.

"Only by accident," Trey admitted as he became uncomfortable and shifted in his seat.

"Nice, I have a little freak on my hands here," Ruby teased as she smiled and looked at Sheldon and Chase in the back seat.

"Wait, I want to hear about this accident," Chase requested as he leaned forward between Trey and Ruby in the front seat.

"My parents had just gotten a computer, and I was searching on the World Wide Web thingy and came across it by accident," Trey explained.

"Mmhhmm," Chase expressed with a chuckle. "Likely story Trey. What did you type into the search bar?"

"Sooo, I was thinking we have time to play some mini golf before dinner," Trey recommended as he tried to change the subject. "I think it would be fun." They all agreed that it sounded like a great plan, letting go of the previous subject and chatting about other things for the rest of the trip.

They pulled into the parking lot of the mini golf course. They walked up to the entrance when Trey stopped. "Hey, Chase, doesn't that look a lot like Tommy Adler's car?" Trey asked as he turned to look at Chase and pointed at a car in the parking lot.

"It sure looks like it," Chase agreed as he looked at the back of the car. "Also, it has Illinois plates. What is the coincidence of that happening?"

Out of the mini golf place walked Ninnie, laughing. Right behind her was Tommy. "What are you guys doing here?" Ninnie asked with a shocked look on her face, like a kid who got caught with their hand in the cooking jar. "I thought you were coming last night."

"What are we doing here?" Sheldon asked with his head cocked to the side and with a just as shocked look on his face. "and why you're here with Tommy?"

"Well, this is awkward," Chase remarked, unsure what to do next.

"Ummm, do you two want to play mini golf with us and then go to dinner and a movie?"

"Yeah, then you can fill us in on what's going on with you two," Sheldon added, pointing his finger back and forth at Ninnie and Tommy.

"I was just about to run her over to the mall," Tommy explained, a bit nervous and unsure. "We could meet you for dinner afterward. Where are you going?"

"We are thinking of Darryl's Steakhouse. We will see you there in about an hour," Ruby answered, trying to hold back a smile as they watched Tommy open the door for Ninnie. Then he got in, and they drove away.

Sheldon was still in shock. He did not see that one coming. "Did you know those two were dating?" Sheldon asked Chase.

"No, I had no clue," Chase replied.

"Did you know?" Sheldon asked, looking at Ruby.

"Well, I kind of had my suspicions that something was up with her," Ruby admitted. "But, I did not know for sure. I'm sure we will find out more at dinner."

"You think they are actually going to come?" Trey asked as he held the door open for them to enter. "That was pretty awkward."

"Yeah, she will make sure they come," Sheldon replied with a half laugh. "She has some major explaining to do, plus she never turns down good food."

While they played mini golf, Trey and Chase became very competitive. It was like one had to prove he was better than the other one when in fact, Ruby was kicking both their butts.

Ruby tried not to rub it in so severely that she beat them. However, she did do a little dance and laughed. "I finally found something I'm good at," Ruby cheered as she strutted to the car. "I'm starving after defeating you two."

"Yeah, I haven't seen you that determined since we went teepeeing," Sheldon commented. He laughed as he got into the car. "This girl has an arm on her."

"Teepeeing!?" Chase exclaimed.

"That's right, I never heard the story from that night," Trey said with a smile as he raised an eyebrow.

Ruby told the story about their teepeeing adventure while Trey drove them to the restaurant. They laughed that Ninnie got pissed about not being able to throw the roll very far. Ruby got so into it that she finished her rolls and started using Ninnie's toilet paper rolls. She freaked out about almost getting caught when they pulled into the restaurant's parking lot. "I don't see Tommy's car anywhere," Trey said, looking around. "We should have taken bets."

"Patients," Ruby requested. "They still have five minutes."

"You would have lost that bet," Sheldon smirked as he pointed to Tommy's car pulling into the parking lot. "I told you."

They all got out of the car and greeted Tommy and Ninnie. It was a little awkward at first. No one knew what to say. They made their way into the restaurant. Trey checked them in with the greeter, who told him their table would be ready in five minutes. Sheldon couldn't wait any longer, so he sat beside Ninnie and stared at her.

"What?" Ninnie asked. "You're freaking me out. Don't worry, he has known about you two for quite some time," She said as she looked at Chase and Sheldon.

"What?" Chase asked, taking the words out of Sheldon's mouth.

"How?" Sheldon inquired.

"We kind of saw you two making out in the gym one day," Ninnie replied shyly. "He was about as shocked as you all are right now. We had gone in there for some, you know, alone time."

"Alone time?" Sheldon queried. "How long have you two been… Whatever ever this is?"

"We have…" Ninnie was interrupted by the hostess, who showed them to their table. The whole group was riveted by this point, waiting to hear what Ninnie would say next. They were all seated at their table.

Ninnie continued her story while they waited for the server to come over. "We have been seeing each other since about the second week of school," Ninnie explained as she looked at their shocked faces. "We didn't start doing, you know what, till around the camping trip."

"That explains where you were going all those times after lunch," Sheldon thoughtfully recalled as he glanced at Ruby, who was nodding.

"Which explains the look on Tommy's face when you kissed one of the Rogers Twins," Ruby added with a laugh. "I wondered why he cared so much."

Everyone looked at Ruby. Chase and Trey didn't know about that part. "Sorry," Ruby said. "Hold on, you said something about camping."

"That's okay. That shock was nothing compared to the shock Tommy got when he saw his Mother kiss Mandy," Ninnie blurted out.

The table erupted at that point, and everyone in the restaurant stared. Chase didn't know about that either. "How is it that I had no clue about any of this," Chase questioned as he playfully elbowed Sheldon. "This is going to be a fascinating story."

"Wait… How?" Sheldon and Ruby were talking over one another and laughed. "How did Tommy see Wendy kissing my Mom?" Sheldon asked, looking at them with a raised eyebrow.

"Okay, Okay, let me explain," Ninnie tried to get them under control while laughing at them. She looked at Tommy, and he gave her the floor to explain further.

"Tommy had come down to the campsite to check in on his Mom, so he says," Ninnie chortled. "Since his parents had separated, he hadn't seen much of her and wanted to see how she was doing. I called it spying. He called it "Checking on," but whatever. He had gotten down there Saturday and saw me sitting by the campfire. It was while the two of you had gone off to find Shawndrea. He crept up on me and scared the holy shit out of me. I thought that was it. I thought I was a goner. The next thing I knew, he was kissing me. I thought he was stalking me at first, but then he explained that the camper was his Mom's. Until that point, I had no idea Wendy was his Mom."

"I was starting to feel bad about calling his Mom a Lesbo etc.," Ninnie added. "That was until Monday…"

"Now we know where you disappeared to on Sunday," Sheldon recalled as he pieced the puzzle together. "Ninnie, how did your Mom not catch you two together at some point?"

"We are just that good," Ninnie chortled. "Plus, I had the best teacher."

"Shawndrea!" Everyone at the table said in unison. They all laughed.

"Okay, so on Monday, Tommy was supposed to head home first. He wanted to beat us back, but for some reason, he was hanging around, and that's when he saw his Mom kiss your Mom. Then, to top it off, a few weeks later, he saw me kissing one of the Rogers twins."

"Ya, you have to go back to the part where you kissed a girl," Trey requested as Ruby elbowed him. "Hey, nothing wrong with hearing a good story about two girls kissing."

Ninnie revealed that as she proceeded to tell them about the night, she had kissed one of the Rogers Twins. "We had decided we didn't want anyone to know about us being together because it felt good to be bad," Ninnie explained. "To secretly date someone was exciting—something our parents could not control. For once, I felt like the bad girl and loved it.

When Tommy saw his Mother kiss Mandy. Then I kissed Alana, or was it, Alicia? Heck, one of the twins. Tommy lost his mind for a few days. I told him that sometimes one's love or desire knows no gender. You love who you love, and you can't help it. We don't always get to choose who we fall in love with. However, we have the choice to accept and support other's decisions and to love one another. It truly isn't our business to tell someone who they can and can't love."

"Wow, I can only imagine what Tommy's Dad is going to say," Chase remarked. "This story sounds like an episode of *All My Children* or *One Life to Live*."

"You know about soap operas"? Sheldon whispered to Chase.

"Yeah, my mom watches them," Chase chuckled.

"Ha-ha, yea, speaking of Tommy's Dad. This story only gets better," Ninnie stated. One night, Tommy and I…

§

Ninnie was at Tommy's house because his dad was at a school event. They had the place to themselves for the evening. Ninnie sat curled into Tommy's side as they watched *back to the Future III*. Tommy would stop watching the screen every few minutes and watch her. He slowly started to run his thumb in circles on her hip where his hand rested. Ninnie shifted; she was beginning to get this heat in her stomach from the way Tommy was touching her. She turned to look at Tommy and found him already gazing at her. He leaned in slowly to let her know what he was about to do and give her time to stop him.

Ninnie closed the space between them. Her lips gently brushed his, testing the waters. As soon as their lips touched, a fire started in Ninnie. She grabbed his face to keep him close so she could deepen the kiss. Tommy put his hands on her hips and pulled Ninnie onto his lap to straddle him. He slid one hand to her neck to deepen the kiss. He flicked his tongue across her lower lip, asking for entry. Ninnie moaned and opened for Tommy. She was so distracted by his tongue and what it was doing that she did not realize his hand had snaked under her shirt and onto her bra clasp. Ninnie pulled back with a gasp when he popped her bra open.

"Am I going too fast?" Tommy panted.

"No, I am surprised at how skillfully you did that. I thought for sure there would be some fumbling. Tommy, have you been practicing?"

Tommy blushed, and Ninnie playfully smacked him and pulled him back for a heated kiss. Ninnie grabbed Tommy's hand and placed it on her breast. Tommy pulled back to look into Ninnie's face to make sure. When he looked into her eyes, he saw hunger. Her face was flushed, and there was unevenness to her breath.

He took all those signs to mean she was ready. He took his hand and slowly ran it up her side to cup her breast underneath her shirt. His thumb brushed over her nipple, and she sucked in a breath. The sensation took her by surprise. The next time he swiped across her nipple, as it pebbled, she let out a breathy moan encouraging him to continue. Soon, that was not enough. She started to squirm on his lap, noticing he was just as excited. He was rock-hard.

"Tommy, please." she moaned.

Tommy pulled her beaded nipple into his mouth through her shirt and started to suck.

Tommy placed his hand on her belly with his pinky slipping into her pants. As he sucked harder, his hand slipped farther into her pants before unbuttoning them. Ninnie felt nervous suddenly. What if he was turned off by how wet she was down there?

Was that normal? She was about to find out when Tommy slipped his fingers into her pants and found the wetness. Tommy let out a gruntal groan. He put his mouth on Ninnie's in a searing kiss.

She got her answer. Tommy brushed the spot that made her wetter and tore a loud moan from her. Unexpectedly, they heard the garage door open. Before they could comprehend what, they heard through their lustful haze, Tommy's dad walked through the door with a bag of groceries…

§

"What happened next," Trey excitedly said realizing it was drooling. By this point, Trey and Ruby were on the edge of their seats. Ruby looked extremely uncomfortable yet intrigued.

"Nothing. Tommy's dad suggested it was time for me to go home," Ninnie replied. "Though - - we picked back up where we left off the following weekend. Tommy had my leg pulled back over my head and…"

"Okay, I don't think they want all the details," Tommy interrupted, extremely red-faced.

"Oh, I think we do," Ruby blurted out, surprising herself.

"Let's just say Shawndrea would have been proud that weekend," Ninnie said, clearing her throat.

They all laughed and finished eating. "We all have had an interesting past six months," Ruby commented as she looked around the table at everyone. "I hope the next six months are just as exciting.

Trey and Chase got up from the table. As soon as they were out of earshot, Ninnie turned to Sheldon. "There is one more thing," Ninnie stated as she looked at Tommy and Sheldon. "The next day after you told me about Laramie, Tommy broke down and told me he had seen what Laramie had done to you. He didn't know what to do, and I didn't know how to tell you that Tommy knew. He knew telling Chase might only make it worse, so he threatened that if Laramie didn't quit bothering you, Tommy would tell everyone that he came onto him too. Well, of course, that got his attention."

"Thanks, Tommy," Sheldon expressed gratitude as he got a little emotional. "I have tried to not think about that incident.

Also, I didn't want to tell Chase because I didn't know what he would do. Plus, Laramie isn't worth it."

"Hey man, no worries," Tommy said. "That is what family is for, right? But you may want to tell him at some point. Things like that have a way of surfacing when you least expect it to."

Trey and Chase were walking back to the table. "Is anyone thinking about going to prom?" Ruby asked, changing the subject, and looking around at everyone. "I think it will be fun. I think Trey and I are going…" She stopped talking about it when she looked at Sheldon and Chase. She realized it was a sore subject and to change it because they couldn't go together.

"I guess we should get going if we're still going to make it to the movies," Trey remarked as he leaned over to kiss Ruby on the cheek. "Are you two coming along?" He asked Tommy and Ninnie.

They both looked at each other. "I think that would be nice," Ninnie replied. "It's going to be strange that you know about us."

"Well, I think this has been really nice," Ruby commented. "We have to do this more often."

Sheldon watched everyone around the table laughing and talking. He was grateful to be seated next to Chase, the man he loved, to be surrounded by friends and a lot of love, and he was amazed at how much his life had changed within a year.

The laughter continued as they settled into their seats at the movies. Ruby was incredibly excited. She had wanted to go to the movie theater for months and loved scary movies.

Sheldon and Ninnie got a large popcorn while everyone else looked at them like they were both crazy. "Man, you guys just ate. Where do you find a room?" Ruby asked, laughing. "But it defi-nitely smells good.

"Hey, no judging," Ninnie demanded of Ruby. Because this is a judge-free zone, thank you very much. Besides, I will just have to work it off later," she winked at Tommy.

"This has been a real eye-opening and enlightening weekend so far," Sheldon laughed as the previews started. "You don't get scared with scary movies, do you?" Sheldon leaned over to ask Chase.

"Psssh, no," Chase answered. "Do you?

"Not at all," Sheldon replied with the most serious expression he could muster.

Halfway through the movie, Sheldon kept thinking about holding Chase's hand and cuddling like the other couples. However, he was afraid to attempt to do so. A scary scene came, and Chase cringed down, hiding behind Sheldon's shoulder. "Tell me when it is over," Chase requested.

Sheldon smiled, and it felt nice to know that Mr. Perfect Chase had fears and weaknesses, too. "Okay, it is over," Sheldon informed Chase with a smile.

Chase looked back at him and smiled his cute dimple smile. They raised the arm of the seat so they could get closer together. They leaned in simultaneously, bumping each other harder than attend, and chuckled.

Then, they began to kiss each other passionately and deeply. Chase took Sheldon's hands and affectionately squeezed them as they continued kissing. Before they knew it, the movie was over.

They walked out as everyone talked about how intense the movie was. "I'm not sure how much of it you two seen with your mouths locked together like that," Ninnie teased Chase and Sheldon. "Man, your lips are red and slightly swollen from all the kissing."

"Whatever," Sheldon retorted, slightly embarrassed as he bumped Ninnie with his shoulder. "Does this mean you two will no longer be "secretly dating" now?" Sheldon said with air quotes.

"I don't know," Ninnie answered with a mischievous smile and locked arms with Tommy. "I guess we will just have to wait and see."

"See you at school," Tommy said as he opened the door for Ninnie. She got in, and he closed the door behind her. He waved at everyone before getting in himself and driving away.

They rushed to get into Trey's car because it had gotten cold while they were in the theater. "Let's get some heat going," Ruby requested as she shivered and rubbed her hands together.

On the ride home, it was quiet. Sheldon was getting very sleepy. He laid his head on Chase's shoulder.

"Did you have a good time?" Chase asked Sheldon as he kissed his head.

"I most definitely did," Sheldon replied as he yawned. "How about you?

"One of the best," Chase remarked with a huge smile.

Sheldon looked out the window, amazed at how bright the moon was. He could hear Chase humming along to the radio as he drifted off to sleep, feeling safe, warm, and loved.

§

It was a frosty Monday morning. A motorcycle with two people on it pulled into the school parking lot. Both wore black leather outfits and helmets, so you could not see who it was. They walked hand in hand up to the school doors and took off their helmets as they walked in. Everyone stared in a state of shock. People whispered to one another. *"Did you know they were dating,"* Could be heard from several students.

"So, Tommy, did you get a new motorcycle?" Trey asked with a huge smile.

"Way to make an entrance, cuz," Sheldon praised Ninnie with a smirk. "A bit theatrical, don't you think? You just HAD to prove that Shawndrea isn't the only Myer that can get attention."

"Hey, you wouldn't expect anything less from us, would you?" Ninnie responded with a big smile.

"Love the leather outfits," Ruby added. "You two look like real badasses now. I bet your dad will be so proud of you, Tommy."

"He already thinks I'm a bad influence on his sweet little boy," Ninnie boasted with an eyebrow raised. "He thinks I'm why he has been acting up these past few months."

"Welcome to the club of misfits," Sheldon chortled. "Setting the expectations low and overdelivering is a good motto."

"Man, they are really putting the pressure on us now, huh," Chase turned and whispered to Sheldon. "Do not worry. They may have raised the bar, but I always fly over it."

Everyone headed to class. Sheldon couldn't help but wonder what Mr. De Longpre had up his sleeve. It scared him to think about coming out to everyone, but it excited him at the same time. He wanted to show his affection to Chase whenever he felt like it without worrying about other people's thoughts.

As the weeks flew by, Chase had become very busy with his band.

Sheldon saw less and less of him. Chase surprised Sheldon by show-ing up after he got off work. They sat in Sheldon's car, catching up.

"I'm sorry I have been so busy lately," Chase offered as he kissed Sheldon. "Trust me, it will all make sense soon. Also, I saw the look you had on your face when Ruby talked about the prom," He pointed out as he ran his fingers through Sheldon's hair.

"It's no big deal," Sheldon said, wanting to change the subject. "How's everything going with you?"

"It is a big deal, and we will figure something out," Chase ex-pressed as he put his hands on either side of Sheldon's face and looked into his eyes. "Trust me, we will figure something out. Ev-erything else is going well. I have decided not to play baseball this year." Sheldon looked at him quizzically.

"I'm too busy with my studies and playing with the band," Chase continued. "We actually booked a few gigs. You will have to come by soon and check us out. I wanted to wait till we were doing well before you witnessed the mess, we were a few weeks ago."

"That would be really nice," Sheldon commented with a huge smile. "I can't wait."

"I better let you get home," Chase stated as he kissed him good-bye. "I really have missed looking into those gorgeous green eyes."

"Wow, you're such a sweet talker," Sheldon flirted. "Now go, I want to watch that sexy ass walk away."

Chase smacked his ass as he headed for home. Sheldon started up his car and headed home. He felt better about the distance that had seemed to creep in the past couple of weeks. Sheldon was so caught up in the moment that he did not notice that someone had been watching them. There was a mysterious truck parked in the shadow of a tree, and the only thing you could see was the cigarette burning brighter with each drag.

Sheldon didn't see Chase the next day at school before his first period, so he wrote a poem and slipped it into Chase's locker. He was feeling good about how things were going and doing better in school. Caring about school and his future for the first time felt good.

A week without you
Is like a desert with no rain.
A day without you
Is like a day with no sun.
A night without you
Is like a night with no moon.
A minute without you
Is like a world with no air.
This is why I choose you.

P.S. can't wait to see what you have up your sleeve with your band.

Chapter Thirteen

A Life of Surprises

Chase was running late for class, as usual. He opened his locker, and a note flitted to the floor. Chase bent over to pick it up. He smiled a little like the Cheshire cat because he felt like the luckiest guy in the world. Chase shoved the note into his bag. He wanted to read it when he got home to savor the moment.

Later that night, Chase was lying on his bed doing some homework. He pulled out Sheldon's note. After reading it, he thought back to his life in California.

Chase remembered well the day he had to tell his best friends Camille Watkins and Glenn Ford he would be moving. Fourteen-year-old Chase was living in Santa Monica, California, and they were sitting outside at lunch. There was only a week left till they graduated eighth grade and went to high school.

Camille and Glenn grew up next door to one another. Both lived in beautifully landscaped, enormous Spanish-style homes in the Pacific Palisades. Camille's dad was an engineer, and Glenn's parents were accountants. They each had a cook, housekeeper, and driver.

Chase lived in a lovely ranch-style home in the Palisades but had no maid, cook, or diver. Their lifestyles were higher end than Chase's, but they still hung out together like it was nothing. The three of them had always talked about starting a band, but everyone had busy schedules, so they never got around to it. He remembered their faces when he told them his dad was moving them to Illinois that summer.

"What will you do for fun there?" Glenn inquired as he fixed his hair in the window of the building they were sitting in front of, "Are there places to shop? Will there be cute boys?" His voice went high-pitched and cracked.

"I'm worried about what you will eat there," Camille inquired. "Who will make you tamales? Hay guey ¿Cómo vas a vivir en LA sin tu familia?"

"Okay, calm down. You two are crazy. You act like I'm going to another country," Chase said as he laughed. And it's pronounced Illinoi; the s is silent. Once we get settled in, maybe you can come and visit us."

"I don't think so. Just the idea of the place makes me itchy," Glenn remarked as he started to scratch his neck subconsciously. Growing up, anytime his parents forced him to wear something cheap, it made him itch. This issue seemed to carry over into places and things, making him feel itchy. "Sounds like a very poor place. They can't even afford to pronounce the s," He joked as he laughed alone because the other two failed to see the humor in his joke.

"I heard there are a lot of cute white boys there," Camille commented, practically drooling. "Cute white meaty boys with big arms that can…"

"Whoa! Camille, we are still sitting here, and we're eating lunch," Chase remarked, laughing at her. "Besides, I didn't think your dad was letting you date till you were out of college."

"Hey, a girl can dream, can't she?" Camille asked as she fanned herself and then resumed eating her tamale. "But you're right. I'm going to save myself for marriage. One day, I will meet the perfect man. We will buy a beautiful house overlooking the ocean and have two kids, a boy and a girl. Oh, and we will have a dog named Scout."

Glenn and Sheldon looked at her with comical expressions as she went about her dream future. "Cute boys or not, it doesn't sound like a place I care to go to," Glenn stated, interrupting her daydream while eating an apple he brought from home. "Why can't you move somewhere nicer?"

"I will be sure to tell my dad that," Chase laughed as he threw his trash away. "It's going to be strange living in a new place. Santa Monica and you two are all I have known my whole life.

"We must have a beach party before you leave," Camille requested as she threw her trash away. "Man, I don't know how I will make it through freshman year without you."

"I know. I feel bad I'm leaving you here with this one," Chase joked, pointing his lips at Glenn. Chase loved teasing Glenn because getting him riled up and watching him spin was easy.

"Hey, what's that supposed to mean?" Glenn questioned with a sour look on his face.

"Don't worry, I will take good care of him," Camille declared as she put her arm around Glenn, teasing him too. "Look out, I think I see grumpy Glenn coming out."

"That's right. You two had better stop it before I turn you both into frogs," Glenn demanded as he pointed his finger and glared at them. He laughed his nerdy laugh. He threw the remains of his apple on the ground.

"Hey, don't litter," Chase scowled at Glenn.

"It's just an apple," Glenn retorted as Camille walked over to pick it up and threw it away.

"Yea, and that's what people say about cigarette butts, but trash is trash," Camille added as they all headed off to their next class.

§

Chase and his friends were standing outside of his old house talking. They had their moving van loaded, and it was time to say goodbye. Chase hugged them as he thought about the times, they had been there for each other. They started kindergarten together, middle school, and now graduating junior high. He thought about the first time they were allowed to go to the mall without their parents. Most importantly, they were there for Chase's first heartbreak. "I will see you two again soon," Chase yelled out the car window.

"Don't forget to…" Camille shouted, but he couldn't hear her anymore as the car turned the corner. They drove past the 3rd Street promenade, where he and his friends used to go and hang out to-gether for hours. Chase was sad to think they would be hanging out there without him. While he rode in the car with his Mom, he had time to think. Chase promised not to fall in love again because his last relationship did not end well. Since they were moving to a small town, maybe he should not date a guy this time. He was lost in his thoughts as Chase stared out the window. He put on his headphones and fell asleep.

When they got to their new town, he threw himself into his studies and sports. He had a goal to make new friends and form a band. He did well at keeping busy, but for some reason, he kept running into this one guy, Sheldon. The more he saw Sheldon, the more he couldn't take his mind off him. He threw himself into football but kept thinking about Sheldon's eyes, hair, and lips. They were always on his mind. He realized maybe it wasn't a good idea to offer Sheldon swim lessons, but he could not stop himself. He started the band with Trey towards the end of the football season, which had been his long-time goal. At first, it was only a two-person band, with Chase playing the guitar and Trey playing the keyboard. Then Tommy joined them on drums, and it made a dramatic difference.

Thinking about his old friends somehow gave him the idea to take the notes Sheldon had written to him and make them into a song. He wanted to surprise Sheldon with a song. Chase started daydreaming about the first day Sheldon almost ran him over. Sheldon's smile was infectious; he made him want to be a better version of himself. That is why he quit smoking a week later, which wasn't too hard since he only smoked a few times a day. Plus, smoking was not good for his endurance during swimming and exercising. Chase pulled out all of Sheldon's notes and started to write out the chorus to the song:

> *Your laugh*
> *makes me smile.*
> *All the while you're stealing my heart.*
> *You don't know what you.*
> *What you do to me*
> *That is why.*
> *Why I choose you.*
> *I choose you.*

Sheldon's words inspired him to be creative, which was a great feeling. He wrote the whole song rather quickly, with most of it already written from their notes. He just had to clean it up and add a chorus. He pulled out his guitar and started to give it a melody. He could not wait to share it with the guys. He knew exactly how he was going to surprise Sheldon with this song.

The next day, after Sheldon and Chase had finished swimming a few laps, they leaned against the side of the pool to catch their breath. "I was thinking we should write a song together," Chase said, watching Sheldon try to catch his breath. I think it would be fun."

"Seriously?" Sheldon asked with a curious look and splashed water at Chase. "I do not know the first thing about writing a song."

"You're more talented than you give yourself credit for," Chase insisted as he leaned down to kiss him and then splashed water on him. "Come on, what's the first thing that comes to mind? I will be right back and give you a second to think of something." Chase ran inside the locker room to get a pen and paper.

"He thinks my backstroke is sexy. It really gets him going. Haha," Sheldon joked, not able to take it seriously.

"Come on, be serious," Chase requested with a sideways glance. "Do not make me throw you in the pool."

"Oh man, this is going to be tough," Sheldon mumbled. "Well, your love is like a ray of sun. It warms me deep to the bone and reaches places I've never known."

"Shit!" Chase exclaimed as he began furiously writing it down. "That was amazing. Keep going."

"I want to stand next to you and not worry about what others think," Sheldon continued his train of thought." Because next to you is the place I want to be."

"Very good, I love these lines. Okay, later I will teach you how to play the guitar so you can write your own music," Chase explained with a big smile while he kissed Sheldon and continued talking and laughing. "I can't wait to hear you sing our song. Did you know you make me a very happy person?"

"Really?" Sheldon questioned as he pulled Chase down into the pool, laughing loudly. "You realize this is where we had our first kiss?"

"How could I forget," Chase remarked as he pulled Sheldon closer. "You practically attacked me."

"Oh no, no, no, that is not how I remember it," Sheldon retorted with a laugh as he pushed Chase backward. "You were the perpetrator in this story."

"Who could blame me," He stated, pulling Sheldon closer. "It was all I could do to keep my hands off you."

"Uggh, you get me every time with those sexy blue eyes and the way you clench your jaw. Stop!" Sheldon pleaded as Chase kept flexing his jaw repeatedly. "Stop, you're driving me nuts." Sheldon leaned over and nibbled Chase's chin.

They wrestled in the pool for a while, laughing, playing, and splashing water everywhere. The rest of the world doesn't exist when two people are in love. All they need is each other.

§

Saturday afternoon, Sheldon and the girls were excited to watch the boys practice their songs for an upcoming gig. The boys were prepared to perform at a wedding reception. Even though Tommy just joined the boys, he caught on quickly. He blended in well with the other two like they had been performing for years. They played a couple of cover songs and a couple of originals they had written together. "We are thinking of calling ourselves Chase the Band," Chase explained as they were playing around with a new song.

"That sounds perfect," Sheldon commented as he looked at the girls. "I love the play on words."

"They are surprisingly good," Ruby remarked, looking impressed at Sheldon and Ninnie.

"They're okay," Ninnie joked when, in fact, watching Tommy playing the drums was turning her on. "Psssh, anyone can pick up an instrument and start playing. Heck, I played the clarinet in middle school, and now that is a sexy instrument, believe me."

Laughing, they continued to watch the boys play. They were still working out a few kinks and getting the sound exactly right. "As coach always says, 'Practice makes perfect boys,' Chase stated as he encouraged them to keep going even when they hit a wrong note.

After they finished and everyone left, Chase turned to Sheldon. "So, what did you think?" Chase asked as he picked up his guitar.

"You guys sound amazing," Sheldon replied, smiling at Chase. He could not believe how one person could be so inspiring. Here is someone who never gives up and keeps pushing forward.

"Pull up that chair. I have something I want to show you," Chase invited Sheldon as he pulled up a stool and started strumming the beginning of the song they had written together. He started singing, and Sheldon looked at him inquisitively. "Is that our song?" Sheldon asked. It's incredible how well it sounds."

"Here, sing it with me," Chase requested as he sang through the song once more. "I only have the beginning of it, but it's a start. When I finish, I will show you a few cords so you can play the song, too."

Sheldon started singing along with him as he picked up the melody and harmonized. Sheldon was amazed at how good it felt to sing with someone else who could sing. It felt as if they were creating magic together. This song was something they created together and was theirs and theirs alone.

"I think we should call it *A Life of Surprises. What* do you think?" Chase asked as he played around with the cord changes.

"I think that is a great name and a very true title," Sheldon declared, biting his lip while watching Chase's fingers strum the cord changes.

"We are thinking of performing it at the wedding reception," Chase mentioned as he sat the guitar down. "You should come and sing with me. We make a great duo."

"I'm not sure I can share something that intimate with the world," Sheldon replied as he started nervously rubbing his legs. "Just the thought of it makes me anxious. I think you would be better off doing it alone."

"If you say so, but I'm not going to stop trying to share your beautiful voice and mind with the world," Chase expressed as he leaned over to kiss him. "Come, let's go for a drive."

"Hey," Sheldon called after him as he grabbed Chase, pulling him closer. "Thank you for the compliments and being very supportive of me."

"Anytime sexy," Chase replied and kissed him, and they got up to head out. "Thank you for being supportive of me too."

It was a typical dreary end-of-winter day in Southern Illinois. It had stopped raining, and there was a slight chill in the air. They drove around, but there was little to look at this time of year. The trees were bare, and most plants died from the frosty winter. Despite the dreariness, it was nice just riding around with Chase. They found an excellent spot to pull over to sit and talk.

"When we lived in LA, my parents knew I was sort of seeing a guy," Chase stated as he started to open up more about his past to Sheldon. "At first, we just started hanging out at school. We would do things after school, and then we started sleeping at each other's houses. After my parents learned that we were more than friends, they stopped letting him stay the night."

"Remember when I told you I have never been with anyone else? To be honest, I haven't even kissed anybody," Sheldon explained, trying not to be embarrassed. "Initially, being around you, I was extremely nervous and never knew quite what to say."

"I had no idea and couldn't tell you had never been kissed before," Chase remarked with a slight sweet smile. "I'm honored to be the first. Come on, let's get more comfortable and relax a bit before we head home."

They climbed into the back seat to stretch out. Sheldon was lying there with his head on Chase's chest as it started to rain again. "I want you to meet my parents as soon as my mom returns home," Chase stated as he ran his fingers through Sheldon's hair. "She went to stay with my grandma in Santa Monica. Grandma fell down the stairs and broke her hip. My Mom was supposed to stay only a few weeks, but Grandma was not better, so it would probably be another month before she could come home. I wish I could have gone because I miss my grandmother."

"Yeah, my mom doesn't want me telling my grandmother about being gay," Sheldon explained as he played with the button on Chase's jacket. "But she doesn't know that Grammy knew before she did. We just haven't had the heart to tell her yet. I'm very close with my grandmother, so I understand you missing your grandmother."

Being there in Chase's arms with the sound of the rain made it extremely relaxing. Sheldon wanted to ask Chase what happened with his ex to make him cautious of dating, but he didn't want to ruin this beautiful moment. They both fell asleep in each other's arms to the sound of the rain.

Chapter Fourteen

Chasing the Band

On Monday at school, they were all seated around the lunch table, laughing about the recent events at the wedding the boys had just played at. The boys excitedly talked over one another, telling their stories.

"Did you see how the bride's brother was giving the groom a serious pounding," Trey asked as he demonstrated.

"No, wait, the best part was when the cousin's husband flew over the table and did a pile driver onto the groom," Tommy added as he jumped up and imitated a pile driver.

"Yeah, it was pretty much over after that," Chase stated as he laughed at Trey and Tommy's reenactments.

"You guys are crazy," Ruby remarked, half laughing at the boys. "Okay, so how did this fight break out?"

"It turned out that the groom had been sleeping with the bride's cousin," Chase began to tell the whole story. "I guess the cousin couldn't take it anymore watching the man she loved be with another woman. That is when she lost her cool at the reception, and the whole night unraveled. We were a few songs in when shit hit the fan. We tried to keep playing while the argument started. We realized when the bride threw her ring at the groom and told him to jump off a cliff and fuck himself that we better wrap it up and pack it up. Despite the unfortunate turn of events of the evening, the bride's father still paid us for our time."

"I think he was more embarrassed than anything," Trey remarked, shaking his head. "He was pissed and embarrassed."

"I think the cousin liked our music," Tommy joked. "Maybe she will ask us to play at their wedding." They all laughed.

Sheldon looked around the table, smiling at his friends. He was amazed at how he had gone from eating his lunches alone to a table full of friends. He could not quite remember how or when Chase, Trey, and Tommy started sitting with him and the girls. It was probably only a short time after their trip to Evansville.

Chase the Band became a hit within the town. An older lady at the wedding saw them playing and liked their sound. She thought they would be perfect to play at her sister's retirement home, so she hired them.

The retirement home was having a dance and wanted live music. The boys did not know many older songs, so they worked on a few. They were unsure what to expect, but they considered it a good opportunity for practice.

§

It was the night of the dance, and the boys started playing songs they thought the older crowd would like. However, the crowd did not seem to be that into the music. "Why aren't they moving?" Trey asked while playing.

"I'm not sure. Why are they just staring at us?" Chase asked as he leaned back from the microphone. "Do you think they can still move at their age?"

Ruby, Ninnie, and Sheldon had come along for the adventure and moral support. They told the people in charge of the retirement home that they were their crew to help set up and tear down. "Oh man, this isn't going well," Ruby sighed as she hid her face. "I can't watch. It's too painful."

"Yeah, it's like they have no life left in them," Ninnie muttered as she looked around at the older people in the room. "I feel the urge to check their pulse to ensure they are still breathing. We need something to shock them into life," She dramatically proclaimed, acting like she was using an AED defibrillator on someone.

"They are playing songs I haven't even heard of," Sheldon remarked as he looked around the room. "I think they are actually falling asleep. These people probably like older country music."

A light bulb went off in Ninnie's head as she grabbed Sheldon. "Come on, I have an idea," Ninnie demanded as she dragged him onto the stage. She whispered something into each guy's ears and then Sheldon's. "I know you can do this. I have heard you sing it a million times," She stated as she looked into his eyes. "Yes, it's like nails down a chalkboard to me, but you're good at it."

"But...." Sheldon started to say, but Ninnie interrupted him.

"No buts, just get your butt to that microphone now," Ninnie ordered him with the stern look her mother would give them when she meant business.

Sheldon stepped up to the microphone, nervous as all hell. He looked out at the small crowd. What *the hell?* It *can't get any worse.* Sheldon opened his mouth, and out came the song *Jolene* by *Dolly Parton, and* the boys started playing along, following Sheldon's lead. Chase smiled from ear to ear as he watched Sheldon sing as he harmonized along with the song. Chase had wanted this moment to happen for some time but did not know how to make it happen. Sometimes, the unexpected events are the best. The crowd seemed to wake up and started to move along with the song. Sheldon sang the Gatlin Brothers *All the Gold in California*, and when he began singing Patsy Cline's, *She's Got You,* they started to get up and slow dance. The nerves that Sheldon had seemed to disappear. He appeared at home on stage.

"Wow, that actually worked," Ruby gushed as they looked around at everyone alive and moving. Good job, Nin. How did you know? They are pretty good at this, too, and Sheldon, who knew?"

"Trust me, I have heard that one singing for years," Ninnie explained as she nodded towards Sheldon. "In fact, I think he was singing before he came out of the womb. He just needed a little shove into the right place."

"Hi, ladies. My name is Janine," a blonde woman introduced herself as she sat beside Ruby. They could tell Janine was not one of the residents. She reached out her hand to Ninnie. "Are you, their manager?" Janine asked as they shook hands.

"Uhhh," Ninnie stammered, looking at Ruby. "We both are,"

Ninnie replied hesitantly. "And this here is Ruby."

"Nice to meet you, Ruby," Janine said, shaking Ruby's hand. "This is perfect. I would like to hire them for my grandson's birthday party two weeks from today," Janine explained with a hopeful look.

"My friend Stella over there said she saw them playing at her niece's wedding and hired them for this event," she said, pointing to her friend, who was sitting there rocking back and forth to the music.

She looked about the same age as Janine, but her hair was all grey and pulled up into a bun. She saw them looking and waved to Janine and the girls. Janine looked more upscale. She did not have one grey hair or one hair out of place. She wore more makeup than one would find at Bloomingdale's.

"I will pay them whatever their fees are. Please tell me. Are they free? In fact, I will double it," Janine offered.

"Hum, let me check," Ninnie stated as she reached into her purse and raised her eyebrows to Ruby with a why the heck not look. She pulled out her planner. "Okay, so two weeks from today," Ninnie said, flipping through the planner.

Ninnie was, in fact, looking at her planner, and Ninnie that day was circled in red, but only Ruby could see the planner. "Well, it looks like they just happen to be free. I will put you down before someone else snatches that day up."

"That is fantastic! Could you give me your number? Here is mine. I will call you next week with the details," Janine explained as she wrote down her contact info. "I'm so excited to have an actual band for the party. My grandson is going to be excited."

Ruby sat there with her mouth hanging open after Janine left. "What?" Ninnie asked, shoving her planner back into her purse. "Someone has to help these boys along the road to stardom."

"That took some balls," Ruby said with a surprised laugh. "I think I could learn a thing or two from you." They both laughed. "You're right. They need to focus on the music and not be worried about small stuff like scheduling. I think we will make a great team."

The boys finished their last song and walked over to where the girls were sitting. "You guys were fantastic," Ruby remarked as she kissed Trey. "It was so cool to see you guys finally doing your thing.

Plus, you looked really hot up there, and it made me want to do things to you, dirty things."

"Boys, we have good news," Ninnie exclaimed as she fanned herself like she was on fire. She had interrupted Ruby and Trey's moment. "You have booked another gig."

What?" Chase questioned, looking at Ninnie and Ruby. "What are you talking about?"

"Yeah, Ninnie booked you guys for a birthday party two Saturdays from today," Ruby explained as she clapped her hands. "I can't believe how popular you guys are becoming. I'm kind of jealous."

At first, Chase was upset by Ninnie booking them without asking, but he realized it would be wise to have someone help manage them. "Thanks, Ninnie. I appreciate your take-charge attitude. Does this mean you're going to help manage us?"

"I... I... sure, why not?" Ninnie replied, surprised because she was only joking with Ruby. I can see this working to my advantage. I get to boss Tommy around even more," she stated as she grabbed Tommy, pulled him down, and kissed him passionately.

They all laughed as Tommy acted like she took his breath away. "Oh, to be young and in love," Crowed an elderly woman as she rolled by them in a wheelchair. "And to able to find someone that can still get it up, yea boy!"

They all busted out laughing again. "Did she actually just say that?" Ruby asked, looking around the room laughing. "Is this real life?"

"Come on, guys, let's pack up and get out of here," Chase requested as he returned to get his guitar. "Sheldon, do you mind grabbing my case?" They loaded everything into the van.

"I want tacos this time," Tommy requested as they climbed into the van.

§

Ninnie got the details for the boys to play for Janine's grandson's tenth birthday party. The party would be at her son's house, the president of one of the only two banks in town. They rolled up to the gate and pushed the intercom button. Janine's voice came over the speaker. "Hello, is this the delivery for the dinosaur cake and ice cream?" Janine asked.

"No, we are the band," Chase replied, leaning out his car window.

"Oh good, come on in," She requested as she opened the gate. "Come on around back."

It was one of the few mansions in town. The mansion was on the outskirts of town. Set back off the road with a long driveway and a private lake. They unloaded the equipment out of the big green van. "It's nice having people to help with the equipment," Trey commented as he smacked Ruby on the ass. "Especially someone that is good-looking to boot."

"Flattery will get you nowhere, mister," Ruby growled as she turned and smacked his ass. "You're my bitch tonight."

"Whoa," Ninnie praised Ruby as she gave her a high five. "I don't think I have ever seen this side of you. Me likie, likie."

They started to take the equipment around back. Janine was already in the back decorating and preparing the place for the party. "Oh, hi, everyone," Janine greeted them as she shook everyone's hand. "It's nice to meet you officially. I was visiting a friend in the retirement home when I saw you boys playing. I knew I just had to have you for my grandson's birthday party, and here you are."

She had tables on the patio and a couple of balloons, and she had started to blow up herself, but she was all over the place. "I want the Band at the far end of the pool. Everyone should be arriving within forty-five minutes."

There was a doorbell sound. "Oh, I bet that is the cake and ice cream. I will be right back," Janine said as she disappeared through the patio door.

When she left, they started setting up their equipment. The boys were talking about how they thought the party would be quiet. The delivery boy carried a large Jurassic Park dinosaur cake and sat it on one of the tables.

Next, he wheeled in a cart with all kinds of ice cream that he plugged in to keep the ice cream cold.

"Would you two ladies be dears and come help with the decorations and balloons, Janine requested of Ruby and Ninnie. "It's so hard to get good help these days. The housekeeper refused to come and help out today. She likes to overreact a bit. Her hair grew back just fine, and the burns were superficial." Janine explained as she walked with them over to the table.

"I often told her not to let the boys play with fire. The kids didn't mean to set her on fire. It was an accident, but for some reason, she refuses to believe that and declines to help with any more of the kid's activities," Janine disappeared back into the house.

Ninnie and Ruby looked at each other with terror as they followed Janine. Ninnie mouthed to Ruby, *"Did she say fire?"* Ruby nodded. They set her on fire," Ninnie croaked out as she looked back at Trey, who was tuning his guitar. He smiled and waved at her.

"I think the boys were wrong thinking this was going to be a quiet kid's party," Ninnie commented to Ruby just as she inhaled some helium and started talking. "I have a feeling this could become quite crazy."

They both laughed at the way Ninnie's voice sounded. "Oh, Nina, darling, would you be a dear and help me?" Janine asked as she waved her over. The kids were arriving, and we still needed to grab the snacks from the kitchen and get the ice for the drinks."

"Nina?" Ruby whispered to Ninnie with a giggle.

"I guess I will be right back, Rudy," Ninnie teased with a chuckle.

The parents started dropping their kids off and seemed too eager to dump them and run. You could hear the collective screams and yells from the kids in the front of the house. The kids were hyper, wound up, and hadn't even had cake yet.

The boys were set up and ready to perform. Ruby had the balloons inflated, and Ninnie had the snacks and ice ready for the drinks. Ruby and Sheldon walked over to standby Ninnie. "Does it feel like we are about to run a race?" Ruby asked Ninnie and Sheldon.

"Yeah, like the calm before the storm. The moment before it hits you all at once," Ninnie agreed, rocking back on her feet.

The boys began to play some songs that Janine had requested. The kids started coming to the pool area to find a place to sit at the tables. Some of the kids started pushing one another. "Where is Janine?" Sheldon asked, looking around. "These kids are going to tear each other apart."

"Don't look at me!" Ninnie exclaimed as she turned around to see she was not there. "She was just here. Sheldon, can you look for her? I think these monsters are about to make a mess."

The boys started popping balloons. They were fighting over party favors and where they were going to sit. Ruby and Ninnie looked at each other; neither knew what to do with thirty wild boys.

"Okay, no fighting over where you're going to sit," Ninnie demanded, giving an ear-piercing whistle. She imitated her mom, and this turned out to be the best idea yet. All the boys stopped, and she had their attention for a moment. Then they continued back to being rowdy but not as rambunctious.

"Hey, who would like something to drink?" Ruby asked as she started putting ice into the cups.

Sheldon walked around the house, trying to find Janine. He went out front to ensure she was not still talking to any of the parents. She was not in front of the house, the kitchen, the living room, or the dining room. He heard a banging sound coming from down the hall.

As he got closer, he thought he heard a muffled cry and someone saying, "Oh God." He started to panic. What if something terrible happened to her? *I watch crime shows and know what happens to rich people sometimes. What if someone came in with the kids and was in the process of attacking her? Should I get help? No, by that time, she could be dead.*

He ran to the kitchen, grabbed a butcher knife, and headed back down the hall. *Oh no, now it was* too *quiet; what *if she was lying on the floor dead?* He reached for the doorknob of the room from which the sounds were coming. Just as he touched the knob, the door flew open Sheldon raised the knife, ready to attack whoever was coming out.

He scared Janine so severely that when she jumped backward, she tripped over the rug and landed face-first onto naked little Jerod. Janine and Jarod had been in the bathroom having sex right after he dropped off his little brother.

Sheldon didn't know what to say, so he slowly backed himself out of the room. Sheldon could not help but look down and see how long and thick Jerod was. *Well, I guess Jerod isn't so little anymore,* Sheldon realized. "I'm so sorry," Sheldon apologized." I thought you were being attacked."

"Believe me, I was! Do you see how big that thing is?" Janine asked, acting like it was no big deal that Sheldon had just found them as she pulled down her skirt. "I mean, I have had a few cocks in my day, but this one here," She remarked as she pulled on it.

Jerod was so embarrassed that he kept fumbling while trying to get dressed. Sheldon didn't know whether to look at it or away.

"Oh my god, the party!" Janine exclaimed as she fixed her hair in the mirror. "I totally got distracted seeing his huge cock flopping around in his shorts. What a naughty boy running around without underwear. I must get back to the kids now." She smacked Jarod on his bare ass as she walked out of the bathroom.

She walked down the hall like she had not just been caught having sex in the bathroom and headed back to the party. Sheldon followed her to the backyard, where Ninnie and Ruby entertained the kids. The boys continued to play despite the children's lack of interest.

"Oh, thank god," Ninnie said as she sat in a chair. "These kids are a handful. This one set that one on fire, and that one there kept yelling drop and roll, and when he didn't listen, he shoved him into the pool. The little boy they shoved in the pool was shivering and wrapped in a towel.

Sheldon could not believe all this happened while he had gone looking for Janine. Well, then again, Janine had time to get down and did dirty in the bathroom with someone his age. "Okay, who wants cake?!" Janine yelled, waving the knife in the air that Sheldon almost stabbed her with.

All the boys started yelling so loudly you couldn't hear the Band playing anymore. Janine walked over to the giant dinosaur cake, put a candle in the shape of a one in the left claw and a candle in the shape of a zero in the right claw, and lit the candles. "Now, everyone, sing along," Janine requested as she started to sing.

The Band stopped playing while they sang Happy Birthday. "Happy Birthday, dear Timmy… Wait, where's little Timmy?" Janine stopped singing to ask as she looked around.

"Isn't this him?" Ninnie asked, pointing to a brown-haired boy.

"No!" Janine exclaimed. "Oh my God! Where could he have gone?" Janine asked in a panic as she took off into the house.

"Oh shit!" Ninnie expressed as she looked at Ruby. "Did we lose a kid on our watch?"

"Our watch?" Ruby questioned, looking at Ninnie in complete shock. "We don't even know how many kids were supposed to be here. We don't know who is who or what this little Timmy even looks like."

"I'm Bobby," said the little boy Ninnie thought was Timmy. "My brother is the one that was wrestling around with Timmy's grandma."

"What?!" Ninnie shrieked as she looked at Sheldon. "What is he talking about?"

"Long story," Sheldon stated as he waved for Chase, Tommy, and Trey. "Come on, guys, let's go look for this missing boy."

"Timmy has blond hair and blue eyes. He kinda looks like that guy," Bobby motioned towards Tommy. "I know where he went," he said, pointing to the water.

Janine was running through the house, shrieking Timmy's name. "Someone, please go and get her. Sheldon and I will go find the boy," Chase stated, looking at Sheldon.

Ruby ran into the house while Sheldon and Chase headed towards the lake. They started to yell Timmy's name. They come across an old boat house, and Timmy was sitting inside looking at the water. The boys were relieved to find him okay. "Hey Timmy, do you mind if I sit here next to you," Chase asked, looking at the boy and then at Sheldon.

Timmy didn't say anything; he just stared out at the water. Chase and Sheldon sat down on either side of him and stared at the water momentarily. "I told her I didn't want a party," Timmy finally spoke. "I don't even like half those guys anyway. They only want to hang out with me because I have stuff they don't have.

Chase and Sheldon looked at each other, surprised by this young kid's character. "I just wanted to spend time with grandma alone, but she always has to have people around. I wanted to see a movie with her. Instead, I saw her going into the bathroom with that guy again. Is my grandmother a whore like my daddy says?"

Sheldon and Chase looked at each other in shock and unsure how to answer. "Again?" Sheldon mouthed to Chase.

"Come on guys, let's go get this over with," Little Timmy

motioned for them to come as he got up. "That way, all these assholes can go home."

"Yes, Sir," Chase said in a military salute-style voice. He shrugged his shoulders as he looked at Sheldon.

They could hear Janine screaming Timmy's name as she ran to the boat house. "Why did you run off again?" Janine asked, shaking him, and then she hugged him so tight that his eyes started to bulge.

"You can't just run off like that. You scare your grandmother half to death when you do that. Let's go cut your cake. Everyone is waiting."

As they were about to head back to the house, Chase grabbed Sheldon's arm, pulled Sheldon back into the boathouse, and started kissing him. They stopped for a moment, and Sheldon smiled at him. "What was that all about?" Sheldon asked, smiling back at him.

"I don't know. This place just seemed like a place where a lot of romance should occur," Chase responded, kissing him again.

Janine started yelling for them to come and get some cake. "Did she say cake? Chase stated as he headed off to get some cake, but Sheldon was still standing there looking at him. "But I really want some cake. Come on, let's go…"

After the party, they packed the equipment and loaded it into the big green van. "Even though we didn't play much, it made for good practice. Plus, it has been quite an entertaining day," Chase commented, shutting the van's back doors. "And she still paid us the total amount.

"Whose turn is it to pick the place to eat?" Ruby asked as she opened the van door to get inside.

"I believe it's Tommy's turn," Sheldon answered, looking at Ninnie.

"Oh, god no," Ninnie remarked, making a sick face and holding her stomach. "Remember, he picked last time, and we all got food poison. But at this point, I don't care. I would hate to be the one to clean up that mess," Ninnie said, pointing back at the house and hurrying to get into the van. "Those kids trashed the place. So, let's get out of here before she comes back out and tries to make us her maids, too!"

They got into the van and headed out. "Ninnie, where are we playing next," Tommy asked.

I'm not sure I will have to check my date book," Ninnie replied. "I'm more interested in hearing about Janine fucking Jarod in the bathroom."

"What!" someone said as everyone started talking at once. The van pulled out of the driveway.

"Hold up! I want to know why today is circled on your calendar," Ruby said, looking at Ninnie, who laughed boisterously.

"Oooh, trust me, you do not," Tommy said. "Not unless you want another Shawndrea toe-curling story. You could hear their laughter as they drove away...

Chapter Fifteen

Chances and Choices

Levin sat in his car as he waited for his prom date to come out. While he waited, his mind drifted back to the first time he saw Charlotte and the events that led to this moment. The first time Levin saw Charlotte, he wanted to talk to her but lacked the courage to walk up and talk to her. Levin being a sophomore and Charlotte being a junior made it even more difficult. He kept waiting for the right moment, but he waited too long, and someone more persistent caught her attention. His blood would boil every time Levin saw them together. Levin knew this guy wasn't right for Charlotte and that this guy wouldn't treat her as well as he would.

At the beginning of the school year, Levin had no idea how small moments could impact and change one's life forever. He did not know at the time, but the guy Charlotte was dating, Laramie, was the guy who had been giving Sheldon a hard time at school. Sheldon never told Levin about the awful things Laramie would do to him.

One day, Levin saw Charlotte crying in the hall. She had just gotten into a fight with Laramie. They had been fighting about the little affection Laramie showed her and how he never wanted to hang out with her.

"Okay, here is your opportunity. Talk to her. Let her know you're here if she needs someone to talk to," he mumbled, psyching himself up.

Levin walked up to Charlotte, and at first, nothing came out when he tried to speak. "What are you looking at," Charlotte snapped at him. "I don't need any more crap from a guy."

"I-I just wanted to make sure you're okay," Levin finally spoke as he handed her a wadded-up tissue. "Here, take this. I just wanted to let you know I'm here if you ever need someone to talk to."

"Thanks, but I don't think any amount of talking will help," Charlotte confessed as she wiped her eyes and nose. "I just need to wake the fuck up."

"From time to time, we all get stuck going down the wrong path," Levin commented with a half-smile. "Sometimes someone comes along and shows us how to get on the right path. I will leave you alone now. I just wanted to let you know I'm a good listener."

"Wait --- don't go," Charlotte requested, trying to force a smile. "Aren't you in my Calculus class?"

"Yeah," Levin replied, excited that she had noticed. "I usually sit in the back."

"That's right, the nerdy guy," She teased. "Maybe you can help me understand differential calculus sometime?"

"Sure, I can do that; just let me know when," Levin offered. Suddenly, Mr. Stevens interrupted them and asked what they were doing out of class. After Mr. Stevens wrote them up, he sent them to class. Levin turned to look back at Charlotte and smiled as Levin kept walking. Levin felt she didn't need help with Calculus, but he was down for any chance to spend more time with her.

At first, they started hanging out in the library, talking about calculus, music, and life. Over time, she started to open up about her relationship with Laramie.

"He doesn't seem to want to hang out with me," She explained. "He seems only to keep me around just to say he has a girlfriend. I thought maybe it was because I wasn't ready to have sex, so one night, I started to go down on him. He stopped me and asked what I was doing. It made me feel like I was unattractive and repulsive that he didn't want to have sex with me."

Charlotte was almost in tears. "I don't think that is the case at all," Levin argued as he stared into her eyes. "You're beautiful; any guy would be honored to be with you."

Charlotte was taken aback and did not know what to say. She had not heard such nice things in a very long time. She leaned over and kissed him, and there was a spark. Charlotte and Levin were surprised by the kiss.

Charlotte grabbed her stuff and turned to leave. Levin grabbed her arm and asked her to wait. He started to kiss her back, but she stopped him.

"I can't, I'm sorry," She pleaded as she turned and left the library.

Charlotte would not even look at Levin for days. He tried getting her attention, but she ignored him. He could not figure out what went wrong.

One day after school, he waited for her to come out. He thought one last try. She walked past him and told him to stop bothering her. He decided to respect her wishes. He finally gave up.

The day Laramie kissed Sheldon was the same day Charlotte decided to stop wasting her time on him. After Sheldon had kneed Laramie and left him lying on the floor, Charlotte had been the one to find him on the floor, writhing in pain. She went over to check on him and tried to help him. Laramie only yelled at her to get away and not touch him.

When he pushed her off of him, she tripped and fell. Even though she knew he did not mean to cause her physical harm, his mental abuse was too much for her. At that moment, she looked at him and realized she did not know him like she thought. Charlotte got up, walked away from him, and decided from the moment she was done with him forever.

The next day, she approached Levin as he got something out of his locker. They stared at each other momentarily, and then she kissed him. Later that day, she explained why she had been avoiding him. She did not want to do to Laramie what her dad did to her Mom, which was cheat on him. She realized in the moment that even honest people make mistakes. Life does not always go as planned, and you have to make the best of the situations before you.

From that point on, the two were inseparable. With just weeks until the holiday break, Charlotte was smiling as she told Levin she could not wait until they had some free time together.

At first, Laramie acted like it was nothing to him to lose Charlotte to another guy, but it was eating at him. He was fighting his internal demons. Laramie was battling with who he really was. Slowly, he turned his attention to Levin.

Laramie would walk by and knock Levin's books out of his hands. "You two are perfect for each other," Laramie said sarcastically.

He would walk by, slamming Levin's locker shut and tripping him any chance he got when going down the hall. Charlotte would tell Levin to ignore Laramie and not to stoop to his level.

One day at lunch, he bumped into Levin's chair. "I'm sorry, queer, I didn't see you sitting there with your ugly girlfriend," Laramie scoffed on his way to the soda machine. "Good luck trying to please that fat ugly whore," Laramie jibed as he walked back by their table, pushing Levin's head forward.

At that moment, Levin lost all control. He could handle the insults to him, but not to Charlotte. Levin stood up so quickly that his chair went flying backward. He lunged at Laramie like a wild animal. He threw Laramie to the ground and started punching him in the face.

Laramie flipped him over, and they started wrestling on the floor, knocking chairs in every direction. Everyone was chanting fight! Fight! Fight!

Charlotte could not believe this was really happening. Part of her wanted someone to break it up. Another part of her wished for Levin to kick Laramie's ass.

Laramie got on top and threw a few punches before Levin flipped him off the top of him. Laramie could see how enraged Levin was. His face was blood red, and he breathed like an animal ready to attack. Laramie took off fast.

Charlotte stopped Levin from running after him. "It's not worth it," Charlotte advised, grabbing his arm.

Charlotte got a napkin and wiped the blood off his lips. "I think you should have the nurse look at this," Charlotte suggested, dabbing the blood off his chin.

"What am I going to tell her?" Levin sputtered, picking up his chair. "Tell her I walked into a wall. I will be fine, so let's go."

Charlotte was highly proud of Levin at that moment. Even though she did not believe in the use of violence to solve a problem, he defended her honor, which was something no man had ever done. Suddenly, she realized she wanted to screw his brains out, which was not something she ever wanted to do with Laramie.

While everyone else was planning their holiday break and what they would be doing, Charlotte was daydreaming about how she wanted their first date to go and how her first time would happen. She figured they would have a lot of free time during the holiday break. She would borrow her Mom's car and drive them back to her hometown, where she had many older friends.

They would be able to rent a hotel room for the night. They would tell each other's parents they would spend the night at a friend's house. She was excited and could not wait for the holidays to arrive.

Levin was so excited to take Charlotte out on their first date that he did not plan it well. He took her to the local Dairy King. Charlotte was trying to hide her disappointment, but Levin could tell. "Are you okay?" Levin asked Charlotte, even though he knew something was wrong.

"I guess I thought our first date would be more romantic," Charlotte replied, looking out the car window. "I guess there aren't any options to go on a romantic date in this town."

"I'm sorry," Levin apologized as he put his hand to her chin to turn her head so he could kiss her. He took her hand and started kissing it. "Next time, it will be better."

"It's okay as long as I'm with you," She replied, kissing him back. "But the next time, I am planning our date."

They smiled at each other and were genuinely happy just being in each other's company. They saw quite a bit of each other over the first half of their holiday break. Charlotte's Mom accused her of hanging out too much with her boyfriend. Her Mom refused to let Charlotte have the car for the weekend.

Charlotte's Mom had heard the Majors boys were trouble and demanded that she stay away from them. Whenever Levin called their house, her Mom would tell him Charlotte was sick. During the last week of vacation, they had no contact. Levin grew worried because, until then, they had not gone a day without seeing or speaking to one another.

On Saturday, while her Mom was at work, Charlotte got her next-door neighbor Duane to drive her to the Majors' house so she could talk to Levin. She explained to him that she had not been sick, that her Mom had kept her home, and that she had forbid her to see Levin. They sat in the car talking. They could not go into the house because his Mom did not like for them to have people over.

"Maybe next week, while both of our parents are at work, you can come back out, or I can come there," Levin suggested with a big smile. You could tell he was pleased to see her. He had grown worried that she had gotten tired of him. He was relieved to find out it was not about him but disappointed that her mother was judgmental. When, in fact, she did not even know him. "I can't believe how much I have missed you," He commented, brushing the hair out of her face as he leaned in to kiss her. "I have missed these lips."

"I don't mind driving you out here when I'm free," Duane interrupted them as he looked into the review mirror. You could tell he was slightly jealous by the way he watched them just a little too long in the mirror while they were kissing. They had forgotten he was still in the car. They met secretly for the next few months with Duane's help.

§

The guilt of keeping two people in love apart was starting to wear on Charlotte's Mom. She could see the glimmer had gone out in her daughter's eyes, along with the bounce in her step. She started to second-guess her actions. Maybe she should give Levin a chance. At least meet him and see what he was like.

When her Mom came home, Charlotte sat in the living room chair reading a book. Her Mom had just worked a swing shift at the hospital, where she had been an RN for years. "Hi, Sweetie. How was your night?" her Mom asked, bending over to kiss her cheek. Is that a good book?"

"Yeah, it's a real page-turner," Charlotte replied, giving short answers, which she had done since her Mom had forbidden her to see Levin.

Her mom went to the kitchen to put some stuff away and returned to the living room. "Sweetie, I have been thinking and I wanted to talk to you about something," Her Mom announced as she sat on the arm of the chair and started playing with her daughter's wild red hair. "I was thinking maybe we should have this Levin fellow over for dinner so I can check him out and make an honest decision about him myself."

"Really?" Charlotte cheerfully queried sitting up in the chair so fast her Mom almost fell onto the floor and stood up. "Wait, what's the catch?"

"Yes, really, and there is no catch," her Mom stated as she stepped closer to her daughter and wrapped her arms around her. I'm sorry I may have overreacted about you having a serious boyfriend. You're my baby. I want to protect you. I know I was wrong, and I'm sorry."

"Thanks, Mom," Charlotte said, smiling and hugging her Mom. "When do you want to invite him over?"

"I was thinking that next Saturday I'm off work, and that will allow me to make us a nice dinner," her Mom suggested, relieved her daughter was talking to her again. "Sweetie, I don't like it when you're mad at me, or we fight."

Charlotte and her Mom had always had a close relationship. They were all each other had, which made their bond even stronger. "You just have to promise me you will take care of yourself," her Mom requested, pointing a finger at her daughter's chest. Do we have a deal?"

"Yes, Mom, I will make sure to be careful," Charlotte replied as she hugged her Mom again. "I love you a lot, you know that right."

"Yes, and I love you too," Her Mom said, hugging her back. "Now go clean up that room and get your laundry ready for me to wash," her Mom said, smacking her on the butt.

"Calm down, Roberta," Charlotte joked.

"Stop calling me that!" Her Mom half shrieked, half laughing as she grabbed a pillow from the couch and chucked it at Charlotte. Her Mom's full name is Roberta Jeannie Roberts Reid. She had always hated being called Roberta for as long as she could remember. She preferred being called Jeannie or Jean. "You know I don't like it when you call me that."

"Whoa, Roberta," Charlotte teased as she dodged the pillow. "Your arm is getting better. You almost hit me that time."

"Go to your room, young lady," her Mom demanded as she returned to the kitchen. "I don't know what I'm gonna do with you."

On Thursday, they went to the store together to get the ingredients for the meal they were making for Levin. "What does Levin like to eat?" her Mom asked. "We could make a roast."

"Honestly, I'm not sure what he eats," Charlotte replied, stopping to look at her Mom. "I should know what he likes."

"It's okay, sweetie. You don't have to know everything about him yet," her Mom reassured her, pushing the cart into the fresh vegetable section. "That is the fun part about dating, getting to know each other's likes and dislikes.

Now, come on and help me pick out some ears of corn. I thought I would make my famous tuna casserole, some fresh veggies and fruit."

"But what if he doesn't like it?" Charlotte asked, putting the corn into the cart, looking concerned.

"Hand me that corn; we need to put it into a bag," her Mom requested, taking the ears of corn from her. And if he doesn't like it, I will just make him pancakes. Now go and get me four cans of tuna.

"Pancakes?" Charlotte questioned as she walked towards the tuna aisle. Her Mom just chuckled and shook her head at her daughter.

They met back up near the frozen section. Charlotte felt proud of her Mom for being cool about her dating Levin and inviting him for dinner. Charlotte walked up to her Mom and kissed her on the cheek. "What was that for?" her Mom asked, shocked.

"Just for you being a cool mom," Charlotte answered, putting her arm around her and giving her a side hug. "I love you, Mom."

"Awwwee, well, I love you too, sweetie," Her Mom responded, looking at her with inquiring eyes. "Are you sure there isn't something else going on?" Charlotte shook her head. "Okay, well, let's go check out."

They arrived at the check-out and put their things on the conveyor belt. Her mom noticed one of the boys bagging groceries and kept looking over at them. "Who is that guy that keeps looking over here?" her mom asked as she looked at Charlotte. She glanced back at the guy as she got the last of the items out of the cart.

Charlotte looked over to see who she was talking about and waved. "That is Sheldon Levin's older brother," Charlotte answered as she looked back at her Mom. Her Mom was eyeballing him like she was looking for his third eye or a tail. "Mom, are you okay? Why are you looking at him like that?"

"No reason," her Mom replied, turning to pay the cashier. They grabbed their groceries and left the store. They did not mention the stare-down again that day.

Saturday night had finally arrived, and Charlotte was as nervous as could be. She could not decide what to wear. "Snap out of it, girl. He is just a guy, and it's just dinner," Charlotte commanded to herself as she looked in the mirror and put on her makeup.

When Levin arrived at Charlotte's, he was extremely nervous, and his palms were sweating. When Charlotte realized he was there but just sitting in his car, she came out to greet him.

"Relax, you're going to be fine," Charlotte reassured him as she leaned in to kiss him. She could tell right away that he was nervous. We are just having dinner with my mom; it's not a big deal."

Charlotte led him into the house and their living room. Her Mom was in the kitchen putting the finishing touches on dinner. "Let me show you my room," Charlotte offered as she took Levin's hand and started towards her bedroom.

"Hold right there," Charlotte's Mom commanded as she entered the living room. "And where might you two be going? You haven't even introduced us yet, Charlotte."

"I'm sorry, Mom, this is Levin. Levin, this is my Mom," Charlotte said, then headed to her bedroom again.

"Not so fast," her Mom said, sitting down in the chair. Come and sit down for a moment. Dinner will be ready in about ten minutes." Charlotte and Levin sat down on the couch next to each other, their hands folded across their laps.

Usually, they would be holding hands, or Levin would have his arm around Charlotte, but they felt it would not be appropriate at the moment, so they sat awkwardly. "So, Levin, what are your intentions with my daughter?"

"Mooom!" Charlotte exclaimed, completely embarrassed. She looked at her mother, surprised that she had asked the question so abruptly.

"What?" her mom asked innocently. "If he is going to date my only daughter, I have a right to ask questions. Well, I'm waiting," Her Mom demanded as she looked at Levin expectantly.

"I have every intention of respecting your daughter like the beautiful young woman she is," Levin replied, looking at her Mom. "I plan on ensuring your daughter is the happiest she can be."

The timer went off in the kitchen. "Dinner is ready," Charlotte's Mom stated as she exited her chair and returned to the kitchen. "Charlotte, will you please set the table."

Levin went to help Charlotte set the table. They placed the silverware and plates for the three of them. They smiled at each other from across the table. Charlotte bit her lip, thinking about being alone with Levin and kissing him later.

She needed to play it PG for their first dinner together. "Charlotte, would you mind grabbing the salad out of the fridge?" her Mom called out from the kitchen.

Charlotte saw a small window of opportunity and lunged forward to kiss Levin. She just could not wait. She almost did not want to quit kissing him, but she knew her Mom would call out for her again soon. She pulled away and backed up, grabbing a chair. "Sit and relax," she smiled at him, unable to take her eyes off him. "I will be right back."

Charlotte and her Mom return with salad, tuna casserole, and corn on the cob. Charlotte immediately starts putting salad onto Levin's plate. She tries not to stare too long, so her Mom does not notice just how bad she has it for this guy.

She passed the salad bowl to her Mom. "Levin, what do you plan to do after you graduate?" her mom asked as she put a small amount of dressing onto her salad.

Levin had just put a mouthful of salad into his mouth. He tried to chew it quickly so he could answer. "Well, I would love to work for IBM. I plan to go to college and study computers."

"Wow, you know I have been impressed with your answers to my questions so far," her Mom boldly stated, giving Charlotte an approving look. "Charlotte told me you grew up on a farm. How was that?"

"The farm was a lot of work," Levin answered and drank water to clear his mouth. "I guess that is how I learned to work hard to get what I want. This casserole is really good, by the way,"

He complimented as he took another bite.

Charlotte remained quiet while eating her dinner and watching the two talk about life and the future of computers. Since Jean worked in a hospital, she knew technology was progressing fast.

"You know Charlotte, this guy is a lot better than that last one you brought home." She pointed her fork at Charlotte while she turned twelve shades of red. "That last guy was rude and had no sense of direction in his life."

The rest of the dinner went well. However, Charlotte did not get the alone time she had hoped for with Levin. Jean had suggested it was time for Levin to head home, and they called it an evening. The weeks passed, and Charlotte was allowed to see Levin more and more, but with some restrictions. They would have to sneak moments of alone time together to kiss and make out. The Prom was coming up and Charlotte asked Levin if he would escort her to the Prom, of course he said yes.

§

"Charlotte, sweetie, I told you I would go with you to pick out a prom dress," Her Mom said. You need to pick it out soon in case we have to make any alterations."

"I want to find something that doesn't make me look lame or clashes with my hair," Charlotte stated. "But you're right. I don't want to wait till the last minute."

"It's okay, sweetie. We will find you something nice," Her Mom reassured as she played with Charlotte's long hair. Just relax; it isn't good for your tummy to get all worked up."

"Maybe I shouldn't go," Charlotte stated. "Maybe I should stay home."

"Oh no, you're going if I have to drag you there myself," her Mom said buttery sweetly. "Now stop mopping around and get your butt in gear because we're going."

"Fine, let me get ready," Charlotte replied as she went to her room.

Her Mom knew getting ready for Charlotte would take at least an hour. She had just come off the late shift and was very tired, and before she knew it, she had drifted off to sleep.

"Mom, Mom," Charlotte called out as she touched her Mom's shoulder after contemplating waking her up. "You want to just stay home?"

"What? Did I fall asleep?" Her Mom asked as she whipped the drool off her mouth. "I'm up, and I'm ready."

"Mom, are you sure? We can wait and go another day?" Charlotte inquired as she looked at her Mom with concern.

"No, I'm good and ready to go," Her Mom insisted as she grabbed the keys. "Let's do this. Oh, my baby is going to Prom. I can't make any promises, but I will try not to cry."

They headed off together to find Charlotte a prom dress. They liked having Mother-Daughter time together.

§

The day of the Prom had finally arrived, and Charlotte was so nervous. The time had come for Levin to arrive and escort her to Prom. Her Mom was pacing the floor, seeming nervous herself. "Why is he just sitting in the car?" Charlotte's Mom asked, looking out the window. Doesn't he know he has to come to the door? He has been out there for quite some time."

Charlotte looked out the window. She had been fidgeting with her hair and was not too worried about him not coming to the door yet. She was worried about how she looked, though. It was buying her more time to get ready, plus he was early. "I'm not sure," Charlotte answered as she walked back into the bathroom, still messing with her hair. How does it look?"

"Your hair looks spectacular," Her Mom responded as she looked at Charlotte's hair and then back out the window. "Stop messing with it; you look great. Now, finish up and get that dress on so I can take pictures. Let me know if you want help getting into the dress."

"Would you mind helping me get it over my head, so I don't mess up my hair? I did not want to get hairspray on the dress, but now I fear my hair is too big to fit through the hole," Charlotte explained as they both laughed. Her Mom was getting the dress ready to slip over Charlotte's head, and Charlotte was making funny faces in the mirror at her Mom.

"Stop. You're going to make me laugh and mess up your hair," Charlotte's Mom chuckled so hard she shook. "Why do you not just step into the dress?" her Mom questioned as she lowered the dress for Charlotte to slip into.

They both laughed loudly. "Now, why didn't I think of that?" Charlotte giggled. They successfully got her into the dress without putting one hair on her head out of place. How much hairspray did you put on there? I don't think it could move if it wanted to."

"Good, then mission accomplished," Charlotte cooed, turning to look in the mirror to double-check if her Mom was correct. She turned side to side, looking at her hair. Once satisfied, she turned back to her Mom, who had begun to cry from watching her daughter swishing around in her dress. "Mom, you promised, no crying."

"I know. I know. But I can't help it. You look so beautiful in that dress," Charlotte's Mom bawled, trying to get herself under control through the sobs she continued to try to speak. "It's just that my baby is all grown up, and you will leave me soon."

"Mom, pull yourself together," Charlotte requested as she hugged her. There was a knock at the door. Besides, who said I was leaving you anytime soon? Do you mind getting the door? I want to make an entrance."

Jean opened the door to let Levin inside and guided him to the living room. "Charlotte will be right out," Her Mom explained, showing Levin to the couch. She is just doing some last-minute touch-ups, you know. Wow, you really do look like a prince." Charlotte walked into the living room, and Levin's mouth dropped open…

Chapter Sixteen

The Prom

Everyone was excited in the weeks leading up to the prom. Well, mainly the girls. Most of the boys could have cared less. The prom's theme was *A Fairy Tale to Remember*—come as your own Prince or Princess. Ninnie and Ruby had planned to dress shop together, but Shawndrea and Ruby's Mom decided to come along. Sue suggested they go into a high-end dress shop, but Ninnie and Shawndrea opted for a more affordable store. They decided to split up for the time being.

Ninnie frowned at the prices. Shawndrea had tried to talk Ninnie into wearing her dress from last year's prom. Shawndrea gave her an "I told you so" look while Ninnie scoffed at the prices.

"My boobs will not fit your dress," Ninnie quipped as she lifted her boobs to demonstrate the severity of her situation. "The girls will be popping out all night. Don't even say it...."

"What? I wasn't going to say anything. Gessssh," Shawndrea remarked with a sour look as she shrugged her shoulders and continued looking at dresses. "So much for trying to help."

"Cause these babies only come out in private," Ninnie continued to defend her decision as she came out of the dressing room, adjusting herself inside a hideous green dress she found. "Besides, if you were going to be Ms. Grumpy Butt, why did you agree to come with us?"

"I'm not being grumpy!" Shawndrea snapped, realizing her tone said otherwise. "Okay, maybe I am a little," she confessed, pinching her fingers to show how much. "I'm just having a horrible day. Okay?"

"Shit girl, are you PMS'ing or what?" Ninnie asked, looking at Shawndrea in the mirror. "Because you're starting to scare me with your range of emotions."

"I don't want to talk about it," Shawndrea insisted as she started to pace back and forth. Ninnie decided not to press the matter.

"It's Steve. He got back with Yesenia," Shawndrea blurted out, catching Ninnie off guard.

"Okay, Ms. I-don't-want to-talk-about-it, come on, share what's really going on," Ninnie remarked as she tried another dress.

"I haven't had sex in over three days. I miss his cock. I'm going out of my horny mind!" Shawndrea blurted out while she waved her hands in the air like a mad woman.

"Okay, when I said share, I didn't mean literally-IN-detail," Ninnie pointed out as she came out of the dressing room wearing an ugly yellow dress and waving her hands in a circle around Shawndrea's face, mocking her. "Cause this here is what we call crazy. Ookay, so it's been three days without sex that is nothing," Ninnie casually stated as she spun around in a dress looking at her reflection in the mirror.

"That dress is even uglier than the first," Shawndrea pointed out.

"Thanks, Captain Obvious," Ninnie sneered. She looked at Shawndrea with her hands on her hips. "You seriously need to get a grip. Besides, how did you think this was going to turn out?" Ninnie asked as she pulled back the changing room curtain to change out of the dress. She was starting to think about why she brought Shawndrea along in the first place when Shawndrea handed her a dress to try. Ninnie held up the dress and realized this was why she had her come along. Despite Shawndrea's lack of class, this girl can definitely pick out a dress.

Ninnie knew before putting it on this was the one. It was a gorgeous blue, but not too bright, but not too light, and fit her body perfectly. The dress was a vintage blue strapless dress with a high-breasted processed corset. She feared the girls would pop out and wanted to cover them as best she could. Gold and brilliant blue stones covered the top of the dress, sewn into the high and low-set corset. The bottom of the dress had many layers of tulle, which gave a soft but bell-like shape to the dress.

It accentuated her body's curves perfectly. The dress looked classic and vintage, precisely what Ninnie had envisioned.

Ninnie pulled back the curtain to show Shawndrea, but she found her crying. "What the fuck are you crying for?" Ninnie asked as she walked over and put her hand on Shawndrea's shoulder. "Hey, this is my day. We are not making it about you."

"I - I - I don't know what's wrong with meee," Shawndrea replied sobbing uncontrollably. "I. I. started to cry thinking of Steve with that bimboooooo."

"Oh dear, let me see how to explain this to you," Ninnie searched for the words, trying to think of a way to say what she wanted without insulting. "These are what we normal people like to call feelings. It sounds like you have feelings for this guy, and this is what tends to happen when you spend a lot of time with someone and have sex more than once."

"What?" Shawndrea questioned as she stood up and wiped tears from her eyes. "I can't have feelings for this guy."

"I might be wrong here, and I'm just spitballing," Ninnie stated, putting her hands in the air. "Do you think about him when he is not around?"

"Yes," Shawndrea replied, blowing her nose.

"Do you wonder what he is up to when he isn't around you?" Ninnie asked, hoping she would come to the conclusion herself or that a light bulb would go on.

"Yes," Shawndrea replied, furrowing her brow, wondering where this conversation was heading.

"Does it bother you to think of him with another woman?" Ninnie asked as she could see nothing clicked yet, so she pushed further. "Does the thought of him putting his cock inside another woman bother you?"

"I'm going to kick her fucking ass and rip her fucking head off. She better not touch my man like that," Shawndrea demanded. When she heard the words coming out of her mouth, it was like someone else was saying them, and she sat down. "Oh my god, I think you're right. I'm having feelings. I don't have feelings for guys.

I fuck them and leave 'em. How the hell did this happen?"

"Well, first off, he was never really your man; you kinda stole him. Secondly, let me remind you this is my day, and we are here to get ME a fucking DRESS! Now get up and save this therapy session for another day," Ninnie ordered as she stood, swishing the dress slightly. "So, tell me how does this dress look?"

"Oh, wow, this is the one without a doubt," Shawndrea gushed as she stood up and pulled the dress up to get a feel. "I'm kind of jealous."

"Why? Because I got boobs, and you don't," Ninnie teased, looking in the mirror, pushing her girls up, and making funny faces. "Yea, baby look at these," Ninnie stated as shook her boobs in the mirror.

"Yea, Yea, you got the tits, and I got mosquito bites. But I have never had any complaints about my tits, okay," Shawndrea remarked, pulling out her blouse and looking at her girls. "I was talking about this dress. It is nicer than the one I had at my prom last year or the dress I will wear this year."

"Wait, you're still going even though..." Ninnie was saying but stopped herself. She didn't want the waterworks to start or make it about her again. She internalized her thoughts about *who she was going to go with.*

§

Meanwhile, Ruby was trying on dresses with her Mom, and things were awkward. Her Mom had been acting suspiciously and saying no to all Ruby's choices without explaining why. Ruby was trying to figure out how to ask her Mom what was happening. Ruby picked out a beautiful Ruby-Red dress that sparkled.

It was a strapless dress with a sweetheart neckline. The top was a processed corset with silver and ruby red beads in a semi-shaped heart that intermittently ran to the floor and sparkled brilliantly in the light. The bottom had many layers of tulle and taffeta with a chiffon layer underneath, making her look elegant. The dress flowed perfectly when she moved, sweeping gracefully just an inch from the floor. Her mom looked at it and grunted.

Finally, Ruby couldn't take it anymore. "Mom, what the hell is going on?!" Ruby snapped. "Every fucking dress you have vetoed, and this dress, well, this dress is fucking amazing."

"Ruby Jean!" her Mom exclaimed, standing up. "Watch your tone, and do not use that language around me." Her Mom sat down, put her head in her hands, and began to cry. She started mumbling. Ruby looked at her, trying to understand what she was saying.

"Mom, I can't understand what you're saying," Ruby explained as she sat down next to her, letting go of her frustration with her Mom. "Mom, talk to me. What's going on?"

"I - I don't want my baby to grow up and leave me," Her Mom blubbered, barely able to speak. "My marriage is over, and this isn't how I saw my life going.

"Oh, Mom, you will never lose me," Ruby reassured her as she put her arm around her Mom and hugged her. No matter what happens, I'm here for you."

"Thank you, sweetie," her Mom said, hugging her back. I don't know what I'm going to do with my life now," she confessed as she wiped tears from her face. And I have been seeing someone. Also, I'm thinking about moving back to New York.

"Wait, what!? When?" Ruby asked, surprised, and completely caught off guard. "And who?"

"I was thinking this summer, but I want to wait until you graduate," her mom explained as she tried to look at her daughter, but she feared that if she did, she would start to cry again. "I don't want to make you choose where to live, so I'm just going to say you're welcome to live with me. I have gone over my budget; with what I will be getting from your father and the job I'm starting; I can afford to get a small apartment. And I love this dress on you, the Ruby Red sparkles, just like you. Let's get it."

Her Mom started to get up to pay for the dress. "Not so fast, Mom," Ruby stopped to look at her curiously. "Who are you dating?"

"Damn, I was hoping you had forgotten that part," Her Mom chuckled and wiped the remaining tears from her face as she watched Ruby tapping her foot on the floor as she sat back down. "Well, dating makes it sound so serious. I like the term seeing each other. Ooooh, I can't tell you," She said, biting the back of her hand.

"Mom? I don't understand. What is the big deal?" Ruby questioned as she looked at her with a raised eyebrow.

"Cause it's your teacher," Her Mom blurted out, putting a hand to her mouth. "I don't want things to get awkward for you or this person."

Ruby already suspected who she was referring to but wanted to give her Mom a hard time. She decided to have a little fun at her Mom's expense. "It can't be Dr. Spangler. He is too old, and it can't be Ms. Wilson. Wait, you're not trying to tell me you're a lesbian, are you?" She asked her Mom. "Because I'm totally cool with it if you are."

"No, no, nooo, I'm seeing Ben Stevens," her Mom finally divulged. "Wait, you thought I was a lesbian? I mean, really. Do I dress like one?" her Mom asked as she examined herself in the mirror.

"Moooom, lesbians don't dress a certain way," Ruby stated. How long has this been going on? Ruby asked as she got up to change out of the dress.

"He is the son of my friend I told you about, and it's been going on for some time, but I'm not quite ready to discuss it with you," Her Mom answered. "Soon, I promise. I'm just not ready to discuss it yet."

Ruby hugged her Mom, and they went to pay for the dress. Afterward, they met up with Ninnie and Shawndrea for lunch.

While the ladies were having lunch, Ruby's Mom started asking Ninnie and Shawndrea about where they came from and what they planned on doing after graduation. Of course, Shawndrea took the floor with this one.

"When I graduate next month," Shawndrea proudly replied while Ninnie rolled her eyes. "I plan on moving in with my boyfriend. He is in the Air Force. He plans on buying us a big house after I graduate."

While Shawndrea was talking, Ninnie looked at her like she had grown a third head. "What boyfriend are you talking about?" Ninnie asked, confused, as she started mumbling to herself. You *were just crying over Steve, but now you suddenly have another boyfriend. Call me confused.* She didn't want to say it too loud and start an argument in front of Ruby and her Mom, but she could not help herself. And do Dad and Mom know that you're moving?"

"Who cares what Mom and Dad think," Shawndrea replied, stirring her glass of tea and focusing the attention back onto her and her future." Yeah, Jack is going to get me out of this small town. We are going to get married and have two kids."

Jack, Ninnie mouthed to herself, still looking strangely at Shawndrea.

"That is great," Sue remarked as she looked at Ruby. "I'm so glad Ruby has decided to attend my alma mater, Brown University."

Shawndrea continued talking about herself while Ninnie stayed quiet. She was annoyed that Shawndrea dominated the conversation, making it all about herself and telling stories that made no sense.

When they got into the car, Ninnie remained silent. She just wanted to end the day and get home.

However, Shawndrea had other ideas. "Why are you being so quiet," Shawndrea finally asked when she couldn't take the quietness any longer.

"Just you are being you," Ninnie sighed. There was a bit of silence, but Ninnie could not help herself. She let Shawndrea have it about crying over a man in the dressing room and then, at dinner, talking about another guy she hadn't even heard of.

"Well, they always say, "Best way to get over a man is to get under another one." That is my moto now," Shawndrea quoted confidently.

Ninnie laughed and said, "Girl, you are a hopeless mess. I don't even know how to respond to that."

§

The night of the prom had finally arrived, and it was time for the guys to pick up their dates. Levin had pulled into Charlotte's driveway and became lost in thought while working up the nerves to go inside. He was surprised by how nervous he was.

He finally got out of his car and knocked on the door. Jean let him in and talked to him. However, it was like he was detached from his body and watching everything moving in slow motion. As soon as Charlotte walked into the room, looking stunning in a pale lavender dress and her red hair curled, he snapped back into his body and reality.

Charlotte's dress was a light lavender strapless dress. The top was a processed corset with dark and light lavender sparkly beads sewn like snow. The bottom had only a few layers of taffeta and chiffon. Charlotte wanted something simple; she did not want to stand out.

The first thing out of his mouth was, "Wow, you simply take my breath away." He walked up to her, kissed her on the cheek, and turned to see her blushing. You're absolutely beautiful," he whispered in her ear. Shall we go, Princess Charlotte?" he addressed her, holding out his arm to her.

"Hold up, I want pictures." Her Mom requested as she ran to grab the camera. They took a few pictures together before heading out.

§

Tommy picked up Ninnie while Shawndrea took their pictures. Trey didn't have to go too far to pick up Ruby. He walked across the yard and knocked on her door. Ruby's Mom greeted him and led him into the living room. When Ruby walked into the room, Trey became speechless and started fumbling for the words. "Let's hope you don't fumble this much next season," Ruby joked, trying to lighten the mood. They were both extremely nervous. She reached up to straighten his tie, looked into his eyes, and they were about to kiss.

"Okay, it's time for pictures," Her Mom interrupted as she walked in holding a camera. You don't want to be late for your prom," she said.

Her mom was holding the camera and taking pictures when she stopped to stare. "Mom, are you done?" Ruby questioned through her smile as she was waiting for the flash.

"Yeah, sorry, I was just thinking back to when you were little and taking your first baby pictures," Her Mom explained as she resumed taking the last few shots. "Let me go and get the photo album. I want to show Trey your first pictures."

"Mom… We are going to be late." Ruby said, picking up the bottom of her dress and walking over to hug her Mom goodbye. "Remember, we will be back late. The after party doesn't get over until 1 a.m."

"Have fun," Her Mom expressed as she hugged her and walked over to the door to open it for them.

Trey put his arm out for Ruby, and they walked out to his car. He opened the door for Ruby and closed it behind her. They pulled out of his driveway. Ruby could not help but look over at Trey, who looked good in his tux. Ruby felt it all seemed too good to be true. He flashed her a beautiful smile, and she melted in the seat.

Tommy and Ninnie were already there talking with Sheldon when they arrived at school. "I'm so glad we talked Sheldon into coming tonight," Ruby remarked, smiling at Trey as they pulled into the parking lot. "The night wouldn't be complete without him here."

They parked, and Trey walked around to open the door for Ruby. "I'm not sure how I feel about you opening my door for me," she teased as she exited the car and stood to face him. "I feel like I am setting back femin..."

He interrupted her mid-sentence with a toe-curling kiss. "I have been waiting to do that since I saw you walk into your living room."

"Well, don't stop," She demanded, reaching up to kiss him again.

"Hey, you two!" Ninnie yelled. Come on, let's go. You can make out later tonight."

Trey and Ruby stopped kissing, still face to face, and laughed. They walked over to join the others.

They stepped into the gymnasium entrance where the prom was taking place. The group hadn't learned what they were about to experience. Ruby doubted the gym would be a suitable venue for the prom.

They entered through an archway designed like an entrance to a castle. They passed through a corridor leading into the gym, which looked like a great hall like you would find in a castle.

The entire gym was surrounded by what looked like brick walls, with black curtains intermittently dispersed around the space. On every other section of the wall was a painted window. The sections that didn't have a window had a crest that you would expect to see in a castle. It was complete with chandeliers and short wooden rectangular tables. They looked around the gym in amazement at the drastic change.

They made their way to their assigned table and seats. Each seat had a name card showing everyone where to sit. Ruby and Trey found the cards with their names and got comfortable in their seats. Charlotte and Levin found their seats next to Sheldon, who was seated beside an empty seat reserved for a guest.

"Well, this is not awkward at all," Sheldon remarked as he looked at everyone and tried to smile. "But I'm going have fun no matter what."

"Oh no, I'm seated next to Tommy?" Ninnie joked. "Unacceptable. Who do you have to talk to around here to get a better seat?"

"Sit down, Mariah. No one came here to see your show," Tommy quipped as he smiled and pulled out Ninnie's seat for her to sit down. "It's too early for your daily spanking."

"Okay, that was an image I was not expecting to have tonight," Sheldon commented, looking around the room for someone. "Speaking of slutty pants, where is your sister sitting."

"Probably on her new boyfriend's face," Ninnie quipped sarcastically, and everyone's mouth fell open while she acted indifferent to her sister's whereabouts. "Sorry, I'm just not talking to her right now. Long story, I will fill you in later."

"The decorations are beautifully done. I love the colors. The purple and gold make it pop," Charlotte remarked, looking around the room. She felt uncomfortable sitting at the table because she didn't know anyone. "In art class, Mr. Howell had us painting these panels for months, but I had no idea the panels were for the prom. I'm amazed at how well they turned out."

"Did you notice the little lights in the ceiling?" Ruby asked as everyone looked up. "They kind of look like stars."

"Oh yeah, I didn't notice that," Ninnie commented, looking up. "I don't even want to think how they got those lights way up there."

"It's very romantic," Sheldon added, looking around. "No wonder the gym had been closed for the last couple of weeks; this had to take a lot of time. There are even smoke machines and plants along the sides of windows. It seems very real you truly forget you're in the gym. I wonder how they got this all put together."

"Oh, look, there is even a throne for the king and queen," Trey teased, elbowing Ruby. "You're my queen," he flirted, winking at her and kissing her head while Ninnie jokingly made a gagging face.

"Are those knights standing over there?" Charlotte asked as she tried to look closer. "Wait, are they moving?"

"Yeah, they are, and it is freaking me out," Ninnie commented, leaning over and looking in their direction.

"Yes, they are moving," Tommy answered, looking at the knights and pointing to them around the room. The chaperons dressed like knights and knightesses. That's my dad over there in the corner."

"Well, that's not awkward," Ruby remarked as she turned around to look at Tommy.

"Eh, he is used to it," Ninnie said with her arm around Tommy, patting his shoulder. "He has grown up with his dad all up in his business, which might be why he turned into a little fire starter," Ninnie teased, but Tommy did not look amused. "But he is my little fire started," She cooed, getting a smile out of Tommy.

"Speaking of awkward, did your mom tell you she would be here?" Tommy asked Ruby with a curious look on his face. "Isn't that her standing on the opposite side of the room from my father," He motioned to where she was standing.

"Wait, what, my mom?" Ruby asked, surprised. She looked to where Tommy pointed. "Who is she standing next to?"

"It's hard to tell, but it looks like Mr. Stevens," Trey commented, squinting to make sure who she was standing next to.

Ruby stood up to get a better look. Her Mom was greeting students as they walked by. When she saw Ruby looking, she waved to her, but Ruby didn't wave back. Ruby sat back down, unsure of her feelings about the situation. Ruby debated walking over to confront her mom about why she did not tell her while they were taking pictures that she would be there. She decided she didn't want to make a scene at prom.

"So, where are you from?" Charlotte asked Ruby. From Ruby's accent, she could tell she was not from around there. She was trying to ease the awkwardness.

"I'm from New York," Ruby replied, looking at Trey and Tommy as they excused themselves from the table. "We moved here last summer. My dad wanted to open his practice."

"Oh wow, I can't imagine living in a big city like New York," Charlotte commented, drinking water. "We moved here from a small town in Indiana, which I thought was small, but this town is even smaller."

"I think after you spend time in the big city, you learn to adapt," Ruby explained, smiling at Charlotte. "That is the great thing about humans. We can adapt to almost any environment. Where did those two go?" Ruby asked as she looked at Ninnie and Sheldon.

"Oh, I don't know," Sheldon replied with a look of confusion on his face. "Sorry, I didn't hear what they said." He was half listening to Charlotte and Ruby's conversation and was wondering what Chase was up to tonight.

"I don't know either," Ninnie answered as she shrugged her shoulders and looked around from them. "I don't think they said where they were going."

While talking, they could hear a guitar tuning up and someone saying, "Test, test, one, two, three."

"Did anyone know there was going to be a band here?" Levin asked, looking towards the stage where the curtains were still drawn and closed. "I didn't even notice the stage. I was distracted by the decorations."

"Umm, no. I thought it was going to be a DJ," Ruby said, furrowing her brow in confusion. She looked at Sheldon and Ninnie, who both looked just as confused as she was.

Suddenly, the curtains opened, and the boys played the intro to *Make Your Own Kind of Music.* Chase scanned the audience until he found Sheldon and started singing to him. The song ended, and Chase stepped back up to the microphone.

"Hey, everyone! How are we feeling tonight?" the crowd cheers. Awesome, we are called Chase the Band," Chase smiles at Sheldon, and the boys start playing the intro to the next song. "Get it, Chase-the-band, ha-ha. Anyway, we will play a couple of songs while you eat. Then the DJ will take over from there so you can dance."

They started playing the next song, and Sheldon had the biggest smile. He was ecstatic to see Chase there, and he looked incredibly sexy in his suit. They played a couple of songs while the servers served everyone their food. Sheldon couldn't take his eyes off Chase.

"Okay, our next song, *I Choose You,* is an original co-written by someone very special to me," Chase explained as he picked up his guitar. The next song started with just Chase playing the acoustic guitar. Chase started singing. Sheldon had no idea who he was referring to and thought the words to the song sounded remarkably familiar, but he couldn't quite put his finger on why.

Chase nodded to Tommy and Trey to start playing as he sat down his guitar. Chase pulled the wireless mike from the stand and started walking down the stage's steps. He headed towards where Sheldon was seated. Sheldon had no idea what Chase was about to do.

Chase walked up to Sheldon, held out his hand, and pulled Sheldon from his seat. He led Sheldon to the middle of the dance floor and started slow dancing with him. "What are you doing?" Sheldon whispered into Chase's ear.

During the instrumental break, Chase turned to look at Sheldon. "I don't know what came over me; this wasn't part of the plan. I saw you in this suit, and something told me this was *our* moment, and I couldn't stop myself," Chase explained, looking into Sheldon's glistening eyes.

"I love you, and I told you I would do something bigger than Ninnie and Tommy," he whispered into Sheldon's ear as he started singing again. He led Sheldon towards the stage. Chase finished the song as they climbed the stage. He turned back to look at Sheldon while everyone applauded and cheered. The cheering was so loud he had to pause before he spoke.

"That song was written by Sheldon Majors and me, who will sing with me on this next song we wrote together."

The audience applauded and cheered again. The look on Sheldon's face was priceless. It was a night full of surprises. As he turned to face the audience, he looked like a deer in headlights. "Just like all the times we did it together," Chase reassured him with a smile. Just jump in when you can and remember it's no big deal."

The boys started playing the intro to their song, *A Life of Surprises*. Chase began to sing the song, and Sheldon joined the chorus. It was evident immediately when Sheldon started signing that all his fears melted away. Sheldon got into singing the song with Chase.

After the chorus, Sheldon starts singing the following line and quickly realizes he is singing alone. Chase let him take the lead. Sheldon wavers for a moment and pulls it together. Chase smiles, picks up his guitar, and plays along. He comes back in during the chorus. They finish the rest of the song together.

Everyone got out of their seat and gave them a long-standing ovation. Sheldon was shocked by the positive response they got from everyone. Well, everyone except one person who caught Sheldon's eye.

Laramie was seated beside a standing Shawndrea and glared up at them with his arms crossed. Shawndrea was applauding and elbowing him to applaud, too, but he did not. The boys performed a few more songs together before Sheldon went to sit back down.

Sheldon made his way back to the table. He couldn't help but feel Laramie's eyes watching him. He tried not to look over at him while sitting at the table. Ruby was about to tell Sheldon they saved a plate of food for him and Chase, but Sheldon directed his attention towards Ninnie.

"Why didn't you tell me Shawndrea was bringing Laramie as her date tonight?" Sheldon asked Ninnie. Her face immediately told him she was just as shocked as he was.

Ninnie stood up, scanning the room for her. "Where is she?" she asked, looking around the room as Ruby tried to get her to sit back down. She knew by her demeanor that this was not going to end well. Ninnie spotted her and marched straight over to Shawndrea. She grabbed her arm and dragged her out of the gym and into the hall.

"Hey, you're hurting my arm," Shawndrea cried.

"What do you think you are doing?" Ninnie snapped at her sister. Before Shawndrea could answer, Ninnie berated her with more questions. "Why are you here with that guy, and what about John, Jack, or Joseph? I can't keep up with the names of the flavor of the week," Shawndrea tried to answer but was cut off again. "First, you were crying over one guy. Then spring on me that you're dating an older man and going to run off with him getting married, and now you're here with that asshole."

"Well, if you would let me explain instead of interrupting me," Shawndrea tried to get a moment to say her piece. Ruby, Sheldon, and Levin were in the hallway by this time. "First off, he asked me because neither had anyone to bring. Secondly, my fiancé couldn't come because he is over twenty-one."

"Hold up, when did he go from being your boyfriend to your fiancé?" Ninnie questioned as she tapped her foot, waiting for a response. "Secondly," Ninnie rattled off sarcastically. "Laramie is a sophomore and couldn't have come unless you invited him." Ninnie could see that he had fooled her on that technicality.

Since Shawndrea didn't respond, she ignored that topic and distracted her with the more significant news.

"Last weekend, he proposed to me at a fancy restaurant in Saint Louis," Shawndrea replied, holding up her hand and showing her the ring.

Ninnie pulled her hand closer to examine the ring. "Why didn't you tell me this sooner?" She asked, her voice cracking a little.

"Because I know how you would react like you are right now," Shawndrea answered with a furrowed brow. "You're always overreacting to everything instead of just living your life. You're not my mother, so you have to let me go. I need to live my life just like you need to live yours," Shawndrea explained as she shoved past her to walk back inside to find Laramie.

"Why does she always have to be so difficult, but right at the same time?" Ninnie queried through gritted teeth as she started to cry. "I can't let go. She is my sister. We have always been close, but I feel her slipping away, and I know it will never be the same again."

Ruby and Sheldon both walked up to Ninnie to hug her. "Thanks, you guys," Ninnie said, hugging them back. "I will be fine. I need to focus on my life and let her live hers, even if I disagree with the direction in which her life is heading."

The boys had finished playing for the night, and the DJ took over. They made their way outside to check on everyone. Tommy walked up to Ninnie and hugged her; she broke down crying as he did. "You guys can go on back inside," Tommy requested, forcing a smile. "I will take it from here."

Chase grabbed Sheldon's arm to stop Sheldon from going back inside. Chase wanted to sneak another kiss because now everyone's eyes would be on them. There was no going back now, no more secretly seeing each other even though almost everyone knew anyway. "Were you surprised?" Chase asked him in between kisses.

"I definitely was surprised by the song, and even more so when you came down and danced with me in front of everyone," Sheldon remarked as he kissed him back before taking his hand and leading him back into the gym. "Come and eat. The girls saved us some food. You will have to tell me how you pulled this off."

While eating, Chase explained that he worked with the prom committee and asked if his band could perform. He also got his dad to help with the construction of the castle. When his dad was younger, he used to work on sets for Hollywood TV and film productions before opening his own business.

They danced a bit, and before they knew it, it was time to change and prepare for the Vegas-themed after-prom celebration. As Sheldon was getting changed, he realized Laramie had been on his best behavior. Maybe he had changed and moved on.

Chapter Seventeen

The After Prom

They were holding the after-prom party in the cafeteria. After everyone changed into comfortable clothes, they met in front of the bathrooms and went to the cafeteria. They had to check in when they entered and were given their poker chips for the night.

Throughout the night, they had the opportunity to win various prizes and chances to win more poker chips. They put their names into a basket, and every 15 minutes, someone drew a name. The winner spun the wheel for their prize. The main prize was a computer, VCR, and stereo system. The rest were smaller prizes like a Walkman, coupons to the local video store, pizza place, and more poker chips.

There were card tables for Blackjack, Poker, and Craps, followed by Roulette tables. "Darn, I was hoping for some slot machines," Sheldon chuckled as he glanced around the room.

"They are on the other side," said a voice behind them. They turned to see Ruby's Mom standing there. Ruby looked at her mom and turned to leave. "Ruby, wait. Can we talk?"

"Can it wait until we get home?" She asked, but she knew by the look on her mother's face she meant now. "Fine, let's go into the hall."

While they headed into the hall, Chase and Tommy headed to play cards, and Sheldon and Ninnie hit the slots.

Laramie sat down beside Chase while he played Blackjack. Chase didn't even notice him sitting there or the way Laramie was glaring at him. Laramie turned to the dealer and asked to be dealt into the game. Trey noticed Laramie and started to look around for Ninnie and Sheldon. He spotted Tommy, who was sitting at a Craps table. They made eye contact, and Trey motioned towards Laramie. They waited a few minutes but sensed trouble brewing.

Trey found Ninnie and Sheldon laughing at how neither knew what they were doing.

"I don't mean to interrupt, but we might have a problem," Trey declared as he looked from Sheldon to Ninnie. "Where is your sister?" Ruby walked up and could immediately tell something was going on.

"I'm not sure why?" Ninnie asked, looking at Trey confused. "Why do you need my sister, and what has she done now?"

"It's not your sister I'm worried about. It's Laramie," Trey answered as he looked at Sheldon, who had a confused look on his face too. "He is sitting next to Chase and looks like he is about to start trouble. We need your sister to get him out of here because I doubt, he will listen to anyone else."

"I haven't seen her since she left us in the hallway, but I will go look for her right now," Ninnie stated, setting down her drink. "Ruby, do you mind helping? Maybe if we split up, we can look faster."

Ninnie and Ruby took off in different directions. Trey and Sheldon stood back and watched Laramie, Chase, and Tommy play Blackjack. Tommy had sat down at the table in case he had to intercede.

"Maybe he won't start any trouble tonight," Sheldon commented, looking hopeful at Trey. "I mean, he has been good for months now, especially since…."

Sheldon almost told him about the kiss and Tommy threatening him. Trey knew nothing about the kiss. "Since what?" Trey questioned Sheldon.

"Since the last time I told him to leave me alone," Sheldon replied, hoping Trey bought it.

Meanwhile, Ruby and Ninnie searched the whole place but did not find Shawndrea. They decided to ask one of the Chaperones.

"I saw her going outside about 30 minutes ago," Mr. Stevens replied. "Your Mom is outside too," he continued, looking at Ruby. "She is pretty torn up about what you said to her. She said she wanted to be alone."

"Let's go outside and check," Ninnie stated as she looked at Ruby. "I didn't know the party had moved to outside." She joked, trying to lighten the atmosphere.

Ruby and Ninnie exited the building, searching for Shawndrea and Ruby's Mom. They spotted Sue immediately; she was sitting staring up at the sky. The building had brick pillars holding up the awning to the entrance. The pillars were massive and had large circular holes in the middle of them. They found Ruby's Mom sitting in the curve of one of the large circles.

"Mom, what are you doing out here?" Ruby asked as she walked up to her mom. She turned to Ninnie. "Go ahead, Ninnie. Find your sister."

Ninnie hesitated for a minute but realized the importance of finding her sister. She had no idea why she had come outside in the first place—it's not like she smokes. She could have caught a ride with someone and gone home for all she knew. When she turned the corner of the building, she saw the back of her sister's head.

Even though she was in the shadows, and it was hard to see clearly, she knew the outline of her sister's big curly hair. *What is she doing?* Ninnie started to walk closer to get a better look.

Back inside at the Blackjack table, Laramie took his attitude up a notch and decided he was over being a nice guy. "So, you think you can do whatever just because you're the star quarterback, huh?" Laramie remarked as he glanced down at his cards to see what he held. Then he looked at Chase with a sideways cocky look.

"What did you say?" Chase asked, looking at Laramie, who now had Chase's full attention. "Do I even know you?"

"Ha! You should. At least your boyfriend does," Laramie smirked as he threw down two cards and asked the dealer to be hit again.

"What is your problem....?" Chase questioned as he turned in his chair to look squarely at Laramie.

Tommy nodded at Trey and Sheldon, who were waiting for a signal to come over. "That doesn't look good," Trey remarked, glancing at Sheldon.

"Oh god, what are we going to do?" Sheldon asked nervously, scratching his head and looking at Trey.

"If he starts any crap, we will do what you do with trash," Trey replied, now glaring in Laramie's direction. "You take it out."

Meanwhile, outside, Ninnie walked closer to see what her sister was doing. She noticed that her sister was not alone. She was kissing someone.

"What the fuck are you doing out here?" Ninnie demanded in a voice that reminded her of her mother.

Shawndrea jumped and wiped her lips with the back of her hand. "Ninn, you scared us half to death," Shawndrea stated, pulling her shirt down. The guy she was kissing took a step forward.

"What the….?" Ninnie was caught off guard and stepped back, almost falling off the curb. "You're… You're the guy she almost ran off the road."

"Yes, and I'm the guy who is going to marry your sister," the man introduced himself as he extended his hand. "Hi, I'm Jack."

Ninnie took another step back, shaking her head. "What happened to the Air Force guy?" Ninnie questioned with her head cocked and seemingly upset.

"This is him," Shawndrea gleefully stated as she placed her hand on his chest, and he pulled her closer. "Isn't he just the sexiest thing you have ever seen?"

Ninnie turned away from them and put her hand on her forehead. "This isn't happening," Ninnie reasoned as she started to walk away. "I'm going to wake up tomorrow, and this is all just going to have been a nightmare," She continued as she dramatically waved her hands through the air from left to right.

Back inside, Laramie stood up, and Chase followed suit. "You're my problem," Laramie stated as he started getting in Chase's face, and Chase pressed his chest up against Laramie's. "Get off me, you fucking fagot!"

Sheldon stepped between them and looked directly into Laramie's face. He could feel Chase pressed up against his back. "Stop it, Laramie. Go home," Sheldon commanded as he pushed Laramie back and stepped closer.

"Get your fucking faggot hands off of me," Laramie demanded, getting in Sheldon's face as he whispered to Sheldon. "You know you want more of this. I know you liked it when I kissed you."

Suddenly, Mr. Stevens jerked Laramie backward. At that point, everything in Sheldon's world went muffled. He knew Chase was close enough to hear Laramie's remark. Sheldon was afraid to turn around. He wanted to stop time forever but knew that wasn't an option. When he first turned around, he could not hear anything. Maybe it was shock, or perhaps it was a coping mechanism.

As soon as he turned around and looked into Chase's eyes, he returned to reality. He immediately saw that Chase was confused, shocked, and mostly hurt. "Is what he said true?" Chase choked out as he looked Sheldon in the eye.

Sheldon was shocked that a tough guy like Chase could have that much hurt in his eyes. "He kissed me, but…" Sheldon tried to explain but could not finish. Chase turned to leave and headed straight out of the building. Sheldon was left there with Trey and Tommy looking at him before they ran to find Chase.

Meanwhile, outside, Ninnie left Shawndrea to her own devices. She decided everyone inside could figure it out themselves and checked on Ruby before heading back inside. Ruby was sitting alone, where she had left her to talk with her mom. "You, okay?" Ninnie asked as she walked up and sat down next to her.

"Yeah, I'm doing surprisingly well," Ruby replied as she turned to look at Ninnie and smiled at her. "My Mom is being really sensitive about dating a younger guy. She is continuously secretive, so I said something that was not so nice earlier, and it hurt her feelings, but I have since apologized, and we are good again. She went inside to check to make sure everything was under control."

"That is good," Ninnie commented as she stood back up. "I have a feeling this party is going to end early. We should go find our men."

"Yeah, I guess you're right," Ruby agreed as she climbed out of the circle. "I just…."

Ruby was interrupted by Chase coming out of the door. "Hey, you okay," Ninnie asked as he ran past her. She started to follow him, but he was heading to his car. "I guess the cat is out of the bag," Ninnie stated as she looked at Ruby.

"I think you're right; we better get back inside," Ruby replied as they started to head back inside. Sheldon came running out, followed by Trey and Tommy. "If you're looking for Chase, he just ran past us and headed to his car."

Sheldon took off in the direction Chase always parked his car.

Tommy and Trey stayed behind to talk to the girls. Sheldon ran to stop Chase from leaving. Chase's car was still in the parking lot and not running.

At first, Sheldon did not think Chase was even in the car. When he got close enough, he could see Chase inside. There was a damp chill in the air. Sheldon tapped on the window, wondering if Chase would open up.

It started to sprinkle. Sheldon looked back to see everyone was leaving. When he turned back around, Chase cracked the window. "You can get in if you want," Chase said in his cracked voice.

Sheldon walked around the car. As he opened the door, it started to rain harder. Sheldon climbed into the car and sat back in the seat, afraid to look over at Chase. He finally looked at Chase, and he could see tears running down his face. Chase tried looking away to hide his hurt as he talked.

"You know I have a lot of feelings going through me right now," Chase stated as he quickly brushed tears away before he turned to look at Sheldon. "One is hurt. It hurt that you didn't feel you could share this with me. Secondly, I felt a little betrayed that I had to find out how I did, which made me mad because I almost got emotional in front of people. That is why I ran out of there the way I did. What I really wanted to do was kick his ass. My strongest feeling is my love for you, which makes me a different and better person. I can't explain it better than that..." Sheldon did not know how to respond. They were quiet for a beat.

"Normally, I would have just kicked his ass. I want to be mad at you, but I can't," He explained, breaking the silence as he put his hand on the side of Sheldon's face and looked deep into his eyes. "Tell me what happened?"

The rain plinked down on the car's roof. Sheldon did not want to talk about what happened. At that moment, he felt extremely awkward, but he had no choice but to tell him in detail. Sheldon started explaining his history with Laramie and what happened the day he kissed him.

Trey and Ruby pulled next to them. "Hey, you guys, okay? I'm going to take her home," Trey stated as he looked at Chase. "Let me know if you need anything."

"Yeah, we are good," Chase answered to Trey as he waved goodbye. "Thank you for checking."

They drove off, and it became quiet again for a moment. The only sound was the sound of the rain. "I guess I haven't told you everything either," Chase confessed as he watched the rain run down the windshield and turned to face Sheldon. "I never told you what happened to make me suspicious of dating, and for a split second, I was right back there in that moment. Though I know you didn't have ill intentions, this situation was different. My first instinct was to fight, then to run and hide."

There was another pause. "Emotions are a sign of weakness, and crying is not considered manly," Chased stated with one hand on the steering wheel. Chase stared straight forward for a second before looking back at Sheldon.

"Anyway, back to what I have wanted to tell you for some time now but never felt it was the right time," Chase explained. "I want you to understand where I'm coming from. Growing up, I had the biggest crush on a boy named Brad. At first, he didn't know who I was until we started playing sports together. We started to hang out more and more. Eventually, he started spending the night at my place. Being a young boy, my mom never suspected anything. She just thought it was two boys hanging out together. Brad wanted to keep our fooling around a secret, so I continued with it. He said he was pretending to date girls to keep up appearances. As time passed, watching him hanging on these other girls grew harder and harder. He promised me we wouldn't be a secret once we got into junior high anymore, but that was when things escalated." Chase expressed and paused before he continued.

Sheldon could tell this was difficult for Chase to share, so he took Chase's hand and lightly squeezed it to show he was there for him.

"He stopped coming over to my place, and we hung out less and less," Chase continued. "One Saturday, someone was throwing a birthday party at the beach. I told him I couldn't go because I wasn't feeling well. At the last minute, I changed my mind. I was feeling better and headed to the party. When I got there, he was making out with some girl. I confronted him about it, and that was when he started calling me a faggot, a queer. That I was becoming too clingy, and it was weirding him out. Everyone there started laughing. I was hurt more than I was embarrassed. I thought he was only pretending to see that other girl. My friends tried telling me, but I would only get mad at them and stop talking to them. The fact is he was only pretending with me. I found out later he had been hooking up with her the whole time."

The car became quiet again, except for the sound of the rain. Sheldon did not know how to respond. He had never been in a situation like that, let alone been in love with someone that deeply. "I can't even imagine how much that would have hurt," Sheldon said, looking over at Chase. Chase's eyes met his. "I'm sorry that happened to you, and I'm sorry I didn't tell you about what happened with Laramie."

"Thank you for saying that," Chase said, leaning over to kiss Sheldon. "And thank you for being sweet. I know you probably wanted to forget the incident like it never happened, but it did, and those things come with feelings. Feelings that are best discussed instead of suppressing them."

"Wow, are you planning on becoming a psychiatrist?" Sheldon asked jokingly. Chase leaned over and rested his head on Sheldon's shoulder as Sheldon continued. "Honestly, I'm not used to sharing things like that with other people, let alone feelings. It's still new for me. It was hard to have a friend to share with, like Ruby, and tell her about it."

"Wait, Ruby knows," Chase questioned as he raised his head. "Does Trey know?"

"I. I don't think so," Sheldon stuttered, unsure. He had not spoken about it again with Ruby, so he was uncertain if she mentioned it.

"Well, it doesn't matter. I'm just glad you're okay," Chase replied, laying his head back on Sheldon's shoulders. They stared out the windshield, watching the rain coming down. "He is just jealous. People tend to want to tear down beautiful things that make them jealous. And yes, I'm thinking of becoming a therapist."

Sheldon ran his fingers through Chase's hair as he lay his head on the headrest. "That is funny; Ruby is thinking of becoming a family Therapist," Sheldon remarked. With Chase resting next to him, the sound of the rain relaxed him, and he drifted off to sleep.

Sheldon woke to the sun streaming through the windshield, and for a split second, he did not know where he was until he felt Chase's head on his shoulder.

The movement must have woken Chase. He raised, squinting, and rubbing his eyes. "Oh man, I wasn't planning on sleeping," Chase stated as he rubbed his neck. "You're even sexy first thing in the morning. How do you do it?"

"Yeah, right," Sheldon chuckled and smiled as he kissed Chase's forehead. "As much as I hate to, I should probably go home. Your parents might be worried about you, too."

"Just a few more minutes," Chase requested as he put his arm around Sheldon and hugged him. "I don't want this to be over just yet."

Sheldon smiled and kissed his head again.

Chapter Eighteen

Mom's New Man

*I*Think We're Alone Now* came over the speakers. Shawndrea squealed, stood up, and grabbed her fiancé Jack's hand, "Come on honey, we have to skate to this song," Shawndrea said, pulling him up. "This was a fantastic way to celebrate my graduation and newfound freedom. No more high school hell yaaaaay!" Shawndrea cheered as she bounced up and down on her skates with immense joy.

Ninnie started imitating her sister, acting bubbly and giddy. Everyone laughed, unsure if they should be laughing.

Shawndrea dragged Jack onto the floor, and they started skating around the rink. They showed off by doing a few tricks. They wanted to skate fast, so Jack slug-shot Shawndrea to go even quicker.

"Promise me that if I ever start acting like that, shoot me immediately. Don't hesitate. Just take me out," Ninnie requested, shaking her head back and forth. "Would you look at that? She thinks she is a gold medal Olympian," Ninnie snarled while she watched her sister with a look of annoyance.

A monitor of the skating rink asked them to tone it down a bit for the safety of all the skaters.

"That's right, show off!" Ninnie yelled, but as usual, her sister ignored her. Shawndrea was in love, and there was no one else but her and her man.

"Hey Ninn, isn't that the guy we almost ran over on Seven Hills last summer?" Sheldon leaned over, asking Ninnie. "When did they even

start dating?"

"Don't even get me started with her," Ninnie said, waving her hands. "Do I smell popcorn," Ninnie asked Tommy, trying to change the subject.

"Yea. What's up with the ring she is wearing now?" Ruby asked as she and Sheldon stared at Ninnie, waiting for an answer.

"I bet they have hot dogs, too," Ninnie remarked as she ignored Ruby's question. She looked over at the concession area. "Let's go see what they have. I'm suddenly hungry."

At this point, everyone was staring at Ninnie. They all had questions, and no one had spoken about prom night. "How about you tell us what happened to you two on the night of the prom," Ninnie said, smirking at Sheldon and Chase. "I heard you two didn't come home all night."

"Don't change the subject," Sheldon demanded, giving Ninnie the stink eye.

"Hey, yeah, what DID happen with you two," Ruby asked, turning to look at Sheldon and Chase. "Laramie was dragged out of school and suspended for two weeks."

"My dad warned Laramie that he was about to be suspended," Tommy added. "It was the final straw in a long list of offenses. He was only allowed to come back and take the finales."

"Yea, he's an asshole that should rot in hell," Ninnie said matter-of-factly. "Anyway, the big news with Shawndrea is that she is engaged to this oooolder man. After high school, they will get married and buy a house closer to his job with the Air Force. So, there you have it, the big story. Now, how about we skate since that is why we came here."

"Sounds like a plan to me," Levin agreed as he stood up and tried to balance on his skates. "Guess it has been a while."

"Guess so by the looks of it," Chase teased.

"Oh yeah, how about I race you around the rink," Levin dared as he stepped onto the floor.

"Hey, wait for me," Charlotte called out after Levin.

He did not get far before his skates went out from under him, and he landed on his backside. Trey, Ninnie, and Tommy died with laughter. Charlotte gave them a dirty look and went to help him up.

"That redhead sure has a temper," Ninnie cautioned Trey.

Tommy smacked Ninnie on the ass with a loud wallop. "Hey! Now that was uncalled for," Ninnie cried out.

"Oh, I'm sorry, are you getting soft in the tush," Tommy taunted her. "How about you come out here and do something about it?"

They all headed out onto the floor while Sheldon was slightly hesitant. "What's wrong?" Chase asked, standing next to Sheldon. "Are you afraid of wiping out, too?"

"Ha-ha, you know me too well," Sheldon chuckled as he played it off.

"Hold onto my arm until you're ready to let go," Chase offered. Being a natural athlete, of course, Chase glided on the skates.

Sheldon and Chase remembered they were in a small town and could not publicly show affection. They tried to play it cool. Chase assisted Sheldon until he got comfortable on the skates.

Anyone watching the two boys could tell they were in love with each other. They were compassionate and caring to one another.

"Fucking faggots," Some redneck yelled as they passed by.

Ninnie heard this and immediately swung around and stopped before the guy. "What did you say?" Ninnie asked with her head cocked to the side and ready for a fight.

Tommy rolled up and tried to pull her away. "Not here, babe; I don't want you messing up these rednecks too bad," Tommy proposed as he got in between her and the jerks. "Do not let them ruin our night."

The Bangles song Eternal Flame started to play. Tommy grabbed her hand and pulled her to start skating again. He turned around, still holding onto her as he skated backward. It was very romantic, with the lights down low and the disco ball reflecting light around the rink. Ninnie put her head on Tommy's shoulder.

"Wait a moment," Tommy countered as he looked at Sheldon and Chase, watching other couples skating together. "Come on, guys. Who cares what other people say? Just have fun."

"Thank you," Ninnie whispered into his ear as she put her head back onto his shoulder.

Chase and Sheldon looked at each other, and both agreed. What the heck? They headed to the floor. Chase immediately decided to skate backward because he insisted, he was the better skater, and Sheldon laughed at him. They stared into each other's eyes as they skated around the rink, getting lost in the song and each other.

"This is an amazing moment," Chase remarked, smiling at Sheldon.

"You're right. It's something you dream of happening," Sheldon said, drawing out his words as he looked at Chase curiously. "Looking into the eyes of someone you love.

"Love?" Chase asked with his dimple smile, staring into Chase's eyes. "You said the L word."

"Awww, isn't that just fucking sweet," Ninnie teased as she and Tommy skated next to them. "The song is over if you two love birds hadn't noticed."

"I don't know why everyone is staring at them," Ruby chuckled from the other side. "You would think these people had never seen two guys skating together."

"I think they should kiss," Ninnie recommended with an evil laugh and a smirk. She stared directly at the rednecks, watching them and glaring at them.

"Maybe that's not a great idea," Trey chimed in. "I don't feel like fighting tonight."

The next thing you know, Chase grabbed Sheldon and pulled him into a passionate lip lock. When Sheldon came back up, he was out of breath. They all laughed, but most of the skating rink was not happy.

A few of the parents went over and complained to the manager.

The manager came onto the floor to kick Chase and Sheldon out for acting "inappropriately" in front of the children.

"What the… Where do these bozos get off saying it's inappropriate," Tommy started to yell at the manager. Ninnie cocked her head backward, looking at him like she did not know who he was. She was surprised that he was yelling.

"Okay, honey. You have made your point. Let's maybe take it down a notch," Ninnie requested as she tried to get his attention back on her and calm him down.

"I will not be quiet. These assholes are being discriminative," Tommy yelled again, pointing toward the rednecks.

"You're all out of here," The manager yelled back. "Take off your skates and get out of here before I call the cops."

"Come on, Tommy, let's do what the guy asked," Shawndrea snapped at him in her Mom's voice as she took off her skates. "The party is over, and it's time to go. Isn't that what you usually say to me, Ninn, when I'm the one getting us kicked out of places? I guess your boyfriend had the honor of doing it today. We have trained him well," Shawndrea cooed as

she patted him on the shoulder and went to turn in her skates.

Sheldon, Chase, Trey, Ruby, Charlotte, and Levin had already returned their skates. Tommy sat down to take off his skates' grumbling to himself. "Call the cops. What a joke, and what's he going to tell them?" Tommy continued as he put on his shoes. He marched to return his skates. Ninnie watched him to make sure Tommy did not go after the manager. Instead, he headed straight for the door as Shawndrea and Jack followed.

There was no other entertainment near the skating rink. Their parents were at a local lodge where a live band was playing. "I guess we could walk over and see if the band is any good," Sheldon suggested as he kicked a rock across the parking lot.

"Maybe if we walk slowly, it will be over by the time we get there, and then we can just go straight home," Ninnie suggested as she tried to think of a better idea.

"Jack is over twenty-one, and he can get us a jack and coke," Shawndrea pointed out as she leaned over Ninnie's shoulder.

"When you put it that way, then lead on our fearless booze card-carrying leader," Ninnie suggested, a little more excited.

As they walked, they laughed about the night's events. The lodge was not far from the skating rink, so it did not take them long to arrive. "Okay, so here is the plan. Everyone orders a Coke. Then Jack will order himself a Jack and coke. He will take turns getting you each a Jack and Coke. A few of you may want to share it. Otherwise, it could knock you on your butt since you guys don't drink often," Shawndrea recommended with authority like it was something she regularly did.

They heard the band playing as they approached the lodge, and people were whooping and hollering. "Wow, it sounds like the party has already started," Tommy pointed out. "Maybe this isn't such a good idea. We could just wait out here."

"Oh no, Tomminator, you're going inside. You were all ready to go back there at the skating rink," Shawndrea remarked as she shuffled her feet around and tossed her head back and forth like a boxer would do. She started to push him towards the door. "We are going to have fun even if it kills you."

Chase looked at Sheldon with an unsure look on his face. "Are you sure this is a good idea?" Chase whispered to Sheldon.

"Yeah, our moms are in there, and it should be fine," Sheldon reassured.

§

Earlier in the evening, Mandy and Letty had dropped the kids off at the skating rink and headed to the lodge to meet their dates. Mandy was meeting her new, much younger, and very sexy boyfriend, Damian. Letty was meeting Damian's friend Trevor. They found Damian sitting alone at the bar, waiting for them. The three of them got a drink and found a table.

"So, how did you two meet?" Letty asked Mandy and Damian.

"We met the weekend we were all camping a few months ago," Mandy replied as she smiled at Damian and leaned against him. "I had gone to the bathroom, and he was having trouble with his horse."

"You see, I was trying to break in a young horse to ride," Damian told the story. He wanted to make sure the story was told so he did not come off sounding like a weakling that a woman had to save him. "I was trying to get the bridal on her, and she wasn't having it. She reared up. I stepped back, tripping over a bucket, and fell on my ass. That was when Mandy grabbed her and kept her from running off."

"Uuuhuh," Letty responded as she started putting the pieces together. She looked at him and then turned to Mandy. "You two met while we were camping?" she said with a raised eyebrow.

"Yes, and then later that night, we slow danced," Mandy replied, acting like a giddy schoolgirl.

"Wait, you were dancing with Ted when I left! How is that possible?" Letty questioned with a muddled yet intrigued look, leaning over the table so as not to miss a word.

"I was dancing with Ted, but he got a Charlie horse and had to sit down. That's when Damian stepped in," Mandy explained as she kissed Damian. "We danced the night away, and then I ensured he stayed warm for the rest of the night. Let's face it. I just wasn't that into Ted, and I doubt he could have kept it up if you know what I mean. Damian and I have been inseparable since that night."

"Huh, well, that explains why I didn't see Ted anymore after that night," Letty commented, still thinking. "How come you never told me this before?"

"I don't know. I guess it just never came up," Mandy answered as the band started warming up. "Oh, hey, I know one of the guys in the band. I will be right back."

Mandy took off and left Letty and Damian alone at the table. "So, this fun," Damian remarked as he tried to break the awkwardness.

"Oh, it sure is," Letty chortled, half amused, looking around, feeling awkward. "Where is your friend that was supposed to be meeting us here?"

"I'm not sure. He must be running late," Damian answered as he took a drink and looked around. "He should be here any minute."

"How old are you?" Letty asked, looking him up and down.

"I'm twenty-one, but I will be twenty-two next month," Damian replied proudly.

Letty looked at him with both eyebrows raised this time. She was speechless for a second. "Wow, no wonder she has kept you a secret."

"Oh, there is my friend. Let me get him. Would you like another drink?" Damian offered.

"Sure, why the hell not? I will make one of the kids drive home," Letty commented as she slapped the table and laughed to cover up her nervousness.

Damian looked at her funny and went to get his friend. *What the hell, Letty? Why are you suddenly nervous? They are young enough to be your kids. You were having organisms before they were even born. Get yourself under control.*

"Where did Damian go?" Mandy asked, sitting down on her stool.

Letty pointed over at the bar. "His friend just got here, good lord Mandy. What have you gotten us into? These guys are young enough to be..." She paused momentarily, thinking of something that did not make her sound old.

"Young enough to be one of our children?" Mandy asked, looking at her matter-of-factly. "Who cares? Who set the rules anyway? Oh, here they come. How does my lipstick look?"

"You look fine," Letty answered as she cocked her head back and to the side, looking at her with a severe expression on her face.

"Letty, this is my friend, Trevor; this is Letty. She is Mandy's friend," Damian introduced the two. "Sorry, I'm not good at this."

"You're doing just fine," Mandy remarked as she smiled at him.

"Oh, for god sake, Mandy," Letty barked as she looked at Mandy, then turned to Trevor. "How old are you?"

Mandy practically choked on her beer, shocked at Letty's question. You would think by now she would be used to Letty's boldness. "I'm twenty-eight," Trevor replied like it was not a big deal, taking a drink of his beer.

"I'm forty-three. You think you still want some of this," Letty said, looking dead into his eyes. "And Mandy here..."

Mandy kicked her under the table before she could finish her sentence. "Ouch, and Mandy here is a very bad girl," Letty announced wide-eyed, looking at Mandy for approval of her statement.

The band started playing, and everyone turned to watch them perform their opening song. "Wow, you're right, Mandy; they are pretty good," Letty nodded approvingly.

"Yeah, my good friend David is the lead guitarist and background vocalist," Mandy said, turning around and explaining to everyone.

The band started their second song, and Letty began to move with it. "Wow, this song takes me back," Letty remarked as she started moving her hips, getting into the song. "But you guys probably don't know it because it was before your time. Hell, I was shooting out babies from this vagina before you were even born, Damian," Letty announced, laughing her loud, awkward laugh.

Mandy gave Letty a shut the fuck up look. "Hey, how about we get up and dance?" Mandy suggested standing up and pulling on Damain's arm.

"Mmmmmm. Okay, how can I resist such an offer from the sexiest woman in the place," Damian replied as he stood up and grabbed Mandy. He swung her around and led her to the dance floor.

"Can you believe those two?" Letty remarked as she sat back in her seat, looking at Trevor, who was drinking a beer.

"I think it's kind of nice," Trevor acknowledged as he watched Mandy and Damian. "They are lucky to have found each other."

"Seriously, the age thing doesn't bother you?" Letty questioned as she looked at him with her head tilted.

"No, most of the women my age are more worried about what they look like and men who drive nice cars. That is why I like older women. They already know what they want, their kids are almost grown, and they are better in bed."

"Well, okay, then," Letty said, downing her drink. Let's go dance," she requested, standing up. But don't get any ideas that this means we will be sleeping with each other tonight."

"Damn, I guess I won't get to try out the new ribbed magnum condoms I just bought."

Letty's eyes got huge, and she tried not to let her eyes wander down to his crotch to gauge if he was full of bull. "Oh really, well, I said we wouldn't be sleeping together because we would not have time to sleep. I plan on keeping you up aaaall night," She stated as she grabbed him and pulled him close on the dance floor.

They danced to a couple more songs before sitting back down. The guys got up to get everyone another round as their kids walked in. "Oh shit!" Mandy exclaimed as she saw the kids walk into the lodge. "What are they doing here so early?"

"What does it matter?" Letty questioned as she lit a cigarette, I haven't had this much fun in quite some time. "Did you see the ass on Trevor, and supposedly he has...

"It does matter because he doesn't know how old my kids are," Mandy answered as she tried not to say it too loudly, but the band was so loud.

"Wait, he doesn't know you have kids?" Letty inquired with a look of curiosity.

"No, he knows I have children. We have yet to discuss how old they are or how old I am," Mandy answered as she watched their kids walk over. "We kept getting distracted by other things if you know what I mean."

"Oh, I can imagine. I hope to get some distraction tonight," Letty snickered as she inhaled smoke from her cigarette. "But you better think quickly because your current sex life is about to collide with the offspring from your past sex life."

"Hey, I will intercept them, buy them something to drink, and have them sit…" Letty looked around for an excellent place to stash them. She spotted an empty corner. "I will put them over there, and we can just say they are friends of my children, at least till you can have your confessional moment with him. You can't hide them forever. I guess you could, but that would require…"

"No, no, you're right. Damn, why did I let this get so complicated," Mandy cursed herself with her hands on top of her head. "Go, go, and thank you."

"No sweat, I may need a favor from you one day," Letty laughed as she headed to intercept their children.

The guys arrived at the table with their drinks. "Where is she going?" Trevor asked, watching Letty walk away.

"Oh, she is just going to say hi to some people," Mandy replied, thinking of a way to distract him momentarily. "So, Trevor, what did you say you did for a living?"

Letty ushered all the little chickadees to the corner table. She instructed Shawndrea and Jack to come with her to get everyone a drink. "Now, don't bother your mom right now because Mandy is on a date," Letty talked to Sheldon and Levin like they were still twelve. Then, she headed over to the bar to get drinks.

"So, are we going to talk about how badass Tommy was tonight at the rink?" Trey asked as he slapped Tommy on the back. "I didn't know you had it in you."

"Ha, ha, I did," Sheldon commented as he ate some bar nuts.

"Hey, where did those nuts come from?" Ninnie questioned as she watched him pop some more into his mouth. "Don't bogart the nuts. How about sharing?"

"I got them right there," Sheldon said, pointing to a glass cabinet full of nuts next to Ninnie.

"Oh well, forget your small bowl of nuts. I have the whole thing to myself," Ninnie marveled as she got up to hug the container. They all laughed.

"You must be remembering that time in the third grade when you called me an asshole?" Tommy asked Sheldon.

"It was bitch, but yes," Sheldon replied with a smirk.

"I felt bad when you got spanked for that," Tommy remarked as he flicked a nut across the table at Trey. "I never thought she would spank you for that."

"Oh, that lady was crazy. You don't even know the half of it," Sheldon stated as he rolled his eyes. "She looked for ways to punish me."

"You didn't deserve it because I was a little prick back then," Tommy remarked.

"Was?" Sheldon teased.

"Hey now," Tommy retorted as he chucked a nut at Sheldon, and they all laughed. "I know I was a little shit back then. Since my dad was in charge of the whole school, I thought I could do whatever I wanted. So, she already had it out for you?"

"Someone told us later that she had a thing for our father growing up," Sheldon explained as Levin nodded in agreement. "She was pissed because it came out that our father was abusing us. She told us that we were faking it and deserved punishment, but I guess crazy runs deep with some people."

"I heard her telling my teacher about it, too. In fact, my whole class was talking about what she did to Sheldon. She was justifying her actions to my teacher," Levin added.

"That is just inexcusable," Tommy stated as he shook his head. "I had no idea."

"Does anyone else find it odd seeing our mothers dancing with men who are not our fathers," Ninnie asked, looking at everyone. Shawndrea was too busy making out with her man to take notice.

"I was wondering if anyone had noticed just how young the guys were," Trey added, watching them sideways. "They can't be much older than us."

"Hey, who are we to judge? You like who you like, right?" Ruby said, defending their mothers.

Wendy walked through the door with some other lady Sheldon did not recognize. She saw Mandy on the dance floor dancing with Damian as if she were auditioning for the next Dirty Dancing movie. She motioned her friend over to the bar.

They got a drink and found a table to stand at. Wendy focused entirely on Mandy, who was on the dance floor with Damian.

Wendy did not even see Tommy a couple of tables over. Sheldon leaned over to warn Tommy, who was at the opposite end of the table. Sheldon got Tommy's attention and motioned with his head to where his Mom was standing.

"What is my mom doing here?" Tommy questioned as he watched his Mom talking to Mandy on the dance floor.

"Wait!" Shawndrea interrupted as she waved her hands in the air. "Wendy is Tommy's Mom? How did I not put this together before now?"

Oh, shit, she was just at the table! How did she get onto the dance floor so fast? Sheldon watched Wendy pull on Mandy's arm, and Letty got in between them.

"You're drunk, Wendy. Go home before you make a bigger scene than you already have," Letty ordered as she separated the two. "Tommy, do you mind driving your Mother home before she gets hurt or embarrasses herself even more?"

Tommy was embarrassed more for his Mom than for himself. He knew she had problems, but he had no idea how terrible things had gotten since she moved out of the house. He put his arm around her and walked her out of the lodge with Ninnie behind them. Wendy's friend stopped Ninnie to give her Wendy's purse. "I will see you at home, Mom," Ninnie called out as she waved at her Mom, and the door closed behind her.

Sheldon could see his Mom was extraordinarily embarrassed and having difficulty looking at Damian. He could see she was talking to Letty and looked over at them. She said something to Damian, and they walked over to where the kids were sitting. Mandy introduced Damian to her children, Shawndrea, and their friends. Sheldon could see right away by the expression on his face that he either didn't know she had children or that they were older than he expected; Sheldon wasn't sure which.

They all pulled up a chair as Mandy proceeded to tell the story of how she and Wendy met years ago. It turned out that Wendy and Mandy went to high school together. They used to sleep over at each other's houses often, and one night, they had a brief sexual encounter.

"I explained to her immediately that I was just experimenting and how I liked her only as a friend," Mandy explained as she looked around the table, ending at Damian, trying to read his reaction. "We would go for long periods fine as friends, but occasionally, Wendy would get like this, and we would stop talking for months, sometimes years. It got to the point where Wendy thought she owned me. She would think we were dating and destined to be together. I don't want to lead her on, but I don't want to stop being friends. I don't know what to do anymore."

"I hope they make it home safely," Mandy remarked, looking sad.

"I'm sure they will. That son of hers is a good kid," Letty commended as she stood up to leave. "Cause if he wasn't, he sure the hell wouldn't be dating my daughter," she added with that crazy laugh that made Mandy laugh, too.

"Hey kids, what do you say we leave these two alone to talk?" Letty turned to leave. She ran right into Trevor, whom she had forgotten was there when things went down with Mandy. Come on, everyone, let's go outside, and you, I have plans for you," she said as she grabbed Trevor by the shirt and led him outside.

Just before Sheldon walked out the door, he turned back to see his Mom talking to Damian. Damian held his hands on Mandy's, saying something to her when she suddenly pulled them back. Chase put his hand on Sheldon's shoulders, diverting his attention, and pulled him out of the lodge.

Chapter Nineteen

Summer of Love

The sound of buttons clinking against the dryer as it dried filled the quietness of the laundromat. Sheldon and Levin were sitting with Ninnie, Shawndrea, and Jimmy at the laundry matt, waiting for the laundry to finish.

"So far, this summer has started off really well," Sheldon commented, climbing onto one of the tables and crossing his legs. "I had no idea the guy Mom was dating was so young!"

"By the look on his face, I don't think he had any idea about you guys or how old you were," Ninnie remarked, laughing as she shoved her hand into Shawndrea's bag of Doritos.

"Hey, get your own bag," Shawndrea scoffed, dodging Ninnie's attempt to get more. "Yeah, I don't know what your Mom was thinking dating someone that wasn't her own age."

They all looked at her, wondering if she was joking because she was dating someone about ten years older than her.

"I'm kidding, guys," Shawndrea said sarcastically while laughing and munching on a Dorito chip; she turned the page to her magazine. You know our Mom is dating a younger guy, too. Granted, he isn't quite as young as your Mom's boy toy."

"Speaking of boy toys, did you ask Mom why his dirty underwear was on *our* bathroom floor?" Ninnie questioned Shawndrea as she flicked the page of her magazine.

"Will you stop aggravating me," Shawndrea requested, smoothing out her magazine and eating another chip. "I'm not sleeping with mom's man."

"Come on, you know you're going to miss me aggravating you," Ninnie remarked as she danced around her and then stuck her finger in Shawndrea's ear."

"Get away from me, FREAK!" Shawndrea shrieked as she swung at Ninnie but missed because Ninnie dodged her swat.

"Ha-ha missed me," Ninnie taunted her. "This is probably our last time doing laundry together, so come on, let's celebrate it."

"It's not like I'm going away forever," Shawndrea retorted nonchalantly, turning the page. "You will see me at Thanksgiving, Christmas, and my wedding."

Ninnie walked over to check the time on the dryer just as the alarm went off. She opened the dryer door and looked back at Sheldon as she checked the clothes' dryness.

"The night we met our Mom's boy toys, you said you saw your Mom and Damian talking, and she pulled her hand away. Did you guys ever find out what that was about?" Ninnie asked as she pushed a basket to the dryer and pulled clothes out.

"Not yet. I thought maybe Damian was breaking up with her, but that ooobviously isn't the case since we can hear them going at it all night long," Sheldon stated making a gross face and trying to shake the sounds out of his head. "I have to leave the radio on just to sleep through the night."

"At least your bedroom is the furthest from theirs," Levin stated with an exhaustive look on his face. "I'm right next to them."

"Trust us, we know the pain you guys are going through because we are living it too," Shawndrea said as she kicked back in the chair while Ninnie folded all the clothes. "But soon, that will no longer be *my problem*."

"Well, Ms. Independent, how about you get your butt over here and help fold some of these clothes," Ninnie demanded as she threw a pair of Shawndrea's panties at her. She pulled out another pair of bright red lacy underwear and held them up to examine closer. "What the hell are these, and why are they split in the middle?"

"Hey, put down my good underwear," Shawndrea requested as she ran over and snatched them from Ninnie's hand. "Wait a minute, these are not mine!!"

"They sure are not mine," Ninnie stated as Jimmy walked up laughing. He had been playing Pac-Man on the arcade machine.

"Oh my god!" Shawndrea exclaimed with a horrified look on her face. "They must be mooooms!" She tossed them at Jimmy, and they landed perfectly on his head like a hat.

"Aagh, that is disgusting!" Jimmy exclaimed as he flung them off his head, and they landed on the floor. "Sheldon, you pick them up!"

"Oh, for god sake, how old are you?" Ninnie asked, glaring at Shawndrea before picking up the underwear off the floor. "Let's get this stuff all loaded up into the van. I don't want to spend what's left of my summer here in this laundromat."

When they got home, Shawndrea went to her room and blasted her rock music. Ninnie turned to Sheldon. "Okay, so tell me again when Susan's wedding is?" Ninnie inquired, still whispering so Shawndrea did not hear. Susan insisted that Shawndrea not be invited to the wedding.

"Next weekend, just make up a story about where you're going—something that will make her not want to come," Sheldon whispered. "Why are we still whispering?"

"I don't know," Ninnie replied as they both laughed. "I will make up something that she will have no interest in tagging along."

"Sounds like a good deal," Sheldon remarked as he grabbed his car keys. "I will see you next weekend then." He said as he and Levin headed home.

§

It was midday, and Mandy and Damian were lying in bed, talking, and laughing. "Maybe we should get up and do something besides lie here all day," Mandy suggested, throwing back the covers as she started to get out of bed again.

"No, let's just lie here for a little longer," Damian suggested, pulling her back under the covers and tickling her. "We have the house to ourselves for once. Besides, we still haven't discussed what happened at the bar."

"I don't think we need to discuss that right now, do we?" Mandy questioned as she looked at him with her face on her pillow beside his pillow and stared into each other's eyes. "Why mess up a good thing by talking about it or thinking about it too much?"

"I guess for me, it's important because I have never had feelings like this for someone," Damian explained, brushing her hair behind her ears. "Honestly, it bothered me when you pulled away."

"Oh, you young'uns and your feelings," Mandy joked as she did air quotes when she said feelings and then laughed.

"Hey, don't act like you don't have feelings," Damian teased as he playfully tickled her, making her laugh and kick her legs.

"Okay, it's time to get up," she said, throwing back the sheets and climbing out of bed.

Damian stayed lying in bed with the sheet draped across his lower half. His perfect bubble butt was halfway showing, and his head propped on his hand. He watched her walk to grab her robe. "Man, you have a very tight ass," Damian commented as he admired her bottom.

"Get up," she demanded, laughing at him as she tied her robe. "The boys will be here soon. Get dress! We don't want to traumatize the children," She teased, laughing as she threw his clothes at him. He grabbed her and dragged her back into bed…

§

There were sounds of summer in the air, birds were singing, and insects were trilling. A warm breeze blew through the loft, bringing in the smell of straw. Sheldon and Chase were lying comfortably on a bed of straw, telling stories of their past and chuckling. "When I was younger, I would lie here and read the latest adventure book, which helped me escape the reality that was my life," Sheldon recounted as they lay in the quiet loft with the sound of a train off in the distance.

"I would get lost in stories, whether it was a story about children living in a box car or a story where your choices guided you through the plot line, thereby deciding one's fate," Sheldon explained as the train passed their house.

"Man, that train is loud. How do you sleep at night?" Chase asked.

"You get used to it actually."

The two spent the summer enjoying each other's company, but as it was ending, they started to discuss what the future held for them.

A few times, Sheldon and Chase met down by the river. They would sit on the riverbank, tossing stones into the river, playfully poking each other, wrestling around, and passionately kissing each other. Sheldon wished these moments would never end because, for once in his life, he felt alive, that things had finally fallen into place. They made each other laugh and would get lost in each other eyes for hours.

One day, Chase pulled out a joint he got from a friend. Neither one knew what they were doing but thought, why not? As Sheldon took his first big hit, he started coughing intensely, and they both busted out laughing. He continued to smoke and became concerned. *I have to work in a couple of hours. How am I going to manage this if I'm high?* He didn't care for a moment, but then he became paranoid. He kept asking.

"What time is it? I can't be late for work," Sheldon stated.

Chase busted out laughing. "Calm down. You're not going to be late. We will head out in a moment now. Shut up and kiss me," Chase requested as he kissed him, but he could tell Sheldon was concerned. "Okay, babe, we will go."

Sheldon still had to stop by his house to get work clothes and drove like an older man because he was paranoid. As Sheldon drove down the road, he could see dust flying in the air from an approaching car. At first, Sheldon thought, please don't let that be someone coming this way. He was already paranoid. He did not want to meet someone because, suddenly, the road seemed narrow.

Then, he thought *Oh God, do not let that be my Mom.* Sure enough, it was his Mom. Sheldon slowed down as he slowly rolled up and stopped beside his Mom's car. He turned to say something but realized the window was still up, so he rolled it down. While he was rolling down the window, his Mom was talking. "I thought you were already headed to work?" She asked.

"No, not yet. Gotta go get my stuff," Sheldon replied in a higher-than-normal voice. Levin leaned forward, and his facial expression said *what the fuck is wrong with you.* But his Mom didn't seem to take notice.

"You had better hurry up, or you're going to be late, especially as slow as you're driving," Mandy remarked as she rolled back up her window and drove on.

Sheldon arrived at work, and everything seemed to be moving in slow motion as he tried to clock in. He shoved his timecard in the wrong way and stamped it backward. *How the fuck am I going to function today.* He kept saying to himself, "Never again, never again." He heard over the intercom, "Bagger to lane one, please."

"You better hurry up. They need you up front," Sheldon's boss said, standing behind him. Sheldon jumped and swung around, heart pounding. He did not know his boss was even there. *How long had he been standing there?* Sheldon took off through the double doors, almost running over an older lady squeezing and tapping a cantaloupe. He made his way to the front. He pulled out a paper bag to start bagging. His co-worker Sesalie eye-balled him.

"Are you okay?" She asked, observing his movements.

"Yeah, I'm good, thanks," He replied to her with his head down and focused on bagging the groceries. Inside he was screaming *fuck no, I'm not okay! You got this. Just don't smash or break anything.* No one else noticed he was taking extra care bagging the groceries.

The rest of the night flew by. Sheldon ended his shift by mopping the floor. *Okay, I'm good now, but I'm never doing that again.* His assistant manager walked by, smacking his ass and making him jump. "Good job tonight," he said to Sheldon.

Sesalie stopped at the end of the aisle. Sheldon was mopping, and she was about to head home. "Are you sure you're, okay?" she asked him again. "Because this was the quietest, I have ever seen you. You didn't have any of your usual crazy stories for me today."

"Yeah, I'm good, thanks," Sheldon replied, smiling at her.

"Okay, I hope you have a great night, Sheldon," she said as she continued.

"You too, Sesalie," Sheldon said as he mopped the floor.

Sheldon headed to his car, where he found Chase waiting on the hood of his car, smiling his usual sexy dimple smile. "I see you made it through the rest of the day," Chase remarked, getting down from the car to hug Sheldon. "I'm sorry, that was a dumb idea."

"No worries, I made it through," Sheldon responded, hugging

him back. "It was definitely an interesting experience," Sheldon re-marked, their faces close to one another. "I really want to kiss you right now. Let's get in the car and drive somewhere."

"I would love to, but I need to get home," Chase said, biting his lip. "I promised my dad I would help him early tomorrow morn-ing since I'm going with you to the wedding this weekend. You can drive me home if you like and kiss me goodnight."

"Deal," Sheldon stated with a huge smile. They got into the car and drove off.

A truck was parked in the shadows, watching Sheldon and Chase. The man in the truck downed his beer and crushed the can. "God damn fucking faggots," The mysterious man commented in a creepy voice as he threw the empty can outside and opened yet another beer.

Sheldon pulled up in front of Chase's house. "I will pick you up this Saturday at 6 a.m.," he said as he kissed Chase.

"I can't wait. A whole weekend with you will be fun," Chase re-marked as he kissed Sheldon back. Sheldon waited until Chase was inside his house before he drove off, unaware that the mysterious man had followed them and parked in the shadows.

Shortly after Sheldon drove off, the mysterious truck pulled out and started to follow him. When Sheldon pulled down the gravel road to his house, he realized someone was behind him. Sheldon did not think much of it until the vehicle was almost on top of his car. The vehicle had its high beams on, blinding him, so he could not see much of anything. The vehicle followed him for a bit. Shel-don hugged the right side of the road, hoping the vehicle would go around him, but it did not.

When the truck finally started to pass him, he was relieved the bright lights were out of his eyes. He did not get a good look at the vehicle; it was just a dark-colored truck as it flew around him, blocking his view of the road in front of him with a cloud of dust. Sheldon had to slow down; the dust made it hard to see the road. He drove home the rest of the way in peace, thinking it must have been some crazy kids out having fun.

§

The whole gang—Sheldon, Chase, Ruby, Trey, Ninnie, Tommy, Levin, and Charlotte—were seated in the front row for Susan's wedding. The wedding was held outdoors at the Ewing Manor in Bloomington, Illinois.

"Wow, front row," Ninnie commented as she looked around to see who was there. "That's right, we are VIP bitches."

"You have a hard time sitting still, don't you," Tommy teased as he smirked at Ninnie, fidgeting in her seat.

"I didn't hear you complaining about that last night," Ninnie replied, making Tommy's face bright red. She always knew what to say to embarrass him.

The seats started to fill up fast. "Um, Sheldon, aren't you supposed to be giving your sister away?" Chase asked as he turned to look at him.

"I guess I should go find her, huh," Sheldon said as he stood up. "I will be right back." He had spotted one of the bridesmaids waving him over. They told him his sister wanted to talk to him before the ceremony started.

Sheldon found his sister in a tiny bedroom on the manor's second floor. "Oh, thank god you came up," Susan stated, looking slightly pale. "I'm starting to freak out." She turned and looked in the mirror. What was I thinking with this dress? I loved the movie The Little Mermaid, but I'm starting to think this dress is taking it too far. Plus, I spent a fortune," she commented as she spun around and looked at the dress in the mirror.

Susan's dress was light ivory and made of tulle. It was a strapless mermaid style with a sweetheart neckline and a beaded band underneath the breasts. She looked absolutely stunning. Susan's friend, LeLe Watkins, did her makeup, which was about to be tested by some emotional moments.

"I think you look gorgeous," Sheldon remarked. "Who knew you could clean up so well? Plus, you only get married once, right?"

"Hey, now watch it," Susan teased. "Okay, we better…

"You're right, you only get married once," A remarkably familiar voice interrupted her. They turned to see their mother standing there.

"Oh my God, you come!" Susan exclaimed. "You don't know how much this means to me," Susan gushed as she hugged her Mom.

"I'm not going to cry," she declared, fanning her face.

"Someone recently pointed out that I was being a stick in the mud," Mandy explained. "Just because I had a bad marriage doesn't mean all marriages are bad."

§

When Damian pulled Mandy back into bed, he had ulterior motives. "You have to go to your daughter's wedding," Damian stated, urging Mandy to look him squarely in the eye. "You have only one daughter, and she will have only one wedding."

"Pssssh right," Mandy remarked. "No one should ever get married. Worst mistake ever."

"I know you've had a bad experience, and it makes me sad to hear you say that, but you can't lose hope in happy marriages," Damian explained.

"I'm sorry, why are we talking about this?" Mandy asked, trying to get out of bed.

"Whoa, I'm not done with you yet," Damian ordered, pulling Mandy back in bed.

"Let's get up," Mandy demanded, giggling. "The boys are here now."

"Okay, but promise me you will at least think about it?" Damian requested as he tried to tickle her through her robe, making her laugh loudly.

"Okay, Okay, I will, gosh," Mandy said, getting up. "Now, get dressed!"

Mandy couldn't get Damian's words out of her head, and she hated that he was right. She decided she would try harder not to be so pessimistic about marriage. At the last minute, she decided to go to Susan's wedding under one condition: no one would make a big deal of her going.

§

"Why do you seem like you're the one about to get married?" Ruby asked, watching Chase squirm in his seat. "You seem very nervous."

"I'm just nervous for Sheldon," Chase replied. The gang looked at him, not sure whether they believed him.

A choir started to sing the beginning of The Bee Gees Song *to Love Somebody* as the bridesmaids began to walk down the aisle.

Ninnie had a sideways smile on her face as she looked at the gang. "This is a strange song for a wedding," She commented as the harp started strumming during the chorus. "Well, okay then. That's pretty."

Sheldon was relaxed about walking his sister down the aisle. Until the moment came when reality hit him. He started to break out in sweat, and his heart started to pound as the choir began to sing *The Rolling Stones* song You Can't Always Get What You Want.

"Seriously?" Sheldon said, looking at Susan with a smirk.

"What?" Susan replied. "It's the song that was playing when John and I first met, and we had a massive debate about it, so now it's OUR song. They both laughed.

As the choir finished the intro, Chase stood up, surprising the entire audience, and started singing.

"I did not see that coming," Ruby whispered to the Ninnie. "That explains why he was nervous."

"Okay, that is our cue," Susan said, looking at Sheldon.

"Always full of surprises," Sheldon stated as he proceeded to walk Susan down the aisle. Before, he was worried about tripping; now, he was so distracted by Chase singing.

"Sheldon," Susan called his name.

"Yes?" Sheldon replied.

"I'm nervous," She whispered to him as they looked at each other.

"No matter what happens, I'm always here for you," Sheldon told her, smiling and placing his hand on her hand, which was holding onto his arm. They walked down the aisle and saw their Mom sitting in the back with Damian. Susan began to cry.

As Susan walked past her Mom, she reached out to her Mom and took her hand as she passed. They smiled tearfully at one another as she released her Mom's hand and continued down the aisle.

They made their way to the front and stopped to face each other. "Thank you," she said as Sheldon lifted her veil. They shared a watery smile as Sheldon handed her over to John. Sheldon took his seat.

The ceremony was beautiful; Susan and John each recited the

vows they had written themselves. Susan kissed the groom, and everyone cheered.

§

"What a perfect way to end the summer," Ruby remarked, looking around the venue as they stood in line to get food. "This is a perfect spot for a wedding."

"Pssh… Yeah, if you're into romantic things like castles, beautiful flowers, and choirs singing as you walk down the aisle," Ninnie commented sarcastically with a snarled look. "I mean, who needs the hassle of getting all prettied up like a princess."

"Bitter much, Ninnie," Sheldon asked, leaning over and getting finger sandwiches for him and Chase. "I think what's really eating her is the fact that Shawndrea is getting married before her."

"Oh, yeah, that's it. You figured me out," Ninnie quipped as she found a spot next to Tommy at the table. "Though, I must say it has been nice not having her around."

"Man, someone must have pissed in your Cheerios today," Ruby teased, looking at her as she took another bite of her finger sandwich. "Tommy, are you not putting out anymore?"

Trey choked on his sandwich, surprised at what came out of his girlfriend's mouth. He expected that from Ninnie but not Ruby.

After they ate, the boys went to look at the outdoor theatre, leaving Sheldon, Ruby, and Ninnie at the table. "So, I haven't had a chance to tell you Susan offered to let me live with her while I attend Illinois State University College.

"What?" Ninnie questioned as she, too, choked on a sandwich. "I figured you would stay local at least until Chase graduated."

"That was my plan," Sheldon responded, looking around to ensure the boys had not returned.

"What are you going to do?" Ruby asked as she took a big gulp of wine. I'm sorry, but this is a cause to have a drink. I don't know what I would do in your situation. Wait, I will be, and I don't want to think about it. I still don't know where Trey is going to go," Ruby said, taking another big gulp.

"I'm hoping once school starts back up, we will be preoccupied with school and deal with it when the time comes, and it will work itself out," Sheldon said, glancing over and seeing the boys return. "Here they come."

"Good luck with that whole it-will-work-its-self-out-bit," Ruby slurred her words a bit.

"Ruby, are you drunk from one glass of wine?" Sheldon asked with a sideways glance.

"A little bit," Ruby answered, trying to stand up. "Okay, now I have to pee."

"She did have one glass of wine," Ninnie said, standing up. One glass, which kept getting refilled. Come on, hot mess, let me take you to the bathroom."

"Hey, I want to show you something," Chase whispered into Sheldon's ear, making him jump. "Come with me."

Chase led Sheldon into the outdoor Shakespeare theatre. He had Sheldon sit front and center while he ran down and jumped onto the stage. Chase picked up a guitar that was lying on the stage. He began to sing to Sheldon a unique version of *Happy Birthday* mixed with their song *I Choose You*.

"I know your birthday isn't until next weekend, but I saw this place; the DJ happened to have a guitar, and this was an opportunity I couldn't pass up."

"That was amazingly sweet. Thank you," Sheldon said, standing up. He ran down and jumped up onto the stage. He walked over to Chase, put his arms around him, hugged him, and kissed him. They started to sway like there was music playing. "That was extremely creative. What an amazing gesture. I will treasure it forever." Sheldon stated as he leaned in and kissed him again.

They stayed in each other's arms for a while longer, swaying and not wanting it to end. "Wouldn't it have been amazing if they had had the ceremony here?" Chase remarked, holding Sheldon close and looking around the theatre. Suddenly, they heard a commotion from the reception and ran to investigate.

Back at the table, Ruby and Ninnie had returned from the bathroom when they heard people whispering and looking towards the entrance. Ruby and Ninnie's backs faced the entrance, so they had to turn in their chairs to see what everyone was looking at.

"Oh Shit," Ninnie said as she craned her neck, and she spotted what everyone was whispering about. "Hey, I didn't invite them," Ninnie mouthed, looking at Susan with her hands in the air as Sheldon walked up.

Susan gave Sheldon and Ninnie the stink eye. Sheldon shrugged his shoulders, mouthing the words, "I didn't invite them," and shook his head.

"Weeeee're heeere, let's get this fucking party started!" Shawndrea yelled as she walked into the wedding reception, grabbing a glass of champagne. On her arm was a very pregnant Laynardia.

"Whoohoooo, Yeeehaaw!" Laynardia shouted, trying to cheer her best, considering how pregnant she was. "Hell, yeah, Mother fuckers, this party has officially started now that I'm in the house. Bet you fuckers didn't expect to see me anytime soon."

"Shit, she's back," Ninnie remarked, sitting down and looking around the table. "You guys thought Shawndrea was bad. This girl taught her everything she knew about being bad. We better buckle up. It's about to get very interesting."

"Oh my, look at all this food!" Laynardia exclaimed, grabbing a plate and filling it with food. "Oh man, look at these tiny sandwiches. Shawn, will you grab me another plate?"

The moment they walked in, all eyes were on the two, waiting to see what they would do next. Susan tried desperately to ignore them and not let them ruin her day. However, they were so loud that no one could ignore them. Ninnie franticly looked around at everyone, thinking what to do.

"I guess the party is over, and I will be tak-ing these two scream queens home," Ninnie commented, looking around the table at everyone and then at Tommy. "Don't worry, sweetie. I won't torture you by making you ride back with us." You could immediately see the relief in his eyes. "I'm going to say good-bye to Susan first and thank her for inviting me."

Ninnie walked over and hugged, kissed, and congratulated Susan and John. "I'm sorry, I had no idea they were coming,"

Ninnie whispered into Susan's ear.

"It's okay, sweetie. Trust me, I know how family can be," Susan responded, holding onto Ninnie's arms and smiling. Thank you for coming."

"It was a pleasure to meet you," Ninnie addressed John as she shook his hand. "I hope to see you two very soon," She smiled and walked away.

"Okay, this is going to be the real challenge," Ninnie moaned, knowing there was only one way to get these two out of there. She walked up to the table, holding her stomach. "Guys, I'm not feeling well. I think I need to go home," Ninnie moaned in a whiny baby sister voice. She knew they could not resist taking care of their sick baby sister.

"But we just got here," Shawndrea started to object, but Laynardia gave her a Letty look. "Fine! I will pull the car around," Shawndrea stated as she got up from the table, shoveling more food into her mouth before running off. She returned to grab her plate of food and some more sandwiches before running to get the car.

Laynardia started feeling Ninnie's head and proceeded to take her pulse. "You feel clammy, and your pulse is slightly elevated," Laynardia commented, putting down her napkin and standing up with a grunt. "Do you think you can walk?"

"Yes, I think so," Ninnie softly said as she started to stand up.

"Good cause I'm going to need help getting to the car," Laynardia said as she leaned on Ninnie's shoulder. As soon as they left, the reception resumed to normal.

"Okay, everyone, it's time for the bouquet toss," Susan ordered, trying to talk loud enough for everyone to hear.

"I wanted to do something nontraditional. My maid of honor had one of the ground keepers take a piece of paper I drew a flower on and randomly stuck it under one of the chairs. Wait! Don't look just yet. The person who gets the paper does not get to keep the bouquet. There is a twist. I don't want anyone immediately disappointed."

Everyone proceeded to look under their seats for the piece of paper. Chase found it under his seat. Susan tossed the bouquet to Chase, who caught it perfectly. "Everyone, meet our very own star quarter-back, Chase De Longpre," Susan announced loud and proud, making Chase blush.

"And my little brother's boyfriend, and hopefully future husband," she said, winking at Sheldon, making him blush this time.

"Okay, enough of that. Now, Chase, I want you to pass it to the right until it reaches a single lady, and since Ninnie isn't here, it looks like Ruby is the lucky lady. Come on, Ruby, stand up. Everyone give Ruby Nash a round of applause. Now you know you must be married within twelve months of receiving the bouquet?" Susan demanded, looking at Ruby with a serious face. Ruby turned from red to white, and her mouth was hanging open.

"I'm just kidding. I love the look on your face, though. Okay, now we will do something similar for the garter belt. Oh, I guess the groom has to take it off first."

She sat in the chair while John lifted her dress to remove her garter belt. "Whoa, a little high there, cowboy," Susan said, laughing and looking at the crowd. We will save that for later."

She stood back up once John had removed the garter. "Now I have drawn a circle on a piece of paper. It, too, has been placed randomly in one of the centerpieces. Everyone started examining the centerpieces.

"We have a winner," Susan called out. "That was quick, too. Everyone, this is John's nephew Stephen. Here's the catch." She threw the garter to Stephen. "Okay, now Stephen, go ahead and pass the garter to your right until it reaches a single male, which I believe will be Pierre`. Everyone, Pierre` is John's cousin from France.

Pierre` stood up and gave a bow to everyone before he turned in the direction of Ruby's table. "Vous êtes une très belle femme. J'espère que vous me ferez l'honneur de danser avec moi."

"What is he asking her?" Trey leaned over, asking Sheldon, Chase, and Tommy.

Tommy and Sheldon shook their heads. They had no clue. "He is asking Ruby to dance," Chase responded, facing towards Pierre but looking at Trey out of the corner of his eye.

"Oui, je serais honoré," Ruby responded blushing.

"Aaand she just said yes," Chase answered, looking like he did not want to be the one translating.

"Hey, you didn't want to dance with me, so a girl has to improvise," Ruby remarked, smiling at him. She liked this jealous side of Trey. "It is just a dance. Besides, I don't think anyone is going to be dancing. Look at those dark clouds off in the distance."

"Okay, now it's time for our first dance. Then, we will dance with our mothers," Susan announced.

The DJ approached Susan and John's table to tell them something. "I didn't think it was going to rain today," Susan commented, looking at John.

"You've got to love Illinois weather. It's about as predictable as…" John said but stopped after seeing the stern look on Susan's face.

"Okay, I guess we should wrap up and get everything in before it rains," Susan said, looking back at the dark clouds. John and I want to take a moment to thank you all for coming to share this very special day with us," Susan announced, smiling at everyone and then turning to kiss John.

The wind picked up and started to blow a bit. "Hey guys, how about we help the DJ pack up his stuff," Chase requested, looking at Trey and Tommy.

"That's a Good idea. Ruby, Levin, Charlotte, and I will go help Susan clean up what we can," Sheldon added as they went to help Susan.

After loading everything into trucks and cars, Susan hugged Levin and Charlotte and turned to face Sheldon. "I will see you soon, and thank you for coming," she says, hugging Sheldon and giving Chase a wink. Come here. I expect to see you soon, too," she said as she hugged Chase. Here, I thought the Myer girls were about to ruin my wedding. Who would have thought Mother Nature would intervene?"

"Okay, it's starting to come down," Susan said, looking up. Are you guys sure you don't want to stay the night instead of driving back now?"

"Thanks, but we need to head home," Sheldon stated.

In the back seat, Sheldon rested his head on Chase's shoulder. Everyone was quiet from the long day. "Thanks for letting me be a part of this," Chase said, kissing Sheldon on the head.

"Thank you for coming," Sheldon said as he snuggled beside Chase. They both fell asleep to the sound of the tires on the blacktop, the back and forth of windshield wipers, and the rain on the roof.

Chapter Twenty

Unexpected Heroes

Sheldon lay in bed, listening to birds tweeting outside his window, thinking about life. He had just awakened from a nap. It had been raining, and he could still smell the rain and how the cornfields smelled after a summer rain.

For some unexplainable reason, he did not want to go to work. He wanted to be like other kids and be free for the summer. *Why did I think it was a great idea to get a job? Oh, yeah, I wanted to buy a new pair of shoes.* Neither of his parents could afford new shoes for him, so he took matters into his own hands. He wanted this pair of fuchsia high tops with unique metal clasps instead of the regular holes for the shoelaces.

Lying there, he started to think back to when Laynardia helped him fill out job applications. He could not believe it was about two years ago when she drove him around in her orange VW Bug, taking him places to turn in his application. She advised him on how to dress appropriately when turning in applications or for the interview and to follow up on the applications.

Before the wedding, he had not seen Laynardia in quite some time. She had been away at medical school. He could not remember what college she attended. He felt terrible. He should know what school she went to. He remembered all the fun times they had in her little orange VW Bug. His thoughts were interrupted by the sound of a vehicle revving up outside his window.

He looked out to see what was going on. He spotted what

appeared to be Laramie's truck sitting in front of their house next to their mailbox. The windows were tinted, so he could not tell. The truck took off suddenly, spitting gravel everywhere and creating a dust cloud. The truck flew up the road. Sheldon could hear the truck turning around and flying past the house again.

"That asshole better stop it with his shit, or I WILL call Sheriff Bolden," Mandy yelled as she pulled back the curtain to see the truck flying past their house again.

"I don't know why that asshole is harassing us." Mandy saw another truck coming. "That's my brother's truck. I wasn't expecting to see him today."

Bob's truck pulled up, and out of it climbed Laynardia. "Aunt Mandy!" She started yelling. "Aunt Mandy, I have come to see you."

She tried to bend over to pet the dog, but it was hard because she was nine months pregnant. Mandy came out to greet her. "I had to drive my dad's truck. I can't get into the Bug right now. I can't fit behind the wheel," she laughed, half laughing, half cackled. You should see Dad driving my car. Ha! It's hilarious. Oh, it's so good to see you," she cooed as she hugged Mandy.

"Wow, look at you! When are you due?" Mandy asked as they walked toward the house.

"I'm due any day now," Laynardia replied.

"I hear you got a residency at Wabash General, which is great." They walked into the kitchen so Laynardia could sit down at the table. "Anything I can get you? Mandy offered opening the refrigerator. "Water or juice?"

"I will take a glass of water, please," Laynardia replied. "Tell me, Aunt Mandy, what's new with you? I hear you have a new maaaaan friend," she asked, laughing boisterously.

"Ha-ha, man, friend, that's a new one. We are doing well, just enjoying ourselves," Mandy replied as she put a glass of water in front of Laynardia and sat down. "So, tell me about the baby's father. I haven't heard anything about him," Mandy inquired while sipping her coffee.

"Would you believe the asshole knocked me up and took off," Laynardia replied, shaking her head and rubbing her round belly. "Fucking jerk, only wanted one thing. You would think as smart as I am, I would have known better.

"When men want in someone's pants, they can be pretty persuasive," Mandy remarked, trying to make her feel better and not feel ashamed. "Just think, if they were to actually put that power to good use, how much better off the world would be.

They both laugh. "Right! The world would be in a better place," Laynardia stated, looking up with eyes that were a little wet from the pain. She rubbed her belly, and a smile came across her face. "But I've got this, and my baby will be better off without that douche-bag. Where is Sheldon?"

"In his room. I don't think he has been out of his room yet today."

"Now he will. Sheldon, get your butt out here," Laynardia yelled loud enough to make the rafters shake while getting up from her chair. "Get your ass out of bed." She waddled her way to Sheldon's room and knocked on his door. She opened it to find Sheldon on the bed with his headphones on, reading a book.

"Hey, I wanted to give you two sometime to catch up," Sheldon explained as he sat up and removed his headphones. "How's the baby doing?"

"She's doing well," Laynardia replied, smiling and rubbing her tummy. "Oh, she just kicked, you want to feel.

Sheldon hesitated for a moment for some reason. Touching her belly felt like he was invading her private space. "Oh man, that is cool. I felt her kicking," Sheldon said, surprised at how hard she kicked."

"Aagh!" Laynardia screamed out in pain. Sheldon thought he had done something wrong and quickly pulled his hand away. "She is pushing on my bladder. Shit, I gotta go before I piss down my leg." She waddled quickly to the bathroom.

"So, you know it's a girl, huh?" Sheldon asked when she came back into the room.

"Yes…" she started to reply when a truck flew by their house so fast it rattled the windows. They were surprised when they heard the truck stop and revved its engine. After a few moments, the truck took off, peeling out and throwing gravel. Then, like a shot, it was gone.

"What the hell is going on?!" Laynardia exclaimed as they both got up to see.

"That is, I'm calling Sheriff Bolden. He is going to hurt himself or someone else," Mandy stated as she went to the phone and called

Sheriff Bolden's personal number. "This is getting ridiculous; this guy drives by my house like this at all hours of the day and late into the night," Mandy explained to Laynardia as she dialed the Sheriff.

"This guy is going to injure or kill someone," Mandy explained to the Sheriff when the truck flew past again and could be heard turning around. This time, when the truck got in front of the house, there was a loud thud, and it sounded like the truck swerved in the gravel.

"Mandy, I think he just hit one of your animals," Laynardia stated, looking out the window and then turning to look outside. She thought the truck looked more like her old boyfriend PJ's truck. She had not seen him in years. Not since she caught Shawndrea fucking him.

Sheldon got on his shoes to join her, but she was already out the door, interrupting her thoughts. "You don't want to see this," she remarked, looking at the animal lying on the road as Sheldon walked up. "You may want to get a shovel, but there isn't much left of the poor thing. Your Mom is going to be pissed."

Sheldon walked to the shed to get a shovel, and his Mom came to see what happened. "The Sheriff, he is on his way out. By the time he gets out here, whoever it is will be long gone, but the Sheriff wants to file a report anyway. Is that Sadie? Is she dead?

They could see the anger come over Mandy, but it quickly disappeared as the phone rang, and she went back inside to answer it.

The Sheriff arrived fifteen minutes later and took Mandy's statement. He explained that after they had gotten off the phone with Mandy, he sent a deputy to Laramie's house to check on him. It turned out Laramie had been sent to a juvenile detention center for the summer and was not due back home until Saturday to start school on Monday…

§

Chase pulled into Sheldon's driveway. Instead of letting Sheldon out, he put the car in park and shut it off. It had started to sprinkle, and the October night air had a hint of chill. They sat there momentarily holding hands, listening to the light rain coming down.

Things had been quiet for months now. They never figured out who was driving past their house. After Laramie returned from being sent away, things settled down, and it was quiet for months. In school, Laramie left Sheldon alone and seemed to turn himself around. Chase and Sheldon developed a routine of going to school and hanging out.

"I love this time of year," Chase finally said, breaking the silence as he leaned over to kiss Sheldon. "I had fun Christmas shopping with you tonight, even though it's only Halloween."

"I love this time of year. My favorite two holidays are Christmas and Halloween," Sheldon remarked as he started to get out. Chase laughed at him, shaking his head.

"Not so fast," Chase commanded as he grabbed onto the tail of Sheldon's jacket. "Come back here."

Chase pulled Sheldon into him and gave him a toe-curling kiss. "I could kiss these lips forever," Chase stated, gently rubbing his finger across Sheldon's wet lower lip. Chase smiled and kissed him again.

Sheldon looked deep into his eyes. "I love you," Sheldon said with a huge smile. "I will see you tomorrow."

"I love you too," Chase replied, kissing him one last time. "See you tomorrow."

Sheldon got out of the car and walked up to the house. When he got to the porch, he turned around and waved goodbye to Chase as he pulled out of the driveway. Chase was driving down the road, lost in his thoughts of the day's events and how truly blessed his life was.

As he turned the corner, he did not notice a big brown truck parked facing Sheldon's house. He continued down the road and was about to cross the tracks when he saw the lights of an oncoming vehicle.

Being the tracks were so narrow he pulled over to the side of the road to let the other vehicle cross the tracks and go past. The truck flew over the hill of the tracks so fast that it went airborne. When the car landed in the loose gravel, it fishtailed into the driver's side of Chase's car. It happened so fast Chase did not have a chance to react.

Suddenly, his car imploded with a loud smashing sound and glass flying everywhere. Chase's car spun around before sliding into the ditch, flipping over, and stopping upside down in about a foot of water.

The vehicle that impacted Chase fled the scene, leaving behind a trail of dust in the air. The car lay there in the ditch with the sound of the engine popping, something dripping, and the uneven breath of an unconscious Chase.

§

Laramie had been sitting around the corner from Sheldon's house, working up the nerve to apologize. He could not decide whether he wanted to do it in person or leave a note on the windshield of Sheldon's car. There never seemed to be the right moment to do either.

He waited for Chase to drop Sheldon off and was about to drive to Sheldon's house. That was when Laramie saw the accident. He dialed nine-one-one on his bag phone.

After hanging up, his first reaction was to take off after the vehicle hit Chase, but something told him to check on Chase first. He turned his vehicle around and drove to check on Chase. He pulled his vehicle up to where Chase's car went into the ditch.

He jumped out of his truck and climbed down into the ditch. He saw emergency lights off in the distance. He bent down and investigated the driver's side and saw an unconscious Chase hanging there with a gash on his forehead. Laramie bent down into the water, put his arm through the broken driver's side window, and felt for a pulse. There was an unsteady pulse.

"Hey, don't worry, man. Help is on the way." He kept talking to Chase as he tried to open the stuck door. He could hear the sirens. They were quickly approaching the scene. Chase was still unconscious. He rechecked his pulse. It was faint. He did not want to move Chase and cause further damage. Help was so close he wanted to leave it to the professionals.

He heard vehicles pull up and the sounds of several doors closing. "He is down here," Laramie yelled, waving his hands to get their attention.

The Sheriff arrived first, followed by the ambulance. To Laramie, it had felt like forever for them to arrive.

The paramedics came down with a stretcher and a medical case. Laramie got out of the way and let the paramedics do their job.

They put a neck brace on Chase and tried to stabilize him the best they could. The fireman broke out the rest of the windshield and cut the seatbelt. They pulled him through the windshield and free of the wreckage. The paramedics loaded him into the ambulance and headed to the hospital.

§

When Sheldon arrived at the hospital, Trey and Ruby were already in the waiting room. Sheldon hugged Ruby as Trey patted him on the back. Sheldon had so many thoughts running through his head. It all seemed like a bad dream he would wake up from in the morning, but it was not, and this was reality.

"He just left my place," Sheldon commented in a daze. "Do we know what happened?

"His Mom said someone hit the side of his car, causing him to go into a ditch. They drove off and left him there," Trey explained, looking at Sheldon, trying to mask his concern. "His parents are in with him now. He hasn't regained consciousness yet. That is all we have been told so far."

§

Laramie sat in his truck, staring at the guy who had run into Chase's car. The guy had pulled into a gas station and was about to go inside. This guy's truck looked almost identical to Laramie's, except for the tinted windows and the now messed-up front end. He was surprised it was still moving.

Before the guy exited his truck, he saw a picture of a younger Shawndrea on his dash. "Soon, baby, we will be together forever," he said, touching the image.

Laramie put his head against the steering wheel and looked at a letter in the seat next to him addressed to Sheldon. He looked through the windshield while resting his chin on the steering wheel. He watched the guy get out of his truck to examine the damage.

Laramie started muttering to himself.

"Hey, fucking cock sucker," Laramie screamed at the guy as he got out of his truck and started to walk up to the guy. The man reached into his truck and grabbed a gun. He said nothing as he put a single bullet into Laramie before getting back into this truck and once again fleeing the scene.

§

Trey and Tommy sat in the waiting room, telling the girls funny stories about Chase and trying to lighten the mood. Sheldon paced the floor, stopping in front of a window. As he gazed out, he could hear their song *I Choose You* playing through his head, causing him to cry. Sheldon reflected on his time with Chase.

The first time he saw Chase walk across the parking lot. The way he smiled that sexy dimple smile and those eyes you could get lost in forever. The first time, they kissed in the swimming pool. The time he watched Chase play football and when he came running up to say hi to him in the stands.

Sheldon wiped tears from his face as he gasped for air, thinking about the time they danced in the hay loft when he thought he was the luckiest person in the world to know such a beautiful soul. He could hear the part of their song, *All the while you're stealing my heart; you don't know what you do to me*, which reminded him of the prom when Chase came and dragged him to the center of the dance floor. They slowly danced together while Chase sang their song to him in front of everyone. At that moment, he felt like he was floating on air, and nothing could touch them. The way he sang happy birthday to him at his sister's wedding.

Chase was lying in bed with his parents on either side of him. The doctor came in to tell them Chase was stabilized for now and that they would be monitoring him very closely. After the doctor left, they sat holding their son's hands. Suddenly, the monitors started making loud beeping noises, alerting the staff that something was wrong. Chase's Mother yelled for a nurse as his monitor flatlined. The doctors and nurses ran into the room…

In the waiting room, Ninnie and Ruby were seated on either

side of Sheldon when Laynardia walked up next to Sheldon. She had been on her way out after her shift when Chase was brought in and decided to stay to help.

Sheldon stood up, and they walked over to a secluded area. She put her hand on Sheldon's shoulder and handed him a piece of paper as she whispered something in his ear. His face filled with shock as he stumbled back against the wall and fell to the ground. The shock was reflected on everyone's faces as Laynardia filled them in.

Life is a journey full of unexpected events. Enjoy every moment because you may never know if it is someone's last...

To Be Continued....

Acknowledgements

I owe immense gratitude to Alex Waters; without her, this book may never have come to fruition. Her encouragement pushed me to expand my imagination and grow as a writer. Every day, I continue to learn and improve because of her unwavering support.

Jana Davis and Kevin Morgan, thank you for keeping me grounded when I lost my way. Your steadfast encouragement has been invaluable.

I am deeply grateful to Denia Andersen, Shanna McDaniels, and Kevin Waters for their insightful feedback and critiques of this novel. Your perspectives helped shape its final form.

To Sam Losher, your encouragement and push to move to California were pivotal. Your belief in me made a world of difference, and I am happier for it.

Kevin, my brother, your constant presence and shared memories have anchored me through life's ups and downs. Thank you for always being there.

Lastly, Glenn D. Pascual, your presence throughout this journey has been invaluable. Your inspiration and support have been a guiding light.

About the Author

Jason George Waters, born to middle-class farmers, worked on the family farm until its sale. Despite enduring childhood bullying for his feminine traits, he found solace in books and was encouraged by his high school English teacher to write. After working at a bicycle factory, he earned a bachelor's in political science from Illinois State University in 2006. Moving to California in 2008, he secured various roles, including at Kaiser Permanente in 2015. He later graduated with an MBA in healthcare. Inspired by his mother's passing, he began writing the Sheldon Majors series in 2015. Now residing in Southern California, he balances writing with his job as a National Account Manager at Kaiser Permanente. Throughout, storytelling remains his passion, aiming to inspire and entertain.

9 781965 338018